Isabella

Isabella

BRAVEHEART *of* FRANCE

Colin Falconer

LAKE UNION
PUBLISHING

Text copyright © 2015 Colin Falconer
All rights reserved.

Published by Lake Union Publishing, Seattle

www.apub.com

Amazon, the Amazon logo, and Lake Union Publishing are trademarks of Amazon.com, Inc., or its affiliates.

ISBN-13: 9781477828489
ISBN-10: 1477828486

Cover design by Mumtaz Mustafa Designs

Library of Congress Control Number: 2014955218

Printed in the United States of America

To my favorite niece, Jayne. For you, a book about a princess. Sheer coincidence.

Chapter 1

Boulogne-sur-Mer, France, January 1308

"You will love this man. Do you understand? You will love him, serve him, and obey him in all things. This is your duty to me and to France. Am I clear?"

Isabella is twelve years old and astoundingly pretty, a woman in a girl's body. She keeps her eyes on the floor and nods her head.

Her father, the king of France, is the most handsome man she has ever seen. In the purple, he is magnificent. His eyes are glacial; a nod from him is benediction, one frown can chill her bone-deep.

He puts his hands on the arms of her chair and leans in. A comma of hair falls over one eye. He rewards her now with a rare smile. "He is a great king, Isabella, and a handsome husband. You are fortunate."

A log cracks in the hearth.

She raises her eyes. He strokes her cheek with the back of his hand. "You will not disgrace me."

She shakes her head.

"Much is dependent on this union."

Her, breathless: "I will not disappoint you."

Philippe goes to the fire and stands with his back to it, warming himself. It is the heart of winter, and this is as cold and drafty a castle as she has ever been in. She can smell the sea. There is ice in the air.

"If he has cause to reprove you, you will listen and obey him. If he is angry, you shall be kind. If he is dismissive, you shall be attentive. Cherish him, give him your attentions. Be sweet, gentle, and amiable. Patience is your byword. You will make him love you."

He stares at her. He can stand like this for an eternity, fix a look on his face as if he were carved from marble. It is unnerving.

"No matter the provocation."

"Provocation?"

"What do you know of Edward?"

"He is king of England. His father was a great warrior. They say Edward is tall and as fine a prince as England ever had." (Though it is hard for her to imagine a finer king than her father, or a more handsome man. She has always promised herself she will have a man just like him: as fair, as strong, as feared.)

"Your new husband disputes Gascony with me. One road leads to war. A less thorny path leads to the day when my grandson-to-be inherits the throne of my most ancient enemy."

"But what provocation might he give me?" Isabella says.

Philippe frowns.

"You mentioned provocation, Father."

"Did I? I meant nothing by it. Tomorrow you will be queen of England. Remember always that you are also a daughter of France. Make me proud, Isabella."

He nods to her nurse and she is taken from the room.

She can barely contain her excitement. She has rehearsed this moment in her mind for years. A handsome prince, a throne, estates—it is what she was born for. From tomorrow she will live her life at the side of a great king.

Happiness is assured.

Chapter 2

Bells peal across the city. The town is hung with banners. Edward of England arrives in a thunder of hooves, his men dressed in royal livery, scarlet with yellow lions. He jumps down from his horse, his cloak swirling, and tosses back a mane of golden hair. He is like a song a troubadour might sing.

He carries himself with the loose-limbed stride of a man accustomed to having others make way for him. He is tall and blue-eyed, and smiles at her with such easy charm it makes her blush. He is a man, older than her eldest brother, Louis, a man in his prime. His manner and bearing take her breath away.

It is love at first sight.

Her father presents her, and as she steps forward she raises her eyes, hoping to see that glorious smile again. But his attention is already elsewhere, on her father, on the bishop, on her uncle Valois.

"We should get to business," he says.

For three days they talk about Gascony. England camps outside the town. A forest of pavilions flourishes outside the walls, as if they were besieged. There is not a room to be had anywhere; beggars and camp followers sleep in porches and gateways. The town is bursting. Isabella patrols the battlements and passages, anxious for a glimpse of him. They cannot be married until they resolve the politics of the union.

She hates it here. Boulogne is gray and cold. She misses Paris, the ceremonies, her ladies, her private *salles*, the roaring log fires. Here the drafts whistle under the doors, and the wind buffets off the sea day after day. Even the banners seem to be fading in the rain.

She closes her eyes and imagines him. He is hers. Her father was right, she is fortunate. He is beautiful, he is a king, and he is all hers.

———

Our Lady of Boulogne has never seen a day like this. Resplendent in a silver gown and wearing a circlet of fine gold, Isabella meets her groom on her father's arm. Isabella's hands shake; she hopes her father will think it is because of the cold. He despises emotion, which he calls weakness.

It is frigid inside the cathedral. Her breath freezes on the air.

Eight kings and queens are present; there are also mere dukes and a handful of princes. Here the king of Sicily, there the French dowager queen, all jewels and velvets, gold and shot taffeta, elbowing for a better view of the twelve-year-old bride. Everyone has heard how pretty she is. They all want to pass their own judgment.

The archbishop reads the words of the marriage. Isabella spares a glance at her father. His expression betrays nothing.

Edward studies the ceiling, his eyes on a cold bolt of sun that angles through the high lancet window. He looks faintly bored. Isabella tries to catch his eye without success.

Finally he finishes with his looking around and sees his bride; he puffs out his cheeks and raises his eyebrows at her. He nods at the bishop. Will this old bore never finish?

Her father frowns, but only those standing closest to him might notice. This is not the behavior he expects from his new son-in-law. But there is no one here who might reprimand the king of England, who now stifles a yawn.

The choir sings the plainchant as they kneel on prie-dieux; the clouds of swirling incense make her gasp. The bishop joins their hands; she squeezes Edward's fingers, hoping for some response. He just sighs and returns his attention to the ribbed vault.

The marriage is contracted on the high altar. She thinks she sees her father sigh with relief when it is done, as if he had thought that even at this last moment Edward might flee the cathedral and run for his ship. The archbishop of Narbonne sings: "Ite, missa est," and they walk hand in hand to the nave to the polite applause of every noble house in Christendom.

No one smiles as she crosses the nave, except for Edward. When they are outside, he leans in and addresses her directly for the first time: "There," he murmurs. "That wasn't so bad, was it? I thought you did rather well."

———

One face stands out from the others as they leave the church; he is one of Edward's men, a bleak man with a black beard and dark eyes. Even a girl as young as Isabella knows when a man is looking at her in a manner that he should not. He scares her. In that first glimpse there is a savagery to his face that is unmistakable even in a crowded and candlelit church.

Yet there is something about him that makes her glance back over her shoulder. There is something thrilling in his stare. The hairs rise on her arms.

Later, at the feast, she asks one of her ladies who he is. They do not know; inquiries are made of the English party. Someone whispers to her that his name is Roger Mortimer, and he is one of

Edward's barons. Once, she catches him staring at her from across the hall. She looks quickly away and never turns back in that direction again.

Chapter 3

Her ladies prepare her for bed. Her hair is brushed through a hundred times and arranged beneath the caul. They rub her skin with rose-scented oil, and set a fire burning in the grate.

She asks Marguerite her advice. Marguerite is married to her brother Louis, and has already been through this ordeal. "What shall I do?"

"Whatever he asks, your grace."

"But what will he ask?"

Her old nurse, Théophania, pats her head. "Now there's no need to be frightened."

"I'm not frightened."

"You should not be a mortal woman if you were not a little frightened," Marguerite says. "But he will not come to you tonight, or any night soon."

"He won't?"

"*Ma chérie*, you are only twelve years old."

"You have not bled yet," Théophania says. "He is English, but he is not an animal."

"How old were you when you married?" she asks Marguerite.

"I was fifteen. Old enough."

"I want to make him happy."

Marguerite finds this amusing. "It is not hard to make a man happy. Be agreeable. Do not vex him. Have his children. Do as he says."

"And will he love me?"

"Love?" The smile is gone as quickly as it came. Marguerite spares her a look she has never seen in her life: pity. "Rest your faith in God, Isabella."

When her ladies are gone, she finds the gift that her husband's stepmother has sent her, a silver casket with the arms of Plantagenet and Capet in quatrefoils. It is lined in red velvet. She wonders what she might put in it.

The door creaks open. She tosses the box aside and lies down again, her arms stiff at her sides. The casket clatters onto the floor.

Edward picks it up and lays it on the bed beside her. He puts his hands on his hips and studies her. "Well, you're a little on the bony side. I daresay you shall put some flesh on your bones as you grow. Pretty enough. But they told me you were beautiful."

Isabella stares at the coverlet. It bears the emblem of France.

Edward sits on the edge of the bed. He reaches for her hand, pats it. "You're frightened of me?"

She shakes her head vigorously.

"Yes you are. Oh, I think I know what it is. But you needn't worry on that account. I'm not a monster, Isabella. The Church says we might lie together as man and wife, but I always try to put kindness and common sense before anything the pope says."

She still does not move.

"What is this you have here? Did my stepmother give you this? I would have thought the old girl might have done better. You might put jewels in it, I suppose. You shall never suffer a shortage of jewels, Isabella."

He places the casket on her lap.

A log falls from the hearth. He gets up and kicks it back into the grate.

"Do you like me, my lord?"

A broad smile. "Ah. She speaks! At last. I heard you repeat the vows in church, so I knew you were capable of it."

"Do you?"

"I hardly know you, girl. Is it necessary for me to like you? I shall treat you kindly either way."

"Are you pleased that I am your wife?"

"Of course. I need Gascony back."

"I mean, do *I* please you?"

Edward frowns and sits down again. "You're queen of England, Isabella. What else is it that you want?"

She cannot answer him. She wants what her mother had—her father's endless tears at her funeral, the years of mourning. The longing. All the things that the troubadours sing about, like love and gallantry. She wishes to be a queen who is loved by the king, and that king must be someone much like her father.

But she cannot tell him any of these things, and so she says nothing.

"You will let me know if you need anything? After the festivities we leave for England. Anything you require, just speak to your ladies, and I shall attend to it." He stands up and shakes his head. "I never expected you to be so young."

"I never expected you to be so handsome."

There, it is said. He is taken aback; he laughs, then tucks the sheet up to her neck. "You should sleep now."

He makes to blow the candle out, but she stops him, tells him she is frightened of the dark. And so he kisses her on the forehead and leaves, shutting the door softly behind him. Before it closes she sees him say something to the guard and pat him on the shoulder; her father never speaks in a friendly manner to anyone less than a duke, and so this surprises her.

She sits up and retrieves the casket. She runs a finger across the velvet. "One day I will have your heart, Edward," she whispers. "One day, Edward. I promise you! One day!"

Chapter 4

The white cliffs appear through a curtain of rain. Isabella pays them scant attention. She has been seasick since leaving the harbor at Boulogne, and now clings to the side with her ladies fussing around her, those who are not themselves bent over the stern rail. A cold wind buffets her burning cheeks.

Dover Castle appears briefly through another flurry of rain. All she wants is to be on dry land again. The narrow sea now stands between her and her father; she feels adrift.

She looks around for her new husband; he patrols the deck, wrapped in a red mantle, his servants getting in the way of his pacing. He pushes one irritably aside and searches the shore. Does he fear pirates? Once inside the harbor walls, the anchor splashes down; the royal barge is already on its way to meet them.

He goes ashore first, with his retinue of barons and bishops. Not a backward glance.

When she finally arrives at the quay, Edward is lost among a crush of courtiers. Her own people huddle around her, protecting her from the worst of the wind, while her uncles, Evreux and Valois, supervise the unloading of the baggage. The puddles are ruining her shoes.

The quay is foul, wet, and reeking of fish. The forbidding walls of the castle appear through the mist of rain. The scarlet flags with their gold lions are the only color on this dull day.

She catches a glimpse of the king, arm in arm with one of the gallants, a fine-looking man wearing more jewels than she has ever worn at one time, even for her wedding.

"Who is that?" she murmurs.

Valois makes a clicking noise with his tongue. "That's Gaveston."

"Is he a baron?"

"He thinks he is."

Their eyes meet. This Gaveston smiles at her over Edward's shoulder. But there is no time for pleasantries. Another flurry of rain sends them all scurrying for the litters.

A blast of trumpets, and their escort clatters into position on the cobblestones. They enter through a massive gatehouse, bumping through a narrow passage into a broad bailey, which is a madhouse of smiths and horses and dogs. She sees a butcher sling a carcass on a hook to drain the blood into a tin bucket, and women toss filthy rags into steaming vats. Noises, smells, and a sea of grim faces. All this way and it is just like being back in Paris.

———

Well, this is not how she has imagined it at all.

He has paid her no attention, none. He spends all his time whispering and laughing with this Gaveston. They are like two mating pigeons. She fights down her disappointment and remembers what her father told her.

"Cherish him, give him your attentions. Be sweet, gentle, and amiable. Patience is your byword. You will make him love you."

The great hall is long and cavernous. Pennants and banners hang from the hammer-beam roof. The windows and arrow slits have been shuttered against the English winter, but it finds its way in anyway, and the flags above her flutter in the draft. They have built up the fire with logs, but she shivers with cold.

The food is announced with heralds and trumpets: a swan stuffed with a turkey stuffed with capons. There are also plates of venison and boar, roasted and glazed. Edward gasps in delight as if he has never seen such wonders before. What does he usually eat at a banquet, stale bread and haddock water?

She is the subject of much attention, as she has hoped and expected. She is the new foreign curiosity. She does not mind; in fact she rather likes it.

"Look at them staring, Uncle. Will they love me here, do you think?"

"You are their queen," Valois says. "Of course they will love you."

She watches the king. At first she thinks there are children crawling all over him; now she sees they are his dwarves and fools. They dress in bright colors, and some even have their heads shaved like monks. They have names like Maud Makejoy and Graybread, and he even lets them eat at the royal table, below the salt. He diverts himself by throwing food at them. He drinks too much and laughs too loudly.

Now Gaveston leans forward and whispers in his ear. Up close he is breathtaking in scarlet-and-gold satin. His crucifix is studded with pearls, and he wears a ruby ring—both among the presents her father gave to Edward as wedding gifts.

"Who is this Gaveston?" she asks. "He has not left Edward's side since we arrived here."

"Every king has his favorite."

I should be his favorite, she thinks but dares not say. *How can I make him love me if I cannot make him look at me? What kind of queen will I be if I serve merely as decoration to the far table?*

A young lifetime of training is in dissolve. Away from her father's shadow, she is no longer as sure of herself and what is expected of her. What was stone beneath her feet is sand; she feels herself slipping.

"You will not disgrace me."

"Do not worry, your grace, he will not be at your coronation."

"You promise me?"

"The barons have made their position clear on it. You are not the only one unhappy about the king's behavior."

This surprises her. No one has ever dared reprimand her father for anything. It is hard to imagine living in a country where a king might not do exactly as he pleases.

Edward takes a morsel from his trencher and places it between Gaveston's lips. They look into each other's eyes and laugh. The whole court sees this happen. Valois finishes his wine; some of it spills onto his beard. He slams the goblet down on the bench and walks out, kicking one of the dogs as he leaves.

As she turns away, she sees Mortimer watching her. It sends a shiver down her spine. But at least someone is looking at her.

———

Tonight the wind shrieks around the castle walls. Isabella cannot sleep. She pulls back the bed curtains and wraps a fur around her shoulders. She gets up and sits on a low stool by the fire, almost hugging the embers in the hearth.

"You will love this man. Do you understand? You will love him, serve him, and obey him in all things. This is your duty to me and to France."

The chamber they have assigned her is huge, as big as Boulogne Cathedral. There are glowing braziers to supplement the fire, but nothing will warm this cavern. Two of her new ladies snore in trundles at the foot of the four-poster bed.

She hears laughter in the passage outside; it is perhaps just a servant, though when she closes her eyes, what she imagines is Gaveston pursued by her husband in some wicked game.

She does not want to be here, in this cold castle, so far from the Palais de la Cîté and her father and everything she knows. *But I must win him over and make my father proud of me,* she reminds herself. This is her duty.

She climbs back into the cold bed and listens to the wind moan down the chimney and watches the log crumble to ash in the grate.

Chapter 5

Two weeks later Isabella prepares to become a queen. "How do I look?"

"You look beautiful, your grace," Isabella de Vescy tells her. She is much older than her other ladies and has taken her in hand, as if she thinks she needs a mother. Perhaps she does.

"Do I look regal?"

Even in the polished steel mirror, she sees the frown of hesitation. "Very regal," the younger one, Eleanor, tells her and earns a frown of rebuke from de Vescy that she thinks Isabella does not see.

Well of course I do not look regal. I look like a twelve-year-old girl, overprimped and overdressed; if not for these ribbons and artifices, I would disappear inside this gown, and my uncles would have to hack a way through the taffeta and velvet with their swords to free me.

"Will Gaveston be there?"

De Vescy shrugs with all the eloquence that a mature woman can muster.

"Why does no one want to talk about him?"

Valois bursts in. Her uncle comes and goes as he pleases it seems, immune to Madame de Vescy's cold stares. He still treats Isabella as a child; they all do.

He regards her gown and sighs. He has done much sighing since arriving in England. "Are you ready to become queen of England, your grace?"

She takes a deep breath and nods her head. She is ready for no such thing.

A timber pathway has been laid through the mud and is strewn with herbs. Bells peal along the misty river, from Saint Paul's to Saint Stephen's. Every church in London joins in. The procession is announced with pipes and drums.

Edward strides beside her, appearing faintly bored with it all. He looks glorious in a scarlet-and-gold surcoat over a snow-white linen shirt. There is a cape of glory on his shoulders, a jeweled crown on his head.

They walk from Westminster Hall to the abbey, the barons of the Cinque Ports carrying an embroidered canopy to keep the drizzle of rain off the royal heads.

Every citizen of London is pushing and shoving for a better look at them. Their guard is heavy-handed in their duties, but it does no good; they are forced to enter the abbey by the back door, and Isabella feels herself jostled. Edward has to step in himself to protect her, and she smiles up at him, grateful for his gallantry. She glances over her shoulder at her uncle, the Earl of Lancaster; he looks as if he would like to use Edward the Confessor's blunted Sword of Mercy on some ruffian with no teeth who tries to pinch her arm.

To distract herself from the push and shove, she focuses instead on trying to remember who is who among the great lords around her. She feels a great need to impress.

The moving landmark with the gray hair, that is Lincoln. He had come to France to help arrange the marriage, she remembers. The one with the dark eyes and sharp beard is Warwick, and she had disliked him on sight. Hereford is Edward's brother-in-law, a little prickly, she has found, but likeable enough.

And then there is Lancaster; you cannot mistake Lancaster.

Warwick shouts at the bodyguard to use the butt end of their lances, but the crush is so great that those at the front cannot retreat even if they wish it. The hem of her gown is spattered with mud. Edward mutters a curse.

Another baron—she sees now it is the one she caught staring at her at the banquet—strides ahead with the royal robes. He glances over his shoulder at her and nods. Perhaps the gesture is meant to reassure; she raises her chin to let him know she is not intimidated in the least by the crowd. It is bravado. She is terrified.

But at last they come to the coronation. Inside the abbey it is no less crowded, but there is not the jostling or the stink. Isabella looks up and sees the bishops waiting for them by the thrones.

And then she sees Gaveston.

He wears silver and imperial purple, a vision in silk and pearls. He has come down from heaven to anoint them perhaps. He bears the crown of England on a velvet cushion.

Isabella's own robes are made from twenty-three yards of gold-and-silver cloth, edged and decorated with ermine and overlaid with mother-of-pearl lace. On her head she has a crimson velvet cap, adorned with Venetian gold and pearls.

Yet beside Gaveston she feels underdressed.

Lancaster, standing somewhere behind her, mutters a curse. "Look at what he's wearing," he hisses. "I should like to spill his guts with the Sword of Mercy!"

The Lord of Lincoln reminds him of Isabella's delicate presence. Lancaster seems unmoved. He is her uncle, her mother's brother, and it is hard to believe. He has so far shown her no sign of familial warmth.

She looks to Edward for an explanation of Gaveston's presence, but Edward is beaming at Gaveston, who grins back. One of the earls shouts something, but Mortimer steps in and warns him to silence. It was Warwick. Gaveston seems oblivious to them; he has eyes only for the king.

It is overwhelming. There are thousands crammed inside the abbey: monks, soldiers, and bishops. The choir and sanctuary are ablaze with hundreds of candles. There are banners and flags everywhere, a riot of color. Two massive wooden pavilions hung with winter roses soar on either side of the steps leading up to the sanctuary.

The crowds surge forward; one of her ladies shouts in alarm. Isabella looks around for Isabella de Vescy, who gives her arm a reassuring squeeze. There is so much smoke from the candles and thuribles of incense that it is hard to breathe. She thinks she is going to faint.

Finally Edward ascends the platform to the painted coronation chair that his father had made to house the Stone of Scone, a sacred relic he stole from the Scots to gall them. But just as the Confessor's crown is placed on his head, a wall behind the altar collapses, and there are muffled screams from beneath it. The bishops look in exasperation at Gaveston. There are too many people inside the abbey, the crowds have not been properly marshaled. This was Gaveston's responsibility, it seems. The ceremony continues, while some knights and officials haul at the rubble. Someone is trapped underneath.

"I have a man who mucks out my horses who could have done a better job of managing this occasion than Gaveston," Warwick says.

"I can hear Robert the Bruce laughing all the way from Scotland," Lancaster says.

———

The coronation banquet is held at Westminster Hall. The food arrives late and is cold, the grease settled. Her uncle Lancaster stands up with a mouthful of goose and shows the assembly that the meat is raw before hurling a haunch of seared and bleeding beef at an usher.

There is no shortage of wine, and several of the guests become bawdy. Her brother Charles approaches her with her uncles and indicates that it is time to leave. Edward has his arm around Gaveston, and their fingers are intertwined. They have eyes for each other only. Gaveston kisses his cheek.

"Have you not a care?" the Earl of Lincoln shouts at him and has to be restrained. The king hardly notices.

They retire to an antechamber. Valois has a servant fetch him wine.

"I was once on crusade in Outremer," her uncle Evreux says. "I was lost in the desert among some brute Germans who could do no more than grunt at each other, and because we were starving, we ate one of the camels raw. Even so, the company and the food were better than it was tonight."

Valois props himself in a window seat and stares at the river, in a sulk.

She hears described how the king allowed Gaveston to prepare both the coronation and the feast. They all count both a disaster. "Did you see the tapestry he prepared for the occasion?" Charles says to Valois. "It had Gaveston's arms beside the king's. It should have been my sister's arms placed there. He has insulted our entire family!"

The door bursts open, and Lancaster barges in. "He couldn't organize a fuck in a barrel full of whores." Valois nods toward Isabella, and Lancaster's face turns pink. "Your grace," he says and bows. "I did not see you." But he is off his stride only for a moment. "Did you see what he wore?"

Isabella stares at the floor. She has never heard language as ripe as this. This has been altogether an interesting day. "I need to get out of this damned country," Evreux mutters.

"Why is everyone so angry?" Isabella asks him.

"No one is allowed to wear purple but the king!" Lancaster shouts at her before remembering himself and lowering his voice. "Look at me! Is gold not good enough for him as well? And he dares hold the Confessor's crown! Is he high born? Is he noble? The privilege should have been mine or Warwick's!"

"We sympathize with your plight," Charles says. "But let us desist. We are upsetting my sister."

"He has insulted her as well."

"I agree."

"Are you not vexed?" Lancaster asks him.

"Vexed? I am ready to do murder. But one wonders if that would be a wise course. This is not our realm."

Lancaster stamps across the room and pounds a fist against the wall, causing it to dent and splinter. "Did you see them sitting there, staring at each other?"

"Will you all please explain to me what is happening?" Isabella says.

They look at her. The child can speak. But how can she understand? There is a long and difficult silence. They all wait for one of the others to do the talking.

Finally Charles sits down beside her and picks up her hand. "We are shamed that he pays his favorite more attention than you."

"Who is this Gaveston, where he is from?"

"He is a Gascon, a squire in the former king's household. They grew up together. They became close friends."

"Close!" Lancaster snorts.

"I heard his mother was burned as a witch," Valois says, still looking out of the window.

"There is no truth in that rumor," Evreux says. "The plain facts about him are bad enough without making up falsehoods."

"Why does the king favor him above anyone else?" Isabella asks them.

More looks. Charles waits for Evreux to help him, but he joins Valois by the window. Lancaster shrugs and turns away. "Do not fret, Isabella," Charles says. "This shall not stand. He shall give you the respect that is your due."

"I shall go to my knees tonight and ask the Virgin for guidance in this," Isabella says.

"Then you shall not be the only one on your knees when the candles are spent," Lancaster says, and he storms out, leaving behind an embarrassed silence.

Chapter 6

My dread and very dear Majesty,

I commend myself to you as humbly as I can. You have heard from my dear brother of affairs here in England. I am hard-pressed at present to meet my expenses; my husband tells me that his Treasury cannot even afford to pay his own.

I do not know how I shall run my household unless the King endows me with those estates he has promised me.

Now that my good uncles have returned to France, I am in lack of good counsel. Edward has provided me with my own retinue of ladies, and one of them, Lady Mortimer, the wife of one of Edward's barons, is unfailingly kind to me.

I shall do my best to be faithful to you and to France in all things, though I find this present circumstance difficult to bear.

May the Holy Spirit keep you always.

Given this day at London.

Isabella

———————

She wakes to a sound as chilling as any she has ever heard. She puts on a fur-lined mantle and goes outside. Lady Mortimer is already in the hall, hurrying to attend her.

"What manner of beast is that?" Isabella asks her.

"It is one of the king's lions, your grace. He has a private menagerie in the barbican. His father brought these creatures back from the Holy Land, or so they tell me."

Isabella dons sturdy leather boots and goes outside to walk in the garden, pursued by her ladies. It is just after dawn. There is mist on the river and frost on the gray roofs of the king's apartments. A crocus pushes its way through the brown earth.

The portcullis is raised. The stench of the river is stunning, and she reels back. Torches flare in the fog. A barge pulls up at the steps. Soldiers run to meet it, their voices echoing around the water gate.

She returns to her chambers in Saint Thomas Tower and sees Mortimer coming out as she is going in. He seems embarrassed to find her awake and on the stairs so early. "My Lord Mortimer."

He bows. "Your grace."

"I did not expect to find you here. You have been visiting Lady Mortimer?"

He nods his head. He seems uncomfortable in her presence.

"Did you hear my lord's lions? They woke me."

"Was that what it was? I thought it was Lancaster."

She had not imagined him to have a sense of humor, and she giggles. But this is unseemly, and she quickly composes herself. "The smell is overpowering close to the wall."

"Definitely Lancaster, then."

He had seemed so fierce in the church and at the banquet, but now he seems almost charming, if not diffident. He is certainly embarrassed at being caught sneaking from his wife's bedchamber. She likes having him at her advantage. "What are they doing at the water gate?"

He looks over her shoulder and sees the barge and the torches. "They're unloading weapons."

"Weapons?"

"Bows, halberds, shields. The king is preparing for war."

"Against whom?"

He shrugs as if it is common knowledge. "Against his earls."

She tries not to appear shocked. Having nothing more to say, she bids him good morning. "Your grace," he murmurs and hurries away.

Civil war? Does my father know about this?

And if it's true, what will happen to me?

——————

They do not stay long in one place; the royal households are large, and even the most well-appointed castle turns foul soon enough, especially in the winter. There are Parliaments to attend, Scots to be harried, Welshmen to be hanged.

Every time they move, it is like a small army decamping.

Edward's favorite retreat is at Langley. He mentions casually that this is where he met Piers Gaveston—or Perro as he calls him. Is this why it is so special to him?

Her treasurer, William de Boudon, begs audience. "Your grace," he mumbles in the studied tones of a man who shudders to raise the subject of such a vulgar thing as finance in the presence of royalty, though that is what he was hired to do. "I count one hundred and eighty persons in your household, and all must be fed and clothed and adequately compensated. Your wardrobe must be maintained. Yet I do not have an adequate purse for the purpose."

"We have no money."

"Precisely."

She has one of the inadequately compensated ladies-in-waiting call for her steward. She tells him to fetch a horse, the queen wishes to go riding. "Ask the Lady Mortimer if she will accompany me," she says.

She goes in search of the king, who has responded to the threat of revolt among his barons by offering to help one of his gamekeepers repair his roof. When she finds him, he seems so contented, she feels a pang of misgiving at disturbing his labor.

He looks like an overgrown boy. She watches him for a while; he has with him several of the lads of the estate, all of them on the roof, clambering over the thatch. He is a neat hand with a shearing hook. He is down to his peasant hose; his body all wiry and hard muscled. It sends a shiver through her. She hears him laughing, sharing some bawdy joke with the men. Gaveston is asleep in the straw below, looking decorous.

The lieutenant of her guard holds the reins, and she slides from her horse. She lifts her skirts clear of the dew. Edward sees her and waves.

He slides halfway down the ladder, jumps the rest of the way, landing easily on the balls of his feet. "Isabella."

"Dread lord."

A servant hands him a cup of wine. Not quite a commoner yet, then. The dregs leave a glistening residue in his beard. "Is everything well?"

"Passing."

"I trust you have all you require."

"My lord, what are you doing?"

He spreads his hands, puzzled by the question.

"A king does not work alongside commoners. Next you will tell me you have been digging trenches," she says.

"Should they need digging, why not?"

"This is not what a king does."

"Not the king of France perhaps. But it is what I do. I can disport myself as I wish."

"I meant no offence, your grace. I am just . . . startled."

"Will here is my groundskeeper and has been since I was a boy. His roof is in need of some new thatch, and the kingdom may spare me for a morning." He hectors her much as her father does. She feels so stupid here in England; everything must be explained to her. "Is there something I might do for you?" he asks her.

She gathers her courage. This needs saying, and she has no one to do it for her: "Your grace, I hope you do not think me impertinent, but I am in dire need of money. I have nothing with which to maintain my household."

Edward laughs. "Madam, it shall be forthcoming." He turns for his ladder. He is missing the straw already.

"Forthcoming will not do, Edward. I need money *at this moment*."

He stares at her. He looks shocked. "I am not accustomed to being addressed in such a manner by a girl."

"I am the daughter of the king of France. I have *never* been a girl."

Gaveston is awake now. He leans on one elbow, watching this exchange with interest as do the lads on the roof. Edward says, through gritted teeth: "Well, I should like to assist you in this matter, but the Treasury is unfortunately sorely depleted—at this moment."

"So you have told me. But as part of my dowry, I was promised the Duchy of Cornwall. The rents from the patronage would assist greatly."

"I have given Cornwall to my Lord Gaveston."

She lowers her eyes as she had been taught. She waits, does not move, listening to the beating of her own heart. "I shall see what might be done," he says and returns to the problems of a good thatch.

Isabella lets out her breath. She has never confronted a grown man before. She would not have dreamed of taking issue with her father—or either of her uncles—on any matter; today she has surprised even herself.

She returns to her riding party, and Lady Mortimer assists her back onto her horse. She thinks she hears her whisper: "Well done, Isabella!" But then, she might have imagined it.

Edward's good humor is quickly vanished when her uncle Lancaster and the Earl of Warwick visit him. They have come to complain about Gaveston, that the king is too familiar with him, that he should not have been granted the Duchy of Cornwall. Isabella watches from the gallery, out of sight, as she sometimes did when her father held audience in the *palais* in Paris.

"And where should Cornwall have gone?" Edward asks them. "To you, I suppose?"

"To the queen."

Choked off laughter comes from a chair by the hearth, where Gaveston warms his stockinged feet and reads a book. "That twelve-year-old schoolgirl? What will she do with Cornwall?"

"I see your bitch is curled nice and easy by the fire," Lancaster says. "I didn't see her there."

Heads turn to the hearth. Edward's wolfhound lies at Gaveston's feet, asleep on the Turkish carpets.

Warwick is more direct; handsome as the Devil, dark, bearded, and frightening, he has the whitest hands she has ever seen on a man. They say he can converse in Latin and keeps a dagger hidden in his tunic. "What is Gaveston doing here? This is our point. Do we never get to speak to the king alone?"

"He is my most trusted adviser."

"Then what advice you must be getting," Lancaster says. "He could not even organize the banquet for the coronation."

"The fault lies with the cooks and stewards," Edward says, and starts to rise from his throne. "I believe they were paid to make him look foolish."

"Why?" Warwick asks. "When they could have *that* for free?"

The audience goes badly from there. There is shouting. Lancaster and Warwick depart, threatening reprisals against their own king. She has never heard anything like this; no one would ever dare raise their voice to her father. Who is king and who is servant in this country?

Chapter 7

Easter Friday, cold and bright. Edward storms in, trailing clerks and advisers, even a dwarf. Mortimer is there, and Lincoln, and Hugh le Despenser, as genial and charming a courtier as she has met since she has been in England. He was one of Longshanks's most able diplomats, she is told. He is even friendly to Gaveston.

Edward has still not given her the dowry she was promised, and as she cannot afford to keep her own household, she now lives in his. She is witness now to all of his moods and travails.

Edward paces relentlessly. He is holding a petition bunched in his fist. "'A higher duty is owed to the Crown over the person of the king?' What do they mean by this? *I* am the Crown."

"They refer to the institution of kingship," Mortimer says, refusing to join in the general air of exasperation.

"The *institution*? There is no institution. I am their king, they should do as I say."

"What has happened, my lord?" she asks him.

For the first time he notices her there. He waves a hand airily at her. "Explain it to her, Mortimer."

He fixes those dark eyes on her, as a dog might appreciate his dinner. She does not mind his impertinence, anything in the way of attention will do right now. "The barons have demanded Lord Gaveston's banishment. They say he has misappropriated funds and has turned the king against his own advisers."

"What funds has he misappropriated?" Edward shouts. "Everything he has I have given him openly. If a king may not give gifts to those who serve him best, what are jewels and land for? They are mine to give, are they not? And yes, I listen to him before I listen to any of that crowd. He has my best interests at heart. They don't."

"Have all the barons signed this petition?" she asks Mortimer.

"Of those not here tonight only Lancaster still stands with us."

Isabella is surprised at this. That gargoyle is no friend of Gaveston, if his remarks about barrels and whores are to be believed.

"What does it mean?"

"It means the king should prepare for war," Lincoln says. He is vast, the Lord Lincoln, with his great belly and quivering jowls.

"It means these upstarts will defy their anointed king!" Edward shouts.

Mortimer is still; old Hugh says, "I am sure it will not come to that." Edward sees his dwarf and kicks him by way of venting his frustration. The jester hurries to the door and flees.

"Would it not be wise to listen to your barons?" she asks Edward.

The king stares at her in shock. "What are you doing here?"

"Your grace, I was here when you walked in."

He looks confused. He puts out a hand as if to block her from his vision.

Mortimer stares at her in surprise, she can see him thinking: *Look at this slip of a girl, she has an opinion!* There is a suspicion of a smile on his lips. She feels inordinately pleased with herself.

Mortimer turns back to the king. "Perhaps if you just give them what they wish for now," he says. "Let this blow over."

"He's right," old Hugh says. "It would not harm our cause to appear conciliatory."

"They would not argue with my father, they will not argue with me."

Mortimer and Lincoln exchange a look that clearly says, *Yes, but you are no Longshanks.*

"What is it that so offends them? If I love Gaveston, so should they."

This is too much for Lincoln. "Your grace, who a man loves is a private matter. I have nothing against wives or whores, but I should not like to see them at council meetings."

"Are you calling Perro a whore?"

A man clears his throat. Gaveston is sitting in a window seat, playing himself at chess. The sun comes out, and for a moment he glitters with gold. There are jewels on all his fingers. He gives them a slow smile. "I am still here, you know."

Lincoln waddles toward the king, lowers his voice. "This is what they mean. This conversation should best be kept private. Whenever we have things to discuss, he is always here."

"I can still hear you," Gaveston says, and checks his own black king with his white knight.

"Can this rebellion stand?" Edward asks old Hugh.

"What makes up a king's power, your grace? The loyalty of his barons, for they each bring their armies to every cause he fights. But if they are on the other side, then what armies does the king have?"

"Do you know how to bring down a wall?" Mortimer says.

"Fifty men and a battering ram," Edward says.

"There are subtler ways. Work a chisel into the mortar and work at it until you release one brick. When one brick is out, the wall is weakened. Soon you have a large hole. Then you do not even have to bring the wall down, you just walk through it."

"Your meaning?"

"For now we should stop running full tilt at the wall. Instead you should sidle up to it, examine each brick, and find the weakest. Then work at it, until you have it loose."

Edward nods. "Perhaps Lord Mortimer is right. I shall pander to their petty grievances for the time being. But there shall be a reckoning." He stares at the petition in his fist. "Institution indeed! There is no higher institution than the king himself!" He holds the parchment to the candle, waits until it is well aflame, then stamps on it with his boot. Afterward he grins as if he has solved the problems of the barons for good.

After they have all gone, Rosseletti appears from the shadows. Isabella's father has sent him to help her oversee her affairs and assist her with her correspondence.

In other words, he is Philippe's spy.

"You heard all that?" she asks him.

He nods, slowly.

"What shall I do?"

"England needs a strong king. Your father does not wish to see you married to a prince who cannot control his own kingdom."

"I just want to go home." She would like to throw herself on the floor and weep, if it would make any difference.

"Things will get better when this Gaveston is out of the country. Your position will improve."

"Do you think he will really send him away?"

"He has no choice, your majesty."

That night she stares at the Easter moon, haloed by high wispy clouds. She hugs her fur mantle close around her shoulders.

When she had imagined Camelot, she had not imagined this.

———

Later that day she is in the hall outside Edward's audience chamber. Mortimer is there, dressed in black velvet and lounging. He is here as Edward's trusted man, the one who has secured Ireland with an iron hand. His eyes unnerve her; they follow her without shame. He reminds her of her father, self-possessed and utterly unreadable. She is frightened of him.

"Your grace," he says and bows.

"My Lord Mortimer. Have you seen the king?"

"He is with my Lord Gaveston. They are walking in the garden."

She looks beyond his shoulder and sees them below, hand in hand, between the fish ponds, twittering like birds. She envies Edward that; there is no one she can talk to like that.

"Do you like him?"

"Who? The king?" A suspicion of a smile.

"My Lord Gaveston."

"He was my ward for some years, when he first came to England."

"This is why you support him against the barons?"

"No, I do it because I support the king. That is my duty."

"The other barons do not see it that way."

"They merely smell a weak king. It has nothing to do with what they believe."

"You think Edward is weak?"

"I think he has yet to prove his strength."

She smiles. *I wish you had been my prince,* she thinks, and it is as if he can read her mind, for he smiles at her. "Everyone thinks you're just a child, but they're wrong."

"And you are impertinent."

"I meant only that I think the king has found a great asset and does not know it yet."

She hears a shrill laugh from the garden and closes her eyes, trying to shut out the image of the two of them down there, cooing at each other.

"Don't underestimate Gaveston either. He's a good soldier."

"I don't underestimate him. I despise him!" To her horror she realizes she has just stamped her foot.

Mortimer pretends not to have seen.

"I am still trying to accustom myself to the politics here, who sides with whom."

"Everyone sides with themselves. That's how I remember it. Aside from that, I ask the hour and the day."

"So on this day and at this hour, why has Lancaster sided with the king?"

"Because when Gaveston goes, he is the highest nobleman in the land and the king's next adviser. This is his chance to get what he has always wanted. He will not stand with the other barons and lose his place in the king's affections." When she looks back at him, she is shocked to see him appraising her in a way to which she is quite unaccustomed. He quickly looks away again.

"You are going back to Ireland?"

"Soon."

"I wish you Godspeed." She picks up her skirts and leaves the room, her cheeks burning. He is an unbearable man. She will miss him.

Chapter 8

Edward keeps another menagerie at Langley, some other curious and disgusting animals from the Holy Land now shut up in pens and cages so that he and his friends can stare at them whenever they wish. There is a lion with a great mane of hair, as well as the most curious horse she has ever seen; it would be impossible to ride, she supposes, for it has a huge hump on its back. She thinks it is deformed, but Gaveston tells her that all its fellows are like this, and this is in fact a prime specimen.

How much does it cost to feed all these curiosities? No wonder the Treasury is empty.

The king is with the common sort again, watching some fellows muck out the yards. He wears just a tunic and breeches, no sign of a king here, but a fine figure of a man nonetheless. A boy says something to him and he laughs and grabs him in a headlock. They roll in the grass, laughing.

Really, is this seemly?

When he looks up and sees her there, he stops laughing and climbs reluctantly to his feet. He looks like a chastened little boy. *And here I am, just thirteen. He makes me feel old.*

"Don't look at me like that," he says to her.

"Like what? I don't know what you mean."

"It's like having my mother trail me about. Every time you appear, the sun goes away."

"Because I remember I am royal?"

"I find kingship a burden. It does no harm to laugh sometimes."

"It does much harm to do nothing else."

"You have that look about you. Can this wait?"

"Not really. You clearly have nothing better to do, your grace."

He looks sulky, leans on the fence. She watches the muscles ripple under his cambric shirt.

"My father raised two hundred thousand livres for this marriage. I have received no gifts from you, no estates. I do not even have the funds to run my own household."

"Listen to you. You're just a girl."

"I am my father's daughter. He raised me to be a queen."

"You are not old enough to be a queen."

"Yet I have been crowned in one of your churches. Have I not?"

He shakes his head. "It is already decided. You shall have Montreuil and Ponthieu. You don't have to be strident about it."

"And what of your friend, Gaveston?"

His manner transforms. He stands straight and glares at her. "He is my friend, and none of your concern."

"You cannot ignore this, Edward. It is clear your barons will not back down. You must listen to them and come to some concord with them, or they will make an arrangement of their own."

He stares at her, then shakes his head and laughs. "Listen to you. How old are you? And you see fit to lecture me about politics?"

"I know how these things work."

"How can you know?"

"From watching my father. Do not let them challenge you, husband. Head them off now until you have a stronger hand."

He frowns and leans on the rail again, peering at her as if he is seeing her for the first time. "Because you want Perro gone?"

"My duty is to you and your throne. I will not have you undermined."

The lion roars in its cage, and the echoes of its rage hang on the morning mist. The camel breaks into an alarmed trot, pursued by the farm boys, who are trying to feed it.

"You must sit down with them and hear their complaints."

"It is their duty to sit down and listen to mine."

"Yes, it is. But right now, you cannot force them to it."

He slaps the fence post with the flat of his hand. He shakes his head, confounded by her. Then he walks away. One of the boys makes a joke, and he ignores him.

Isabella tiptoes back through the mud. Another gown ruined.

———

She can see them from the window, arm in arm, heads together, laughing at some private joke. It is no secret that they share a bed. It is not that she wishes to have him in her own bed, not yet . . . the thought terrifies her.

She just doesn't want him in anyone else's.

What do they do together? She does not even know the secrets of a man and a woman, so she does not want to contemplate what joys he might find with another man.

The trouble is, she is lonely despite the large household that is assigned to her. Isabella de Vescy has taken her under her wing; and Edward's favorite niece, Eleanor le Despenser, is touchingly obsequious, when she is not busy being pregnant. There are others who come and go, attending her as family obligations allow, chiefly Lady Surrey (she must remember not to say anything about her husband for she will burst into tears; it seems he is a great lover of women as long as they are not his wife), and Lady Pembroke (do not talk about children in front of her; she is unable to have any).

She still has her old nurse, Théophania, which is a comfort, and a gaggle of others—she cannot remember all their names—of lesser birth.

She is sitting with her ladies, embroidering garments for the poor, a task that makes her want to fling herself into the moat even on her best days. Seeing Edward so intense with Lord Gaveston makes it impossible to concentrate. The other women have stopped their chatter and are staring at her.

She flings aside her handiwork and leaves them sitting there, walks to the end of the passage, finds something of interest in two pigeons nestled on a branch.

She hears the rustle of skirts and draws herself up straighter. She does not want them pitying her.

"Do not let it disturb you, your grace."

It is Lady Mortimer. Isabella does not turn around, afraid that her face may betray her. "They are very familiar."

"They have been friends since boyhood."

"It is more than that, isn't it?"

"Whatever could you mean?"

"You all treat me as a child, and in years I suppose that I am. But you forget whose daughter I am."

"You are very young to be thrust into such a position."

"The barons think he is too familiar with Gaveston, Lady Mortimer."

"This is not your concern, your grace."

"Anything that concerns my husband concerns me." She turns around and fixes her with a stare. *I shall be patronized no longer.* "The barons want this man gone, and Edward has appealed to the pope to intervene on his behalf. Is this not so?"

Lady Mortimer lowers her eyes.

"Do you miss your husband?"

The question catches Lady Mortimer off guard. "Miss him?"

"Lord Mortimer, yes. He has been sent to Ireland, I believe. Do you miss him?"

"Yes, your grace."

"And when he is home, does he consort with other men, as Edward does?"

"He has many friends."

"Friends like my Lord Gaveston?"

There is a twitch in her cheek. Is she hiding a smirk?

"It will be different for you, for all of us, when he is gone."

"Perhaps," she says, and returns her gaze to the window. The pigeons have flown away to nest elsewhere. They do not like being stared at, it seems.

Edward and Gaveston come into view, walking arm in arm. Edward kisses his friend since boyhood on the cheek. *I should like someone to look at me as tenderly as that,* Isabella thinks. She is no longer disgusted, just jealous.

One day I will make him love me like that.

See if I don't.

Chapter 9

Every night, two of her demoiselles sleep at the foot of her bed in trundle beds that are stored beneath her own. They are in their nightgowns and are combing out her hair when they hear Edward's voice in the antechamber.

Isabella panics. He has not been in her bedchamber since that first night in Boulogne. She sends them scurrying from the room and jumps into the vast four-poster bed. She brings the covers up to her chin and lies rigidly, staring at the ceiling, as if recently buried. Her heart is beating too fast.

I am not ready for this. Her hands clench into fists. She takes a deep breath and waits.

Will it hurt very much?

The metal rings that hold the leather curtain over the door rasp as he pulls it aside.

Her beautiful husband stands in the doorway, flushed and harried. He barely looks at her. He strides across the room and kicks the logs in the grate, puts both hands on the hearth, and stares into the flames.

"I need your help."

"Edward?"

"I have asked nothing of you until now. I can't stop thinking of you as an eight-year-old. That's how old you were when we were betrothed. Do you remember?"

She nods her head.

"You're still just a child in many ways, but you seem to see things clearly enough. Well, all right then, let's see."

"You want my help?"

"I know you don't think much of Perro, but this is important to me, no matter what you think."

She had always thought that being a queen would be easier than this; she does not mind being asked for her counsel, she welcomes it, but she never expected that he would barge into her chamber as she was readying herself for bed, and then bark out the first thing that came into his head.

She stares at the ceiling. He looks at the hearth.

"They want to send Perro away. Exile him! They all stand against me on this. It will be war if I don't."

She wants to say: Well then, do it. It's not worth going to war over, is it? Write down a list of the names of everyone who has stood against you and memorize it while you are building your own power. Then one day, when you are all sharing a cup of wine and smiling at each other, have them all thrown into a dungeon and keep them there until they grovel or their bones rot.

That's what my father would do.

"I am their king! How dare they! I choose who will be at my hand!"

"You are king while you behave as their king," she murmurs.

"What was that?"

"You must come to an accord."

"The accord is this: I am their king, by God and by law. I want you to help me."

"How?"

"Talk to your father. I know you have your spies here. Don't look so surprised. They carry letters between you once a week, do they not? Well, now I wish you to write a letter for me. Tell him I need him to stand with me on this. If the barons know I have his support, they will run back to their bogs in the marches and remember their place."

"They are nobles, your grace. No one can teach any of them their place."

"How would you know? You're twelve!" He turns from the hearth and glares at her.

"I have thirteen years now, and I know this from observing my father's court and yours."

"Will you help me or no?"

"I will ask him, your grace. But my father will not commit his wealth or his army to an English war."

"Tell him that these ingrates threaten my throne. It is your throne too, so he must come to know the importance of this."

"I will serve you as best I can."

He looks satisfied with this. "Your grace," he says and leaves the bedchamber.

She throws back the linen sheet and lets out a breath. Well. She wonders what her father will do when he hears of this.

He does exactly as she thinks he will do; he says it is none of his affair, that the king of France cannot be seen to meddle in the affairs of England.

———

At Langley they are set for a beautiful summer; the woods are full of honeysuckle, the breezes bring with them the scent of fresh-cut grasses. There are daisies with fragile white petals ready to be plucked: *He loves me, he loves me not.*

The hawthorn is in blossom in the hedgerows when the king finally comes to his senses. Old Hugh agrees with the king that the barons should one day face censure by God, if not the law, but it is Lord Lincoln who keeps Edward from a civil war that he cannot win.

The king decides to come to an accord.

He makes Gaveston Lieutenant of Ireland. It is like exile, but with honor. He travels with him to Bristol. It takes three days to load the ships; Gaveston has a vast household with chamberlains, confessors, clerks, falconers, archers—he even takes old Mathilda the washerwoman.

Just who is queen of this country?

———————

The summer had promised so much; but for three days, ever since her king has returned from Bristol, it has rained. The middle of the afternoon and it is as gloomy as midwinter. She hears a bell ringing for nones. Edward, the whole great length of him, is sprawled on a throne under a mural of knights in gold and vermilion riding to a tournament.

He has sent his servants away, all the lickspittles and cupbearers, the dwarves and lute players, all the whisperers and flatterers, all banished so that he might sit here and stare at the shields lining the vast hall, watch the shadows creep across the chamber and mope.

Her footsteps echo on the flagstones, and the shutting of the oak door behind her sounds as if they have dropped the drawbridge without its chains.

He does not move. She believes he is crying, but in the shadows it is hard to tell.

The only time she has seen grief like this was when her mother died. On that occasion her father did not eat for almost a week. But that was his queen; this is Gaveston.

"Well, you have what you wanted," he says finally.

"I did not want this, your grace. Your Lords Warwick and Hereford wanted it."

"The archbishop, Winchelsea, says he will excommunicate him if he comes back. Why do they hate me so?"

"It is not you they hate, or even Gaveston. They just wish you to be their king."

"But I am their king! How can I be otherwise?"

"A king has obligations."

"No! I have no obligations! It is they who have obligations—to me!" For hours he has not moved, but now, suddenly, he is animated. Rage sends him bounding from his seat. "They have obligations to me!" Every word staccato.

She lowers her eyes. He frightens her when he is like this.

He stands over her, breathing hard. "You're like this evil little doll. Everywhere I go, there you are. Look at you. A breath of wind will knock you over, but you come in here when no one else even dares peek through the door."

"I wish only to help you."

"You're just a girl. How can you help me?"

"You were ready to ask my help from France."

"And what good did that do me?"

"My counsel may be of more use to you than all my father's bluster and threats."

"So you tell me."

She ventures to put her arms around him, pats him on the back, and murmurs, "It's for the best. You and I, we might start anew from now."

But it is as if he has not heard her. He stares into an impossible future, one with just him and Gaveston in it. "I am sick of all these demands, listening to all this endless moaning and whining. Everyone wants something from me. I sometimes think Perro and

I might find a snug house in the hills and plant vegetables in the sun and drink wine and live out a peaceful life."

Did he really say that? "Edward, that can never be."

He sinks to his knees. He makes a sound like a dog choking on a bone and covers his face. "I cannot live without him." And then he wails and curls on the floor. She watches him, wishing she were not here. She cannot run from the room, but having to watch this horrifies her. She wants to pull him to his feet, but even touching him is something she cannot bear to do at this moment.

Finally he stops, exhausted. He looks up at her, his face wet, and seems surprised to find her still there. "Just leave me."

"You must turn the tables on Warwick and the others. You must be more discreet and more cunning in your ways. And you must subdue the Scots."

"What has this to do with what I have lost?"

"Everything," she says and sweeps from the room. It seems so clear to her.

At least she knows now how she will make him love her.

Chapter 10

My dread and very dear Majesty,

I commend myself humbly. My situation here in England these days is much improved. Edward has become most attentive since my Lord Gaveston has left these shores for Ireland, and requires me in his presence constantly. I believe it may be that before he thought me too young to be his helpmate and confidante, and all that was required was the opportunity for him to see my worth to him.

It seems that my Lord Gaveston has excelled himself with some honor in his new post in Ireland, and my grace the King hopes that one day he shall be allowed to return, but that day seems very far away in England's present mood. I believe that by the time he does return, I shall be well established at Edward's right hand. He tells me daily how much he appreciates my good counsel, though I am yet green in many matters of state. He treats me with great kindness of late, and has awarded me many estates with which to finance my household.

I trust this finds you well. I remain your faithful daughter.

May the Holy Spirit keep you always.

Given this day at Windsor.

Isabella

———————

Empty fields and woodlands stretch far into the distance. The river snakes grease gray through Edward's rebellious countryside. Her ladies' gossip grates on her nerves: who has eyes for whom, children, petty scandals.

She has left the king sitting at a table with piles of paper before him and clerks at his elbow, her uncle Lancaster berating him for spending too much money. The king had looked like he wanted to leap out of the window to escape. It had reminded her of a father reproving a child for eating too many sweetmeats. But the child was not listening. The child was looking out of the window, thinking about his lover.

On cue, she hears the sound of children laughing. She looks into the garden below and sees Mortimer with his broodmare and his brood. He lifts one of his little girls in the air and makes her laugh. Isabella feels a pang.

An unworthy thought invades upon her: *He would make a fine husband, wouldn't he?* He is strong to sire, ruthless to war, calculates seamlessly, and has no fancy friends.

She hears him running up the stairs and composes herself.

He seems disconcerted to see her. Her ladies twitter. She wonders if he has bulled any of them, and if Lady Mortimer knows of it. It seems likely.

"I was looking for the king," he says.

"His grace is with the Earl of Lancaster," she says and inclines her head along the passage to the great hall. Her ladies have stopped their twittering and are staring at them. She walks away from them, out of earshot. He considers a moment and follows her.

She can feel their eyes on her.

She lowers her voice. "I hear you are to go to Ireland."

"To assist my Lord Gaveston, yes."

"Does he need your assistance? I have heard he has become the hammer of the Irish. If he is not putting down revolts in Munster, he is terrorizing the Wicklow Mountains. As accomplished as you are, my lord, I wonder why the king is dispatching you."

"It is not for me to question the decisions of the mighty."

If a French courtier spoke to her like that, she would clout him. "Is he coming back to England?"

"That is impossible. He risks excommunication from Archbishop Winchelsea."

"Nothing is impossible. My uncle Lancaster believes that he is scheming for such a return."

"You believe everything Lancaster says?"

"He's my uncle."

"He's no one's uncle."

She smiles at that. He says these things without changing his expression, and it takes her off guard. For some reason she imagines him kissing her the way he just kissed Lady Mortimer. Her new husband has not kissed her that way yet.

There is something in the way he looks at her. She likes it, though she would think it insolent if he were not Mortimer.

"May I speak plainly? I hear so many rumors. I need someone to tell me the truth."

"The truth, your grace? A dangerous thing. I should hesitate to be caught telling the truth anywhere within a king's palace."

"I hear that he has bribed the Earl of Gloucester to support Gaveston's return, that Hereford and Lincoln have likewise been paid off with promises. If he wins over my Lord Warwick as well, the rest will follow like sheep."

"For one so young, you have an uncanny grasp. My own daughter is your age and concerns herself chiefly with sewing."

"Your daughter is not the queen of England. One grows up very fast."

"Even if Gaveston should return, you have no reason to fear him. The king is seen with you everywhere now."

"Do you think so?"

"Edward is a complex man. But I think you have his measure." He spares an apprehensive glance at the gaggle of women in the hall. He tugs at the neck of his tunic as if he were being strangled.

She dismisses him with a nod. He seems taken aback by this. She is half his age and half his size.

He bows and goes in search of his king, and she returns to her ladies. So it is true, Edward is agitating for his lover's return, just as she and Edward had at last begun to act like king and queen. They had taken a pace forward, and now Edward has taken two steps back. What is wrong with the man? Even from Ireland, Gaveston pulls the puppet strings. Mortimer is going to Ireland because the king knows Gaveston is coming back and he needs a strong soldier to replace him.

Why will he not tell her this himself?

Does he think that she is stupid?

Chapter 11

The king is jaunty. He lopes into the chamber, trailing minions like froth off a galloping horse. All he wishes to talk about is the banquet they have hosted to woo his recalcitrant magnates. He wages this campaign like a war, throwing largesse at his barons like heavy cavalry.

"You made an impression," he tells her. "Your presence at the banquet was a great success! Richmond says you are the most charming dinner companion he has ever kept. Gloucester calls you the greatest gem in my crown. Who would have thought?"

"Your grace?"

She is genuinely puzzled by this pronouncement. *Who would have thought—what?*

"Well, you are so young. So . . ."—he waves a hand airily—". . . thin."

"In France they say I am beautiful."

"Well you are quite pretty." He smiles broadly. "I am proud of you."

Thin and pretty. *You will hunger for me one day, Edward. You will burn for me.*

"We have concord again in England."

"There is still Warwick. And my uncle Lancaster."

"Lancaster," he says and frowns as if he has bitten down on something foul. Something moves in the rushes underfoot, and he stamps on it. "Your uncle was with me once. Now that Perro is gone, he has turned on me."

Well, of course he has. Is it not obvious to you? She is disturbed that she can understand these petty maneuvers, and he cannot.

"You have heard that I have ordered the arrest of a dozen more Templars?"

"My father will be pleased to hear it. So will the Holy Father in Rome."

"You will write to your father again? I would value his support."

"Your grace, however it pleases you. But do you think it wise to bring my Lord Gaveston back so soon? You are just winning the barons back to your side."

"They should never have left it. I am their king!"

"But we have worked so hard to court them. We should strengthen the bonds before we test them."

The room turns dark as the sun slips behind a cloud; the king's good mood evaporates. "I cannot live without him, Isabella. You don't understand."

She feels this like a slap. She draws herself up, composing herself. "Is Gaveston to return then?"

"It will be different this time, Isabella. He will be more circumspect. You have nothing to fear from him. You are my queen. When you grow up, you will understand."

He hurtles from the room, all energy; he wishes to hunt and calls for his falconer and his grooms and his dogs. *"When you grow up, you will understand."*

I know there is much to understand about men and women. But I already know this much: that I will not rest until you love this thin, pretty girl as much as you love Gaveston.

———————

"He says it will be different this time," she tells Rosseletti. "He gives his word."

Her spy stares at the floor. He looks gloomy.

"I have been at his side constantly these last nine months. Things have changed between us, I am sure of it."

"He has written to His Holiness in Rome, asking for the threat of excommunication to be lifted. It is all that is keeping him from bringing this Gaveston back from Ireland today."

"Let him come. He is no longer a threat to me."

"But he is a threat to the king. The barons will not abide him any better now than they did before. Will he not learn?"

"He wishes my father to support him in this."

"Your father will not be drawn into a civil war in England; he has problems enough of his own. He wishes only that Edward keep his own house in order."

"And meanwhile he lets Edward arrest the Templars and make more concessions in Gascony."

Rosseletti shrugs. "Edward offers to do these things. Your father is of no mind to make him relent. Having Edward malleable suits his purpose well enough. But if your king thinks your father will intercede with his barons, he is quite misled."

"What shall I do?"

"Only what you are doing now. Be patient, Isabella. Your time will come."

His sad gray eyes meet hers for a moment, then look away. They both can see what will happen; everyone but Edward can see it.

In the spring, Parliament meets at Westminster and refuses his request to bring Gaveston back to England. Archbishop Winchelsea repeats his threat of excommunication. She thinks Edward will be furious, but he returns from the Parliament quite calm.

They remove to Kennington Palace, on the other side of the river, and she is there that day in June when two emissaries from the pope arrive. He meets them behind closed doors, and she does not know what is said. But she is present the next day when he reads the pope's bull to the assembled barons and bishops of the Parliament. The Holy Father has overruled Winchelsea.

The archbishop is humiliated. He listens white lipped and leaves without a word.

The barons know they have been bested. Some of them look at Isabella and wonder if she has had a hand in this. They give her too much credit. She does not want the barons to hold sway over her husband and king, but neither does she want Gaveston back in England.

Edward has outmaneuvered them all. He is more adept at this game than any of them believed.

———

They remove to York, that cold and godless place, where not even the devil could get warm. A fire burns in the central hearth, but they might as well be standing naked on the moors for all the warmth that comes from it. A moan of wind raises the rushes on the floor.

It is All Souls' Night, and to celebrate, Edward has brought in some minstrels from Aquitaine. They play lutes and sing about love and chivalry, all those things that once seemed so important to her.

She does not see Gaveston sidle up to her until he is there at her elbow. He is quite beautiful to look at—it is disconcerting. He is dressed all in white, a lascivious angel with a scarlet belt low on his snake hips and rubies glinting on his fingers. "So, your grace, you would like to hate me, would you not?"

"I bear you no ill will."

"But we both love the same man," he whispers.

"I am queen."

"And so you ever shall be. He only ever speaks of you in glowing terms." She does not like the look on his face. She does not want his sympathy.

"I do not understand why you have come back. The barons are united against you."

"Not quite united. Just Warwick and that old hog Lancaster. Burstbelly does not like me, but even he would not stand against the king."

"My Lord Lincoln should not like to hear you call him that name."

"I am sure he speaks highly of me also."

"Could you not provoke them so? It only incites them to further hatred. Our peace is a fragile thing, and my grace has done much to mend things with them. As have I."

"I appreciate your efforts on my behalf, even as I find them surprising."

"You find me unpredictable?"

He smiles. "You are not quite the spoiled little brat that people say you are."

"You mean Edward?"

"Edward is terrified of you."

"Now you are making fun of me."

He squeezes her hand. There is nothing in it; it is like something one of her uncles would do. Yet this sudden familiarity shocks her. "We should be allies, you and I."

"How so?"

"We understand better than most that beauty is a curse."

A flurry of rain comes through the chimney, spattering the fire, which sizzles and smokes. The musicians in the gallery lay down their lutes as the room is prepared for the banquet. Pages with silver ewers file in to wash the company's hands, a chaplain says the grace. The *nef*, a golden ship studded with jewels and containing expensive spices, is announced by the herald's fanfare.

Isabella is impatient to know more about why Gaveston thinks them so alike, but first the squires must carve the meats and bring silver plates for dining. It is only below the salt that they use trenchers.

Finally she has her chance to interrogate him further. All innocence, he pretends not to remember what he has said. She almost shouts it at him: "You think me beautiful?"

"The whole world says it. I find no reason to disagree."

"Edward does not think me beautiful."

"He thinks you are nothing else."

She feels her cheeks burn. How dare he?

"Do not take offence, your grace. I understand your predicament."

"Predicament?"

"His barons think the same of me, Joseph the Jew and the rest."

"The Lord Pembroke knows you call him that. You should guard your tongue more."

He shrugs. "Why should I when they speak of me as if I am one of the Devil's minions? I despise them. Do you think they shall ever like me any better, no matter what I do? Would you have me fawn to them?"

"I am just a girl, Lord Gaveston, but my father has coached me a little in these matters, and he taught me not to break any peace unless you are also sure of winning the war."

"Edward is king, not Lancaster, and not that dog Warwick."

"I agree with you. But kings have lost their kingship before now, and Edward risks much for you."

The war in him is written plain on his face. "Do you know what it is like to love? How can you, you're just a girl. You are given to this man you do not know and then you are asked to make the best of it. But you do not know *love*." This spoken so fiercely that she shrinks from him. He is right: she has never loved like that. By now the smile has dropped away, and he fixes her with a stare of withering intensity. "Do you know what it is to have someone who understands your very soul? This love your minstrels sing of, must it always be a knight and a lady? Who made this law? Was it God? Then God is a trickster, for there is no one else will do for me."

Gaveston says all this without pausing for breath. The king looks querulously in their direction. Isabella has never seen Gaveston like this, has only ever seen him in his usual guise, with the knowing smirk and the lofty tilt of the head.

He realizes he has said too much. He turns away, murmurs something to Edward to make him laugh. Edward claps his hands for his dwarves and his tumblers.

That night she slips down the stairs from her bedchamber and leans against the cold stone, watches their shadows on the walls as they sit by the fire drinking spiced wine. The last thing she sees is the silhouette of a kiss.

The next day Edward summons a Parliament, but Lancaster and Burstbelly—she smiles at Gaveston's description of Lincoln— and the other magnates refuse to attend because Gaveston is there. And then there is the Earl of Pembroke. He looks like a walking cadaver, but Mortimer calls him the only principled man in England. Edward listens to him, sometimes.

He tells the king that it is only Lincoln that keeps them all from civil war. *Are things really this bad?* It seems they are. Lancaster and Warwick would go to war against Edward, but they listen to Lincoln, who yet pleads moderation.

She and Edward spend the Christmastide at Langley.

One night Edward and Gaveston do not return from a hunt. She takes squires and rides out, wrapped in furs, to search for him by a rising moon. The frost glistens and wolves howl. She finds him in a glade in Langley Woods, dancing around a fire with people from the village, celebrating the old Yule. One of the women of the village is dressed as the Green Man in a verdant robe with a garland of berries. As the moon rises cold over the trees, she sees Edward and Gaveston kneel before her, as people did in the days of the old religion.

They have not seen her approach, and she rides away. Later, her discovery sends her hurrying to the chapel. What has she married? Is he utterly godless?

Before, he had been at her side constantly; now, she hardly sees him at all. He had promised her that things would be different, but already they were just the same as before.

Chapter 12

He is watching some of his lads break a horse. She picks him out because he is taller than the others by half a head, otherwise no one might know him for the king. The way he is dressed, he might be a smithy or a carpenter.

One of the boys stands on the saddle and pulls a fool's face. He falls off and makes them all laugh. Edward sends one of his lackeys to give him a sovereign.

They cheer and huddle around. Look how they love him. He has an easy charm with stable boys, at least. He glances in her direction, and she sees him sigh.

He turns and lopes toward her through the mud. "Your grace. A fine morning. Chill, but blue skies always lift the spirits."

"I did not expect to find you here."

"You think I should be at court worrying over Lancaster and Warwick? They are wearisome men, are they not?"

"What are you doing here, Edward? You are facing revolt. You know what they say about you. You are accused of keeping evil counsel—"

"They cannot be talking about Perro—"

"—that you have lost Scotland, and that the country's chief enemy lurks in your chamber. Their words."

"If they want war with me, they shall have it."

Her horse nickers and tosses its head. She brings him under control with a sharp tug of the reins and a dig of her heels. She wishes sometimes that Edward were a horse.

"Isn't this what you want? If they have their way, you won't have to worry about Gaveston anymore."

"I do not want to see them take your power. You are the king above all else."

"There is nothing to be done. I know what they want, and they shall not have it."

"You will not forestall them by laughing with stable boys."

"What else would you have me do? I have asked your father for his support, and he sends me letters full of puffery and little else. Perhaps you might shift him."

"*You* are king here, not my father."

"Just so. Then you should go back to your dolls and leave such matters to men."

"I am fifteen years old, and you will stop treating me as a child." She stares right into his eyes. "Besides, do I look to you like I have ever *in my life* played with a doll?"

He stares back. Then he throws back his head and laughs. "No, you do not, your grace." He bows, and she turns her horse's head.

As she is about to ride away, he calls to her. He pulls himself up in the saddle and kisses her. "I love your temper," he says, and runs back to the horse yard. The boys cheer him. For all that he infuriates her, she loves him too.

———

But he loves no one as he loves Gaveston. He is even prepared to go
to war for him. The more the barons defy him, the more he goads
them by giving his Perro gifts of land and titles and jewels.

The barons make their move. She hears about it first from one
of her ladies: old Hugh's daughter-in-law, Eleanor. Her brother is
the Earl of Gloucester, and he has told her that he is thinking of
adding his name to a piece of paper called the Ordinances.

They wish to castrate their king, not with knives but with
rules and restrictions. A select council of twenty-one has been
appointed to tell the king what he may or may not do. They say it is
to uphold the Magna Carta, right the general wrongs of the realm,
and "reform abuses within the royal household."

Isabella goes in search of Edward, but instead she finds
Gaveston, sitting alone in the great hall, warming his boots by the
fire and drinking spiced mead. He looks splendid on such a gray
day, in a tunic of blue velvet trimmed with silk thread and pearls,
one of his men rubbing his feet.

"Your grace," he murmurs and jumps to his feet.

"Where is Edward?"

"He is hunting. There is a great stag in the forest, and one of
his sheriffs saw it near the lake this morning." He sips his mead. "I
see from your face that you have heard about the new Ordinances."

"How dare they?"

"They are concerned for the welfare of England. So they say."

"Is my uncle a party to this?"

"All of them, even Richmond, and he would love Edward even
if he were Beelzebub. They say they cannot keep faith with a king
who does not keep faith with them."

"You have brought him to this!"

"How so?"

"He does all this for you. Why don't you leave him be?"

"I could as soon leave him as he could leave me."

"But if it were not for you, they would not challenge him."

"You really think things would be different if there were no Piers Gaveston?" He replaces his velvet slippers and sends his man off with a coin for his troubles. After he has gone, he says: "Do you hate me also, Isabella?"

"I do not understand why he would risk everything for you."

"If he did as much for you, his queen, would you not think him the bravest king in the world? Would the whole world not applaud him for it? But he does it for me, and they call him weak and a fool."

"Because you are not his queen."

"I am his best friend."

"So you say."

"I am the only one who understands him. Do you know that?"

The words haunt her for months. Edward and Gaveston ignore the council and instead take their army into Scotland to bring the Bruce to heel and the barons back to their side. Such army as it is, for only Gloucester, Richmond, and Surrey show up, while the rest stay home. Bruce chooses not to fight, and retires into the highlands, destroying crops and taking his livestock with him. Edward's army starves and has to retreat.

Isabella is summoned to Berwick to spend the long winter with her king and the only man who understands him.

Chapter 13

Her demoiselles have been banished for the night. Edward has informed her just that afternoon that he will visit her bedchamber tonight. This is the moment she has hoped for and dreaded, and she is as nervous as any new maid would be. She perspires, though it is midwinter. All that day she cannot catch her breath.

She wants to ask Isabella de Vescy what she should do, but she cannot find the nerve. She supposes it is like going to your own execution, that same dread and nervous exhaustion. You can only hope the hangman knows what he is about.

A single candle burns at the end of the bed. The door inches open, and Edward pulls back the furs and climbs into the bed beside her. She watches him remove his nightshirt and is suddenly hungered by the smooth bands of muscle and the leanness of him. He is beautiful.

She lies there and waits. He kisses her forehead and cheek, and she feels his hand touch her breast through her nightdress.

Outlandish thoughts tumble through her mind; she remembers seeing two horses do this. She had wondered at the length of the stallion. Will Edward be as mighty? Has a woman ever died during a coupling?

She likes him kissing her like this. She likes looking at him, and the warmth of his body. She hesitates, then puts a hand on his arm, then his shoulder.

He kisses her on the lips. She kisses him back, unsure if this is how it is done. His hand moves to her belly. A thought: *What does he do with Gaveston?*

Does he do this?

He pulls up her nightdress, forces her thighs apart. She is too terrified to move. He kisses her again. She wants to tell him he is beautiful, but she dares not. He rolls on top of her, kisses her neck, and squeezes her breast.

His weight crushes her. She braces herself. But then he rolls off, gathers up his nightshirt, and goes out.

The door opens again. He leans over her, kisses her once more, and whispers that he is sorry, and it is not her fault.

Then he goes out, slamming the door so hard, it extinguishes the candle.

———————

He is gloomy by the fire the next morning. He dips his bread in his wine and tears at it with his teeth. Gaveston makes space for her. He calls for a servant to bring her wine.

At first she thinks Edward is in bad spirits because of her.

"There is bad news from London," Gaveston tells her. "Burstbelly died two nights ago, in Holborn."

"The Earl of Lincoln is dead?"

"He was the last one who stood for me against the barons. As his son-in-law, Lancaster now inherits all his lands, and with those estates comes the largest standing army in the realm. Your uncle is now the most powerful man in England, next to me."

They stare at the fire. A log burns through and flares briefly, crumbling into the grate.

Gaveston drains his cup and goes out.

"If he loved you, he would leave you," she says.

"He loves me and that is why he will not leave me."

"Does he mean more to you than your throne?"

"He means more to me than anything."

She shivers inside her mantle. The morning is colder than any morning she remembers. She feels like crying, but she will give no one in the world that satisfaction.

One day he will say that about me: she means more to me than anything. *For now I am still a girl, but when I am a woman, I will change his mind.*

"I do not understand you, your grace."

He shakes his head. "I doubt you ever shall. But that is not your fault," he adds, for the second time that day, and they lapse into gloomy silence.

Chapter 14

A boar has gone to ground somewhere in a thicket. As they wait for the hounds to flush him out, she walks her horse beside Gaveston. He smiles when he sees her at his shoulder. He has a brilliant smile, though the barons have never seen it.

The wind burns her cheeks.

"You cannot hope to win. Why do you fight them?"

"What else is there to do?"

"They will kill you if they can."

"Would that make you sorry?"

"Yes and no."

He laughs at that. "I understand why you would say no. But why yes?"

"I don't know."

The dogs are howling, but they cannot see them. They are closing in on their quarry down there in the brambles. When they flush him out, Edward will take him first. The boar has no chance, there are too many of them, and they have him trapped.

"We fight for every moment, even when we are doomed," Gaveston says, and at that moment the boar appears, and the king's arrow takes him in the throat. Four more bolts thud into him, and he goes down. He dies, belly heaving.

———————

The king waits until summer to go down to London and meet his tormentors in the Parliament. She joins him later.

It is a long journey, and she has endured a week of bumping along in the back of her horse-drawn charet with her ladies. But when she arrives, Edward is not there to greet her. He is busy with more important affairs.

But Rosseletti is there. She meets with him privately, and he tells her all that others will not. The barons have presented Edward with a list of forty-one ordinances; if they have their way, Edward will not be allowed to grant land, go to war, or even leave the realm without their consent. His bankers, the Frescobaldi, have been ruined and banished, thus cutting off his source of private funding.

"What does this mean for me?" Isabella asks him.

"Your fortunes are tied to his, and his prospects are fraught unless he bring his barons to heel. But unless he sends Gaveston away, they will continue their defiance of him."

"Because he favors him or because he loves him?"

He blushes at the queen's forthrightness. "That is not for me to say, your grace."

She speaks to the servants, who say the king is much changed. He spends all his time gambling and drinking. He is in a fury most days. He beat one of the stable boys who was slow to fetch his saddle. It is not like Edward.

That evening he storms into her quarters and sends the servants scurrying out. He reaches into his tunic and pulls out a crumpled parchment. He thrusts it at her, without greeting.

"You have heard what they have done?"

She takes the document and glances at it. *The king must not, the king must not . . .* The list of prohibitions is endless.

"Forty-one clauses in all. They say I should live more wisely and avoid oppression of the people. Oppression of the people! Which people, Isabella?" She smells wine on his breath, and his eyes are unnaturally bright. "They restrict my right to issue pardons. All royal incomes to be paid directly to the Exchequer." He leans in. "Read ordinance twenty."

She does as he tells her to do. *"Because Piers Gaveston has misled and ill-advised our lord the king, and enticed him to do evil in various deceitful ways . . ."* She pauses and looks at Edward, who is pacing the hall like a hungry lion. *"—that he be exiled, for all time and without hope of return, as a public enemy of the king and his people."*

"Public enemy! They say he led me to hostile lands—Scotland— where *they* urged me to go! That he put the king in danger—is a king not meant to lead his armies? And that he must be gone from England, Scotland, Ireland, and Wales by November. There is scarce a kingdom they do not exclude from their prohibition. I doubt there is a place left in the known world where Perro may now safely abide."

What can she say to him? Did he not anticipate this?

"Before you celebrate his destruction, note that your good uncle has seen fit to attack you as well. He wants one of your ladies banished."

"Who?"

"Isabella de Vescy."

"But why?"

"Because she's French."

"She was born in England!"

"Not good enough for Uncle Lancaster. She and her brother are back to Yorkshire and the sheep."

"What can you do?"

"What might I do? If I do not sign it, they will make war on me, and who will stand for me then? Old Hugh le Despenser is the only one who has not abandoned me."

"If today brings no hope, we should plan for tomorrow."

"I cannot plan for tomorrow unless I give up Perro. And without Perro what use is tomorrow to me?"

And then, unexpectedly, he throws himself at her feet and buries his head in her lap. She strokes his hair while he weeps. She does not know whether she should feel pleased or horrified. Not far past her sixteenth birthday and already she feels as weary as a crone.

———

The Ordinances are publicly proclaimed on the twenty-seventh day of September in Saint Paul's churchyard, and Archbishop Winchelsea announces that anyone who dares violate them will be excommunicated from the Church.

Gaveston leaves shortly after All Saints' Day for the Brabant, where Edward's sister Margaret is married to the duke. They have agreed to give him refuge. For weeks Edward is inconsolable.

But one morning his mood lifts. He appears at court with a jaunty air, and even greets Isabella with a smile. She goes at once in search of Rosseletti to discover what mischief the king has been up to now.

"Gaveston is back in England," he says.

"Here? In England? How could he be so stupid?" Gaveston has been gone scarcely a month. A month!

"He was sighted first at Tintagel, then at Wallingford. He has come with Edward's full knowledge and consent. The barons have knowledge of it now and have ordered a search."

Isabella stands up, gathering her skirts. "Where is Edward?"

"It would not be wise to offend the king," he tells her.

"Really, Rosseletti," she murmurs, though she is ready to burst. "Have you ever known me to lose control of myself?"

"No, your grace."

"Nor shall I, then," she says and sweeps from the room.

———

The king retreats to Windsor for the Christmas season. His high spirits are now explained. She smiles and says nothing.

There are biblical murals in her apartments: one depicts the parable of the wise and foolish virgins, which seems a cruel joke. *I have been ready for my bridegroom for a long time,* she thinks. That night he asks her to leave a candle burning in her bedchamber, and sometime after the bells have rung for compline, the door creaks open, and he slips in. This time she wraps her arms around him in a tight embrace, determined to do more than just lie there, wishing for something more.

———

Gaveston has a wife, Margaret. She is the younger sister of one of her other ladies, Eleanor, and is barely older than Isabella herself. Her first baby is not long to be born, so her husband has clearly not spent every night in the king's chamber. Isabella feels a kinship with her, because of their unique situation, but she is not easily drawn into conversation.

But one morning, as she is combing out her hair, Margaret bends to whisper in her ear: "The king came to your bed last night," she murmurs.

"How did you know?"

"The servants gossip about everything. If you sneeze in the upper ward of the castle, by the time you come down to the great hall someone has fetched herbs and warm honey."

"There was blood on the sheet this morning. I expect all England will know by Christmas Day that I am no longer a maiden."

"Did it hurt you?" Margaret asks.

"It hurt a little. But he was gentle."

"You are disappointed?"

"I thought there should be more than discomfort to my wedding night, if that was what it was," Isabella says.

Margaret bites her lip, and Isabella senses that she would like to say more. She has already uttered more words this morning than in the past three years. "What is it like . . . for you?"

"Piers is a kind man and a good husband, for all that they say about him." Margaret puts a hand on Isabella's arm. "Don't expect more from them than they can give, it will only make you unhappy. At least he does not bull every servant girl in the castle like . . ."

"You were about to say 'like your uncle Lancaster.'"

"Forgive me. But I think that would be worse."

There is a commotion at the gate. They go to the window and look down on the cobbled yard. It is Gaveston, returned from his exile. He wears a red cloak with a gold clasp, and a jaunty red hat with an emerald jewel winking in the sun. He looks dapper even as an outlaw.

He leaps down from his horse into the embrace of his king. They laugh and walk arm in arm back into the great hall, the king calling for spiced wine and beef.

Margaret squeezes her arm. "I only ever see him smile like that when he is with Edward," she says.

Later, she sees them sitting together, staring at the Yule log smoldering among its bed of holly, Gaveston on the carpets leaning against his king's thigh. Margaret is right. It is the only time Edward ever looks content. The wolfhounds are curled around them, all legs and yawning and snoring. The king bends to kiss Gaveston's head.

Everyone is secure in their affections except the queen. She might stand under the kissing branch of the mistletoe and its bright red berries all Christmas Eve and not draw a single glance from dog or man.

Chapter 15

Edward avoids her bed and her person after Gaveston arrives at Windsor. Perhaps he anticipates her petulance.

It is more than petulance, and he cannot avoid her forever.

She finds him sitting in his bathtub. A servant is scrubbing him with rosewater as he sweats in the steam. Gaveston is sitting at the window, watching. Edward's back is toward her, but Gaveston makes a face as she enters to warn him.

"Why have you done this?" she asks him, dispensing with pleasantries.

"I find it relaxing," he says. "And I was starting to smell."

"I don't mean the bath. Why did you bring—" She glances at Gaveston, and he makes an elaborate bow. "Why did you bring him back?"

Edward sends his man scurrying to the door. He leans back in the tub, the sweat pouring down his cheek in rivulets. "The question should be: Why did I let him go? My father would never have allowed the barons to dictate to him like this."

"You are not your father."

This is the wrong thing to say. Even Gaveston raises his eyebrows.

"I am the king of England!" he shouts and stands.

He glares at her, fists clenched at his sides. Hard for a man to look regal or righteous when he stands naked in his tub. Gaveston hands him a towel. Edward hurls it back at him.

Isabella has never seen him naked; their lovemaking to this point has been conducted in candlelight, under linen sheets. Her eyes travel the length of him. Even when wet, he is an impressive man. She feels her cheeks burn.

Gaveston widens his eyes in mock horror and grins at her. His expression is so lascivious she wants to slap him. Has he no shame? Flustered, she turns on her heel and leaves.

He returns all of Gaveston's forfeited estates and signs a public proclamation, to be read at the Guildhall in London, that the good and loyal Piers Gaveston has returned at the royal command, after his exile contrary to the laws of England.

He then orders his sheriffs all over England to fortify their castles and take in provisions, and sends to Gascony for more troops. His barons conduct musters of their own. Archbishop Winchelsea finally declares Gaveston excommunicate.

Having thrown his gauntlet in all their faces, Edward flees north to Yorkshire. He takes with him his chancery clerks and a cartload of documents. It is clear that he does not intend to return to London with his government anytime soon.

———

Gaveston takes his wife, Margaret, to York as well. By the time Isabella arrives, the child is born. Margaret returns to her service, and Gaveston finds a wet nurse for the infant.

Isabella hates the castle; she hates the north. Even this late in the winter, there is still snow on the north tower. Her apartments are dull and drafty, unlike the vibrant burgundies and royal blues at Windsor and Langley. She misses most the hooded fireplace with a plentiful supply of logs from the scullery and charcoal braziers glowing in every room.

Her demoiselles warm the bed sheets with pans of heated charcoal. What she wants is a man to warm them with her.

"Am I ugly?" she asks Margaret. "Is there something about me that does not please him?"

"It is not you. You are beautiful, your Grace."

"Then why does he not want me?"

"Only Edward can tell you that."

They flee again, this time to Tynemouth Priory. Edward charges Gaveston with the defense of Scarborough Castle. That night, after he has gone to take up his commission, Isabella leaves a candle burning in her bedchamber.

Her joining with Edward doesn't hurt anymore. In fact, she looks forward to it. "I am so happy you are mine," she whispers that night as he lies panting on top of her.

He jerks away. "I am not yours!" he hisses and leaves her lying alone in the dark.

But he is in her bed again that following Easter Monday morning when her maidens burst in and take him prisoner. It is a traditional prank; he is prepared for it and wears breeches for when they throw back the covers. He takes it in good humor, laughing along with them as they drag him out of the bedchamber in his nightshirt and tie him to a chair in the kitchen with ribbons, threatening him with their hairbrushes if he moves. Edward shouts that he will die before he will dishonor himself, but then he has his steward pay them all a gold coin to release him. He then calls for hot wine, and drinks it with her in front of the fire while the servants prepare the tables for the holy day feast.

When it is over and everyone has left the hall and he is tired from laughing, she tells him that she is going to have a baby, a royal son perhaps, and he picks her up and tosses her in the air, laughing out loud. If she could keep this moment forever, she would slip it in the little silver casket and lock it with the key.

But later that day Gaveston returns from Scarborough with news that the fortifications there are ready. That night she sleeps alone once more.

———

She finds Gaveston patrolling the battlements in his scarlet cloak. He looks gaunt. Perhaps the reality of what they are facing has hit him at last. He and Edward have been chased around the northern counties by Lancaster until their bones ache. This is not so much a civil war as the corralling of a troublesome horse.

She fastens her ermine cloak more snugly about her and goes outside to join him.

"I am surprised to find you out here," she says.

"Perhaps you expected me to be with my familiar, sticking pins in a wax effigy of your uncle Lancaster?"

The wind buffets her, and she puts out a hand to the cold stone to steady herself. She huddles deeper inside the furs.

"Is any of it true?"

"About my mother being a witch? Of course. Everything they say about me is true."

"You enjoy being notorious, don't you?"

"You have all made me so. What I enjoy is baiting you all, out of spite."

"Is it spite to bring Edward down? Please don't let him do this."

"Don't let him do what, your grace?"

"Don't let him lose everything for you. He will, you know. For you."

"Because that is what he wants."

Storm clouds gather over the moor. Above them the flag of England whips in the wind. "You hold his destiny in your hands.

They will make war on you both, and they will not relent until you are dead. Unless you do something to stop it."

For the first time since he has returned, he does not try to laugh this off. "Would it be different were I his queen? Then the whole world would call him a great hero for defending my honor."

"But you are not his queen. It is up to you now, Piers. If you love him, prevent this. He has shown his love for you, now you must show your love for him."

"I would die first," he says. Or does she imagine it? The wind is fierce up here, and it is hard to hear anything that is not shouted at the top of the lungs. She leaves him and returns to the great hall and the hearth.

Edward gives Gaveston his orders: he must hold Scarborough against all comers and relinquish it to no one. Edward gives him all the men he can spare, three score at most, and rides with him to prepare the final defense.

He returns a week later to busy himself with raising an army to relieve their situation. But they all stand against him now: Lancaster, Warwick, Hereford, even Pembroke. He tells her he is the noblest man in England, for he is the only one who fights for love, not politics. She thinks he is sordid and foolish, but she cannot say this to the king of England, so she keeps her peace and nurses the hurt, privately and meekly, like a small and wounded bird.

Chapter 16

The child kicks.

He must feel her agitation. She is exhausted from the journey down from Tynemouth. Already she feels she is the size of a castle. Even climbing the stairs to her bedchamber leaves her breathless.

Lancaster's army has now chased Edward all around the north of England. She has spent most of spring at Tynemouth Priory, with the mice and the drafts, staring at the gray sea. Edward has been forced to run like a felon in his own country. He still has no army with which to face his enemies.

Isabella is angry to see him so reduced; angry at Edward for his stubborn refusal to see reason; furious at her uncle Lancaster and the Earl of Warwick for their disobedience. She is a daughter of France, and she did not marry the king of England to endure this.

Edward paces the great hall, drinks more than is necessary, and shouts at the servants. He sends supplies to Gaveston but discovers that they have been intercepted by Pembroke's army, which now has Scarborough under siege. Gaveston smuggles missives out of the castle. It seems they are reduced to eating cobwebs and rats.

Edward upturns tables and rips down tapestries in his frustration. The most powerful man in England is now powerless.

The final message from Scarborough: Gaveston has sued for terms with Pembroke and has agreed to let himself be taken. He believes the earl to be an honorable man. It was this, or starvation.

And within days Gaveston is back at York, marched into the great hall under guard. The Lord Pembroke stands aside, the king's subject gives leave for his king to embrace his lover. It is awkward for them both, Isabella supposes. How is one meant to behave?

Only after they have done commiserating is Margaret allowed to intrude, and Pembroke then allows Gaveston to hold his son.

She understands now why Gaveston calls him Joseph the Jew, although he does not do so on this occasion. Pembroke is olive skinned with a beak of a nose, though he fervently denies Semitic ancestors. Gaveston has made fun of him in less burdensome times, but never with the venom he reserves for Lancaster and Warwick.

There are three days of negotiating final terms. Pembroke's soldiery patrols the abbey while their masters parlay a peace, but when it is done, Edward emerges well pleased. There will be a Parliament called for early the next month; Gaveston will be allowed to put his case to the barons; and if nothing is decided, Pembroke agrees to escort him back to Scarborough and allow Edward to supply him with provisions. Until then he will stay with Pembroke at his castle at Wallingford, under guard.

"I have your word on this?" Edward asks Pembroke.

"I pledge my estates and my honor," Pembroke answers solemnly. "The Lords Ordainers act under law," Pembroke sniffily adds. "We are knights of the realm, not animals!"

This is not enough persuasion for Edward. He has him swear on the Bible that he will keep his prisoner safe.

Next day she watches from the window as Edward says his farewells. The king and his dearest cling to each other desperately. Finally Gaveston pulls away and jumps on his horse.

Then he is gone, surrounded by a squadron of armed knights in Pembroke's colors. Edward runs alongside the troopers for as long as he can and then waves after him until he is out of sight.

Surely a king does not behave this way.

Chapter 17

Old Hugh le Despenser comes to York, the only one of the earls to remain unflaggingly loyal. He shuffles into the great hall with sweat on his upper lip. He has a letter from the rector at Deddington. "He is my son's man," he says. "My son, Hugh. You remember Hugh?"

The king stares at him, as if he were mad. He has not heard of Deddington, and cares for its rector even less, particularly at this moment.

Isabella puts a restraining hand on his arm: *Hear him out.*

"The Earl of Cornwall has been taken by my Lord Warwick," he says.

Edward frowns, leans forward. What is this old fool saying? "Perro is at Wallingford. Pembroke has him under house arrest."

"I only know what the messenger tells me. I thought your grace should know."

The king jumps to his feet. He calls for a messenger to be sent to Pembroke immediately. It is two days' ride, perhaps three. His eyes are wild. Warwick? The Black Dog has Gaveston? How is this possible?

It is just some foul rumor, surely. But he is panicked.

Isabella shudders to think what Warwick would do to Gaveston if he ever had him in his power. Yet she is torn. She wants Edward's favorite out of the way; without him she is sure she would have the Edward she has always desired.

She puts a hand to her belly and the restless son of England. One does not know which outcome best to wish for.

Edward begs her on his knees to appeal to her father. What if this perverse news is true? He promises he will return to France half of Gascony if Philippe will save Gaveston's life. What can she do? She sends the letter as he asks, in the cold certainty that no one across the sea will lift a finger to save Edward's favorite. Even a sixteen-year-old girl can see the inevitable. He has got in everyone's way. Edward's love is the kiss of death.

The king cannot sit still, even for a moment. He has barely slept since old Despenser brought his news. He sits on the throne in the great hall, cursing the servants if his wine cup is ever less than half-full, and has his clerks dash off letters to every prince and nobleman he can think of.

It is summer and the days are long, a violet dusk clings to the dales. Six days after the messenger was sent, she hears a rider enter the castle gates. The shouts and the ring of hooves on the cobbles stir Edward from his wine-rosy lethargy; he drank too much at dinner, and was presently asleep at the table. She runs to the window.

In fact not one messenger but two; their horses have been ridden almost to death, and there is foam on their flanks. The couriers themselves are covered in sweat and dirt, evidence of a hard ride indeed.

She turns to Edward, sees the fear in his face. The servants sidle up to the walls, keeping to the darker corners. She can see it in their faces; they feel sorry for the man who bears the message, and not one of them wishes to be in Edward's sight when the fateful words are spoken.

Old Hugh intercepts them at the door. There is a whispered conversation, and then he comes in quietly. "These men have news for you, your grace."

"Who are they?" Edward says.

"They say that they are . . . they were in the employ of my Lord Gaveston."

They throw themselves in the rushes at the king's feet.

There is a long silence.

He finally gives them leave to speak. "Tell me," he says, finally, in a strangled voice.

The men look at each other. Neither of them wants to be the one to say it. "My Lord Gaveston has been brought to trial," the braver of the two says.

A muscle in Edward's cheek twitches. "Trial?" He is absolutely still. "Who presided over such a trial?"

"The Lord Lancaster, your grace."

"But where was Pembroke? I don't understand."

"He was at Wallingford, your grace."

"Wasn't Gaveston at Wallingford?"

"He was taken from there by Lord Warwick."

Edward shakes his head. He does not seem to understand. "But this is impossible. Pembroke was sworn to protect him!"

"Lord Pembroke was not there. He had left the castle overnight to visit his wife. That's when Warwick came and took him."

The blood drains from Edward's face. But he is in no hurry to hear what must be told. While it is not said, it is not done. "On what charge?"

"That he had contravened the twentieth ordinance."

"An ordinance I have since revoked! There was a trial, you say? And what did my Lord Gaveston say in his defense to this *charge*?"

"Your Grace, they did not allow him to speak."

"But Pembroke gave his word to me!"

"The others of your nobles would not honor his negotiation. Not even Gloucester."

There is the sound of choking; it appears to come from Edward, but she cannot swear to it. His face is implacable.

"What have they done?"

"Your grace, he is beheaded."

Edward sinks into his seat as if he has been struck by a mace. "You saw this?"

"We were imprisoned, we heard of it when we were freed."

"Where is he?"

"The monks took him to Oxford."

"To Oxford? They killed him in Oxford?"

"No, in Warwick."

"In the castle?"

"On a hill."

"Hill? What hill?"

"Lancaster came for him late one night and took him from the dungeon and brought him in irons to Blacklow Hill. It is a mile from the castle, on Lancaster's land."

"On Lancaster's land? But where was Warwick?"

"He stayed behind, at the castle."

"He had the venom for this act, but not the stomach." Edward mutters this to himself, into his beard. His eyes look mad.

The messenger is breathing hard. He wants to finish this and get out but must wait for the king's leave to speak again. It is a long time before he receives it.

"And then?"

"He was handed to Lancaster's guards and taken up the hill in full view of the crowds—"

"The crowds? He made this a public occasion?"

"There was a large gathering. It was festive. Some blew horns."

Isabella closes her eyes. *Do not say that to him! Think fit to leave out such painful embellishments, you fool. Because he asks you for such details does not mean he needs to hear them. Do you not have sense enough to lie to him, man?*

"Lancaster observed all this?"

"And Lords Hereford and Arundel."

"And what of Perro . . . what of my Lord Gaveston?"

The man looks to his companion. *It is your turn now,* his eyes are saying.

The other takes up the rest of the story. "He begged Lancaster for mercy, your grace."

"You saw this?"

"We heard of it later."

"Tell me what you heard. All of it."

Isabella shakes her head: *No, don't.* But the man is not looking at her.

"He begged Lancaster for mercy on his knees. He wept."

"And the crowd saw this?"

"They seemed all the more happy for it."

Isabella wants the story to end. *Edward, Gaveston is dead, let this be over with.* Edward sighs deeply and regards the ceiling. "How was it done?"

"One of the guards pierced him through the chest with his sword. The other cut off his head and showed it to Lancaster."

Edward taps a forefinger on the arm of the throne. Isabella waits for the outburst, but there is none.

"Who told you this?"

"One of the shoe menders."

"Shoe menders? What would a shoe mender have to do with this?"

"He was charged by the monks with sewing the head back on."

The silence stretches for an eternity. Old Hugh thinks it is politic at this point to tap the men on the shoulder and point to the door. Never has she seen two men more relieved to leave a room.

Edward is absolutely still. He hardly seems even to breathe. His eyes are fixed on some point high in the ceiling.

Finally he shakes his head and says, in a quiet voice: "By God's soul, he acted like a fool. If he had taken my advice, he would never have fallen into the hands of the earls. This is what I always told him not to do. I knew this would happen! What was he doing with the Earl of Warwick? He never liked him." He gets to his feet. "Make sure those men are fed and paid for their service to us."

He leaves the hall. No one moves. Isabella hurries after him, but he has already gone to his bedchamber. She hears him, though, on the other side of the door. It sounds as if someone is slaughtering a pig.

She sends the servants away. She wants none of them hearing this.

She wishes the messengers had been less honest. *Did they have to tell him about the shoe mender?* Once something is imagined it cannot be unimagined.

She hears his dogs on the other side of the door, yelping and scratching to get out. They are clearly terrified. She edges the door ajar to release them, and they flee scampering down the passage. She glimpses Edward, drooling like a lunatic. He overturns an oak table it took four men to move the day before. He tears down a recess curtain and breaks a holy picture over his knee.

She shuts the door and sits in a chair, listening to him rage. She sends orders to old Hugh that no one is to be allowed entry to his chambers.

She finds him the next morning among the wreckage. It looks as if his apartments have been ransacked by marauders. Edward lies in the middle of it, clutching a goblet, wine spilled on the carpets and all over his clothes.

She goes out again, lets him sleep.

For days he wanders the halls and gardens, mindless in grief. Once, from her window, she sees him sink to his knees in the rain, then keel onto his side there in the mud. Grief owns him totally.

She feels the child kicking in her belly. *It will be all right,* she tells him. *Gaveston is gone. Everything will be all right now. We will just get through these dark days, and then all will be well.*

Chapter 18

Isabella, by the grace of God, Queen of England, Lady of Ireland and Duchess of Aquitaine, to our well-beloved the mayor and aldermen and the commonalty of London, greeting. Forasmuch as we believe that you would willingly hear good tidings of us, we do make known to you that our Lord, of His grace, has delivered us of a son, on the thirteenth day of November, with safety to ourselves, and to the child. May our Lord preserve you. Given at Windsor, on the day above-named.

———

She lies under the bedcovers, too weak to move. She manages a smile. They tell him the birthing was difficult, she so small in the hips, and this her first, a lusty boy, and carried long.

"Isabella . . ."

"Your grace."

"You have given us a son."

"I hope it pleases you."

He leans over the bed. She has not seen him smile like this since the year before, when Gaveston returned from Brabant.

There was a time she thought never to see him smile again. If this was what it took, then it was worth it.

"They say you lost much blood."

"You have your battlefields, I have mine."

"And you were valiant on it."

"Once it has begun, a woman has no choice but to bear it. What shall we call him?"

"I was thinking . . . Piers."

She looks at her baby, better arranges the blanket around his face. The room has turned cold.

"Your suggestion?" he asks her, finally.

"I thought Philippe, after my father."

He stands up, crosses his arms. "What about Edward?"

"Well, he is your son."

"So he shall be Edward, then."

He smiles and kisses her. She closes her eyes. If he would only tell her he loves her—as she had once heard him say to Gaveston—the moment would be perfect.

———

The threat of civil war has ended with Gaveston's death. The manner of his kidnap and execution brings Pembroke, outraged and humiliated, back to the king's side, Surrey and old Hugh's son with him. It horrifies even those who despised Gaveston, and many call it murder. Warwick sulks in his castle and Lancaster returns to Kenilworth, snarling with contempt at any who dare question his motives.

Edward meanwhile decamps to Oxford, where he pays for cerecloth to wrap the body and then has it embalmed with balsam and spices. He commissions an elaborate coffin for Gaveston's body, for he will yet be awhile above the ground. He died excommunicate, so he cannot be buried in hallowed ground.

"You know they left the body there in the open?" he shouts at her, as if she is to blame. "Some shoe menders took him on a ladder to Warwick Castle, and our good earl turned them away!"

"Will there be war now?"

"If I could not defeat them before, how should I do it now? But the wheel will turn. Lancaster will part with his head and so will Warwick. I shall swear it on my father's tomb. They will pay for every drop of blood, by God's soul they will!"

The king makes overgenerous financial arrangements for monks in Oxford to keep Gaveston's body at their friary and to pray for his unhallowed soul. He hires two men to watch over the coffin night and day. Margaret and Gaveston's former servants are all awarded pensions.

Lady de Vescy returns, no longer outlawed, and then Winchelsea dies. "More good news, then," Edward says, clapping his hands in delight when the messenger brings him the missive. Edward makes his friend Walter Reynolds archbishop of Canterbury in his place, with the pious hope that his predecessor will moan everlasting in hell on the end of a hot pitchfork.

Hereford and Arundel come sniveling back, and old Hugh encourages the king to make peace with Lancaster and Warwick, for the good of the realm.

"I cannot do it," Edward tells Isabella. "I cannot forgive them."

"Just make a show of it," she says. "You have the other barons on your side now. If you were to take an army and defeat the Scots, your kingship would be unquestioned. You could then turn the army on them. Hold your hand till then."

"But I have vowed to see them dead!"

"Vengeance cannot be rushed. Have patience, take their submission, and when you are stronger, then you can make them pay you in full measure for what they have done."

The birth of her son thaws the frosty relationship between her husband and her father. Gaveston's death does no harm to it either.

Now Philippe sends the king a letter, inviting him to Paris so that he can see his new grandson and talk about Gascony.

Edward is delighted. He senses the possibility of concessions. As soon as his wife is recovered, they will take ship to France.

Chapter 19

Paris, June 1313

"He is so handsome!" Marguerite squeals, peering between the curtains.

Pentecost Sunday, and Isabella's brothers are to be knighted by their father, Philippe. But it is Edward who attracts the attention; tall, strong, and handsome, it seems at last Isabella is envied, as she never is in England. And he does carry it well; working on a roof or a field may not be regal, but it has made him a physical specimen to be admired.

She thinks Marguerite should instead have eyes for her husband, Louis, for it is his day; but she and Charles's wife, Blanche, have always been this way: flighty girls, though pleasant company. The silk purses she has made for them warrant barely a glance. Once they treated her like a little pest, now they behave as if she is all but invisible.

Neither do they try to hide the looks they give the two young men on the other side of the church. Isabella makes a point to find out who they are; they are brothers by the name of d'Aulnay, both knights and outrageously handsome. They pretend not to notice that the two sisters are watching them.

They do not pretend very well.

Her sisters-in-law's gossip is about the Templars—all arrested and put to the torture, at the pope's behest. Marguerite and Blanche are not concerned about the politics of it, their talk is of how the Order encouraged their members to have sexual dalliance with a cat and worship a disembodied head.

Really, she could have more intelligent conversations with her horse.

Neither Marguerite nor Blanche has many kind words for her brothers, their husbands. "All Louis ever wants to do is play tennis," Marguerite says.

Her father has not aged at all. His nickname is Philippe the Handsome, and he still is, frighteningly so. He actually smiles when he sees her, a rare compliment indeed.

"You have grown beautiful," he says and nods with approval. This she did not expect.

They are in the White Chamber, so named for its pure white walls. The windows of thick stained glass bear the armorial insignia of the royal house of France, a wheel of candles burns overhead. Théophania enters, holding the new prince for the king's inspection. He pronounces himself well pleased and then calls for wine to celebrate. She has waited five years to make him so proud.

Afterward her father takes her aside, and they talk in whispers beside the roaring fire. He is much consumed by the state of her marriage to Edward. "Things go well between you now?"

"They could not be better."

"There are no more . . . favorites?"

"He is as attentive a husband as a wife may hope for."

"I hear from Rosseletti that Lancaster and this Warwick still disobey him."

"Gaveston was just their excuse. They wish to undermine his rule and have the power for themselves. But killing Gaveston was very bad for their cause."

"But very good for yours." He fixes her with one of those famous looks, as if he could see into her soul. She has never flinched under Lancaster's or Edward's gaze, but she feels her cheeks grow hot now. Suddenly she is twelve years old again.

"A new necklace? It looks expensive."

"A gift from Edward." She fingers the pearls at her throat. Forty pounds they cost him, and he had to borrow it all from his new Italian banker. She thinks she will never take them off.

Philippe nods approvingly. A very good sign. Once, Edward's gifts were only for Gaveston.

"He has several requests to make over your dispute in Gascony," she says.

"And he has sent you to discuss them with me?"

"He trusts that I understand such matters. After all, I had a good teacher."

"Now you seek to disarm your father with flattery. I raised you well, did I not?" His mouth curls into something like a smile. The second in an afternoon! They should hold a feast day to commemorate it.

"He will need your help to teach the barons their place."

"Does he want money as well as treaties? And I thought he came here to show me my new grandson."

"It is more than a grandson, your grace. It is a dynasty, and your blood is in him."

Philippe's gaze is ironlike. "You do not have to remind your father of the importance of your son by the king of England. It was the whole purpose of the marriage."

There is a royal banquet. Edward and her father sit side by side on the dais while stewards bring out dish after steaming dish on silver platters: a pig with the wings of a swan and the tail of a peacock, soup of ground capon thickened with almond milk, kid cooked in cream, pears fragrant with cinnamon and red wine. There are jugglers, minstrels, and fools.

There are private negotiations over Gascony; her father makes concessions, though not many. Still Edward pronounces himself well pleased. He spends a week gambling and dancing and drinking Philippe's wines.

For the first time since Gaveston's murder, he seems to be enjoying himself.

Philippe travels with them to Pontoise, outside Paris, on their way back to Boulogne and England. Isabella allows herself to be happy at last. It is a new beginning for them, she is sure of it.

She wakes to the sound of screaming.

Two of her ladies are standing over the bed, shaking her. She can smell smoke and hear the horses stampeding. "There is a fire," Isabella de Vescy says. "We must leave, madam."

"Where is little Edward?"

"He is safe, madam. The Lady Eleanor has him. Please, your grace, we must leave the pavilion."

"I have to dress."

She hears men shouting, panicked. There is a glow creeping up the silk of the pavilion, and men outside running with torches. Her ladies help her with her clothes, but they fumble with the laces, their hands shaking.

Théophania is almost jumping up and down on the spot with fright. "We must go! We must go, your grace!"

How did this start? A torch perhaps, a flame touching the silk. It will all burn before anyone has a chance to fetch buckets from the river. Where is the king? She hears him outside, yelling orders. Her women finish. Lady de Vescy grabs her hand and drags her out, forgetting her manners in her haste.

She feels cold air on her shoulders, heat on her cheek. Chaos, the whole field is on fire, orange flames jumping into a black sky.

Men try to keep horses from bolting as they lead them away, eyes wide. Others, slipping in the mud, struggle to carry treasure chests.

She tears free from Lady de Vescy and runs back into the pavilion.

"Your grace! What are you doing?"

She thinks she has plenty of time to find what she is looking for, but the pearl string has fallen from its table and she has to search for it on the carpets. Flames roar at the silk, and by the time she reaches the entrance again, the embers have caught her dress, and the sleeve starts to burn. She tries to put out the flame by shaking her arm about, but that makes it worse.

Someone throws a cloak over her, smothering the fire, then picks her up easily and carries her out.

Edward.

He shouts for assistance, then looks back at the royal camp. If Robert Bruce had done this, they would call it a massacre.

"Are you hurt, your grace?" He examines her arm. A strip of skin is laid back and peeling. "By God's soul, what made you go back?"

She holds up the pearls he gave her, still clutched in her fist.

"For those? I would have bought you ten strings to replace them."

She shakes her head. These were her first gift from him. They are irreplaceable.

He puts her easily to the ground, and her ladies fuss around her. He calls for his physician and leaves her to their care.

She looks after him as he strides back toward the ruin of the camp. It seems he at least cares for her enough to come back for her. She smiles over the pain. It is just a little burn; if it meant he would rescue her again like that, then she would give her whole arm.

———

The night before they leave Boulogne, they lie abed, side by side, staring into the dark. The palace is quiet; a guard calls the all's well.

He holds her and kisses her. All is indeed well. Once, she had dreaded having his body on top of her, now she longs for it. It is a new appetite, one she has not anticipated. Eleanor and Lady de Vescy had whispered to her about their intimate dealings with their husbands, and blushed and twittered as if they cared for it, and now she supposes she cares for it also.

She only wishes he would care for it as much.

"What troubles you?" he whispers.

She cannot tell him the truth, so she tells him the first thing that comes to mind, which is the behavior of her brothers' wives.

"The two French knights who have accompanied us from Paris? They are handsome enough fellows. Are you sure?"

"Their names are Philippe and Gauthier d'Aulnay. Did you see the purses they wore at their belts?"

He shakes his head.

"I embroidered them myself and gave them to my sisters-in-law as gifts."

"They may have given them over as knightly favors. You know how they are in France."

Too late, he realizes what he has said.

"Yes, your grace. I know how they are in France."

"I mean only that it is chivalry and no more."

"Perhaps."

"Why does it bother you so?"

"I think they may have taken their chivalry too far."

"You mean they are sleeping together?"

"For a prince to take a mistress, this is . . . well, it is the way of princes. But it is very different for a princess, and if her husband may one day be king, then it is simply unthinkable. She pollutes the royal blood, and this is the greatest sin there is. She will be at fault before her country and before God."

He reaches for her hand and squeezes it. "I am sure it is nothing. Marguerite and Blanche would not be so foolish, surely?"

"I hope not," she murmurs. She rolls toward him, and tries to rouse the king's servant to life, but he will not rise.

My father and my brother's wives all say I am beautiful. Everyone says I am beautiful but my husband. What must I do to win his heart and arouse his passion?

Chapter 20

Lancaster stands beneath the vast timbered ceiling and its shields and flags of all England. "While you have been on your pleasure jaunt, the Bruce has been at work. Stirling is the only castle left in our hands on this side of the border, and now his men have it under siege. If you do not rouse yourself, I have it on good authority the governor will surrender that to him as well." It's as if he is hectoring a child.

Edward grips the arms of the throne. Beneath him is Longshanks's great prize: the Stone of Scone. It's a constant reminder of what true greatness means—in the eyes of his barons at least.

When Edward finally speaks, his voice is slick with contempt. "It was not a pleasure jaunt."

"I have seen the bill for wine you handed the Exchequer. If it was duty done, then you drank your way to it."

Edward tries to keep himself from rage. His eyes glitter, but his face remains a mask, though the blood is much drained from his face.

"We shall attend to the Bruce presently."

"When he takes Berwick? Or when he is at the gates of York?"

"Presently," Edward repeats and storms from the chamber. She follows him into a chapel and watches as he hurls a prie-dieu across the pews, where it lands with a crash, startling a friar. Edward falls on his knees before the altar and leans on all fours, growling like a dog.

She needs to help him. This will not do. "How dare he speak to you so," she says to let him know she is on his side.

"That is the man who killed Perro!"

"It is the man who wishes to usurp your power."

"I would have his ugly head on a pike."

She dares put a hand to his shoulder. "One day. But that day is not yet."

She thinks he might try to shake himself free of her, but instead he takes her hand and kisses it and lays it on his cheek. "Every time I look at him, I see Perro lying at his feet, shaking in terror. What mercy did he get from that dog?"

"This must wait for another time, your grace." She kneels beside him. "You must take back your power first. Everything else comes from that."

He nods, his eyes wild. He needs her now; she is all that keeps him from madness. "I will do as you say," he murmurs.

———

Her uncle Evreux comes back to England to mediate. He and Gloucester and the pope's emissaries go to Lancaster and sue for calm yet again. They get nowhere and ask Isabella for her help. She sits down with her uncle and with Warwick and makes a plea for peace.

She begs Warwick and Lancaster to ask the king's forgiveness for Gaveston's murder.

"It was not murder!" Lancaster barks at her, offended at being upbraided by a girl, even if she is his queen. "It was the law."

"They are just words, Uncle," she says and smiles. "For the sake of my son, let us bring peace back to our country."

He thinks about this. He looks at Warwick, at Hereford, at the others. The king has a son now, he is not as vulnerable as he was, and the barons are divided. Hugh le Despenser the younger, Pembroke, Gloucester, Richmond, they have all returned their allegiance to the king.

Perhaps they listen to her because she is no threat to their pride, they can back down and appear gallant rather than weak. When they finally accede, the pope says it is the prayers of his envoy Cardinal Arnaud Novelli that change their minds, and Philippe says it is the work of his man Evreux, but Edward tells everyone it is Isabella.

An agreement is reached, and the barons submit to come back to Westminster. There are rumors that Edward intends to arrest Lancaster as soon as he enters London. Other whispers talk of Lancaster coming armed and seizing the king.

But the king's peace is maintained. They come to it: Lancaster, Warwick, and Hereford kneel before Edward in the great hall at Westminster, though Lancaster is red-faced and looks as if he is swallowing back his own bile. He begs the king's forgiveness for Gaveston's death, and Edward pardons him.

They give each other the kiss of peace, and after it is done, they all stand and glare at each other, Edward's smile frozen on his face. "Your pardons," he tells them, "have been granted through the prayers of my dearest companion, Isabella, queen of England."

Afterward she is attended by two of the king's physicians, Peter and Master Odinet, and two more sent by her father. Her arm is swollen and hot and is weeping fluids. They apply herbal plasters and a lotion of rosewater and olive oil. Edward storms in and sheds his good humor like scalding armor after a long battle.

"Did you see his face? I would sooner have taken out his eyes than kissed that man!"

"It is done now, Edward. You need his truce for the moment."

He kicks over a stool. Then he sees the physicians around her and comes himself to take a look at her injury. "Isabella, you are suffering. Make her well," he tells them, "there is reward for all of you in it."

"We are doing all we can," Master Odinet says.

Her physicians fuss around her. They tell her she should rest. But while Edward needs her, she will not rest. She is his queen and he is in trouble.

She sees the fever in Edward's eyes. These days the king is not himself, whoever *himself* is.

"I will have my revenge," he tells her when they are finally alone. "He may be your uncle, but he is my enemy now. Both he and Warwick, they will pay for this, by God's holy soul, I will not rest until they pay!"

Isabella smiles. For a time she had been afraid he would be too consumed with his grief to remember to be a king. Lancaster was an uncle, but not much of one, and no one would weep for the Earl of Warwick when the day came. She prefers him vengeful to besotted.

He sends her back to France to present his case again over the disputed Gascon lands at the Paris Parliament. "How can your father ever resist his own daughter when even Lancaster gives in to you?" he tells her.

He does not know her father.

But he trusts her, and so she will go.

She makes a pilgrimage to Boulogne, to Amiens, and to Chartres, accompanied by Gloucester, Henry de Beaumont, and another magnate called Badlesmere. It is a passable show of strength.

The night before she arrives in Paris, Jacques de Molay, the last grand master of the Templars, is burned over a slow fire on the

Île aux Juifs. As he dies, he invites her father and Pope Clement to meet him at God's judgment before the year is out.

When she arrives, everyone in Paris is talking about it.

"The ravings of a madman," Philippe says and dismisses the episode out of hand.

They walk together through the royal cloisters. There is frost on the grass and mist curls around the gargoyles perched on top of the pillars. Isabella shudders, imagining one of them to be the writhing spirit of Jacques de Molay.

She presents Edward's petitions and asks for her father's favorable opinion of them, but Philippe is more concerned about the wounds on her arm. He summons physicians.

The next day a messenger arrives at the court from Rome. The pope is dead. The Templar's curse has been swift, though her father seems unperturbed. "Clement was an old man," is all he says. She stares at Philippe and imagines him dead. What would the world be like without him? She cannot imagine it. He has been the touchstone to duty and achievement for so long.

What will I do when I have only my own conscience as guide?

Chapter 21

Berwick

Edward is no longer the man who sat shrunken and abandoned on his throne when they brought him news of Gaveston's death.

He has now amassed a great army; just one victory against the Bruce, and he will have the barons in his thrall, and there is nothing Lancaster can do about it. She sees Pembroke in attendance. These days he cannot do enough to appease the king, though she knows from her private conversations with Edward that he does not blame him over Gaveston's death. Mortimer is there, too. His looks are smoldering, but she ignores them. She is a wife now, not a simpering girl.

Surrey, Richmond, the Despensers, father and son—they are all there; only Lancaster, Warwick, and Arundel have not appeared for the mustering of troops. "They say I have to wait, that I may not move against the Scots without the consent of the Parliament, or I am in defiance of the Ordinances! The Ordinances! They still wish me to bow and scrape to them for permission to visit my own privy!"

She is resting in the rooms he has put aside for her in the castle. Her arm is healing at last, though she fears it will leave a permanent scar. But no one will see the disfigurement except her husband, and even he sees it seldom enough.

After the journey home from France, she had gone from Dover directly to London, then on to Doncaster and Pontefract, and finally here to the wild borderlands. The traveling was hard and difficult, but she is Edward's queen, her place is beside him.

"Thank you for coming," he says when they are finally alone.

"I would be nowhere else at such a time. Win this one battle, and everything will be restored to you."

"The die is cast. I will make Lancaster regret what he has done."

He cannot lose. Even without Lancaster and Warwick, his army outnumbers the Scots by three to one. The king's only fear is that the Bruce will run and deny him the victory he needs.

"I have heard disturbing news from France. Is it true?"

She nods. "The adulteries were proven. Jean, their sister, was a witness. I was right in my suspicions. The d'Aulnay brothers were convicted of treason and will suffer their fate accordingly."

"What has your father done to your Marguerite and Blanche?"

"Marguerite has had her hair shorn and is sent to Château Gaillard, her marriage annulled. Blanche as well. I fear they will never see the sun again."

"And Jean?"

"Under house arrest. My brother argues her case. I do not think she had any part in it, but she is disgraced for not speaking out sooner."

"As you said yourself, a royal lady who commits adultery knows the sin she commits in God's eyes."

"Indeed, your grace. They knew the risk."

She thinks of Marguerite, that stupid giggling girl, how she had stared at her doomed knight through the curtain that day in the Notre Dame. *"All my husband ever wants to do is play tennis."* A woman might have private longings, but if she is royal, she cannot indulge them, no matter how she burns for more. What had happened to Marguerite was not Isabella's fault. She had been obliged to tell her father what she knew.

That night she keeps a candle burning in her chamber and waits for Edward to come to her again, after all these months and so many letters. But he stays awake, drinking and gambling and laughing at his tumblers and fools. The nights are cold in Berwick, and she shivers alone.

Chapter 22

He is a common foot soldier, Humphrey or Hubert, she does not quite catch the name. He stands bedraggled and covered in mud, shivering from his exertions and from the cold. She tells him to get up off his knees and has a servant bring him wine, which he gulps down. She watches it leak into his beard.

He has lately come from the battle that her husband must not, cannot, lose. The battle he had so ardently wished for, fearing that the Bruce might flee.

She knows the news is bad, or why would Edward send an infantryman? It now appears Edward did not send him at all. He is a straggler, discovered by one of her patrols.

She braces herself for what he has to say.

"Tell us your news," she says, finally.

"They were waiting for us, your grace."

"Who? The Bruce?"

He nods. "He dug pits in the carse so that our army was all pressed together on the battlefield. Then one of our knights saw him and charged him with a lance."

"Which knight?"

"Sir Henry de Bohun, your grace." One of Edward's best knights, then, and Hereford's nephew.

"What happened?"

"The Bruce killed him. With just one blow. He split Sir Henry's helmet in two and broke the shaft of his axe."

Isabella winces as she imagines what had happened to Sir Henry.

"It was a sore thing to see."

"I suppose it was," Isabella answers mildly, dreading the rest of the tale. She composes herself. "What was the outcome of the battle?"

Humphrey or Hubert stares at the stone flags. He mumbles something. It sounds as if he is saying that Edward has fled the field and that Bannockburn is littered with English dead.

Her hands tighten around the arms of her seat. This is not possible.

She makes the peon repeat his tale; the Earl of Gloucester has been killed and the Scots have captured the Earl of Hereford. The battle had turned into a rout. Bruce's tiny army has massacred thousands of Englishmen.

She goes to her room to pray. She wishes her father were here. He would know what to do.

But then her father would never have his army destroyed by a minor Scottish baron like Robert the Bruce.

———

The next day a fishing boat docks at the castle. Isabella and the rest of her women rush down the narrow walk to the Tweed to meet it. Pembroke, Lady de Vescy's brother, and Edward himself are both on board. Old Hugh is there as well. He carries his son up to the castle on his shoulders, gore leaking down the front of him.

Edward does not even look at her. His eyes are glazed, still fixed on the battlefield.

Later she dresses his wounds as he sits immobile in a wooden tub, not speaking. Afterward she and her ladies wash his armor; they must scrape off the mud and dried blood with stiff brushes. They say the king fought well, but whether he fought well or ran like a girl, it will not matter now.

He had believed nothing could stand in the way of heavy cavalry; they had all believed it. They were all wrong.

———————

"And you!" Lancaster dares point a finger at his king. Some gasp inside the Parliament at his presumption. "If you had honored the Ordinances, we should never have suffered this humiliation. An army of twenty thousand defeated by a dozen peat boggers with sharpened sticks!"

Edward is forced to listen to this abuse. Isabella stares over her uncle's head. She will not look at her husband for fear that should he look back, they will see it as further sign of weakness.

And she will not look at Lancaster, for she has come to despise him.

He relishes this moment. He has the king on his knees.

"We must press on with this war," Edward says. "If we desist now, the Bruce will have his crown, and we shall never have Scotland."

"Is eleven thousand dead not enough for you?" Lancaster hurls at him.

"We cannot let them win."

"We didn't. *You* did."

Edward subsides into his throne, shrunken in, as if they have removed all his bones and left just breathless flesh and half a heart.

"I never wanted to be your enemy, Edward," Lancaster says. His long sleeves rustle against his velvets as he parades before the Parliament, like a peacock before a mate. "But you planned to lead your victorious army against me, is this not so? You thought to vanquish the Scots only so that you might vanquish your own cousin." He shakes his head, appears disappointed rather than angry. "But you are not your father, you are not Longshanks. You are weak and stupid and easily led."

Edward flinches, as if struck with an open hand, and struggles to recover his composure. His hands ball, white knuckled, into fists.

"You made me kneel to you at Westminster. For what? To be forgiven for a righteous act. I should kill Gaveston again if I could, send him to a traitor's death just to hear the bitch scream."

Now Warwick is on his feet, the great resenter, the great complainer. "You have led us to disastrous wars and bankrupted the Treasury. We demand a purge of the royal Exchequer and a limit to the royal purse of ten pounds per day."

"Ten pounds!" Edward is on his feet. "I would not keep my dogs on that."

"Then get smaller dogs," Lancaster says.

He cannot refuse. He no longer has power over England, though he is the king. It is Lancaster who is regent now, in all but name.

———

It is just after the Feast of Saint Saturninus when a messenger arrives at court from France. Her father is dead. She knew he had been ill, but this is unexpected. It is not possible to attend the funeral, for a crossing of the narrow sea at this time of the year is not advised. Besides, Edward tells her that he needs her with him to help deal with the revolt of his barons.

She hears Jacques de Molay laughing, perched like a gargoyle on the roof of the palace. When he died, he cursed Philippe's line for seven generations. She wonders what her own punishment will be.

It is hard to imagine him truly gone. Yet in many ways he is not gone at all, he is still there with her every day, wagging a long finger in her face: *"You will love this man. Do you understand? You will love him, serve him, and obey him in all things. This is your duty to me and to France. Am I clear?"*

———

Edward works tirelessly to have the anathema that Winchelsea laid on Gaveston's head reversed. His man Reynolds makes sure it is done, but it is not easy and costs money. He has said to her that he will not bury his friend until he has been avenged, but common sense prevails. He cannot have him moldering in a priory chapel in Oxford forever.

He decides to inter him at Langley. It is a perfect day for such a homecoming; crows perch on skeletal trees, the wagon bearing his bones splashes through puddles of freezing mud, the friars that accompany it splattered to the waist. How much is he paying the Order for this?

Edward stays with him that night so that his Perro does not sleep alone. From her window she sees the candles flickering in the chapel, and once, she thinks she hears a noise over the moaning of the wind. Was that Edward wailing? No one has ever loved like this. *It should have been me, I want a man to love me like this.*

So many lords are there the next day for the funeral: Pembroke, the Despensers, even Hereford, who was one of those who dragged Gaveston off to Warwick Castle. The clouds of incense are so thick it is hard to see the grandees on display, but she counts an archbishop, four bishops, thirteen friars, fifty knights, and the lord mayor of London. There is Mortimer, of course, with his wife. She catches him staring, and wonders what goes on behind those black eyes.

The occasion is mostly marked by who is not there: Lancaster and Warwick.

Today they are saying masses for Gaveston in every church in England. This does not come cheap, but Edward does not care. He refused Gaveston nothing in life. He is disposed to do no less in death.

The tears come, she feels her control slip; it starts with a choking at the back of her throat. She cannot hold it back. She sees Edward give her a questioning glance. He thinks the tears are for Gaveston.

She never cried for her father. Perhaps she still expected to see him there when next she went to Paris: stern, strict, the one sure thing in the world. Her eldest brother is king now, though her uncle Valois makes all the decisions, while Louis plays tennis.

They lower Gaveston's gold-draped coffin. *What a sight we are! Me howling, the friars chanting, and Edward on his knees, shoulders heaving. And the whole of England watching. What they must think of us!*

She rides back to London in her carriage, bumping over muddy roads. Her ladies cry out at every bump, every rut in the road. She peers through the curtains at a sodden and starving world. Human scarecrows scavenge in the fields. The rains ruined the autumn harvest, and it has not stopped raining since. She sees a cow lying bloated on its side in a flooded field, then another. She cannot stand to look further; she flicks back the curtain and submits to the jolting of the carriage.

They have seen me cry once today; they shall not see me weak again.

She stares at Eleanor le Despenser, who winces with every bounce.

You have your duty, Philippe whispers. You know what you must do.

But what if I fail you?

You will not fail me.

But what if I cannot make Edward love me?

Love is nothing. You are my daughter. You were not born to trouble yourself about love.

But it's not fair. You know what love is like, I saw you at mother's funeral. And look at Edward. In the church, he could scarcely breathe. What is it like to love so much?

Just remember your duty.

"My duty."

"What was that, your grace?" Eleanor asks her.

She realizes she has spoken aloud. She shakes her head. "It is nothing," she says.

My duty. Is that all there is for me?

Why should I complain? He is not cruel to me. Yet if I was to die before him, would Edward wrap my body in gold cloth and have all England's churches say mass for me? Would he sob over my tomb like a child, as he did for Gaveston?

He is more like a brother than a husband, pleasant company but never a kiss or an embrace, and comes to my bed for procreation only, like a good Christian, but not like a red-blooded man.

But this she promises herself: one day she will have his heart. He will love her like he had loved *him*. She could not bear it if she were to live her entire life and never know what it was like to be Gaveston and be truly adored.

Chapter 23

Lancaster's star is in the ascendant; Edward is under his heel. He needs her now, and she will remember these as their best times.

While Lancaster skulks in his castle at Kenilworth, issuing proclamations and demands, the king holds his councils at Westminster. Isabella is invited to attend. Does he do this to irritate Lancaster, or because he is beginning to trust her?

Old Hugh's son now becomes a regular petitioner at the court. The king says he does not like him. He refers to him as the Despenser, in a dismissive tone. Lancaster and his fellow dissenters forced him on the king as their chamberlain for a time, and Edward has not forgiven him for siding with Lancaster when Gaveston was murdered. He tolerates him for old Hugh's sake.

Now he wants the king to ratify some estates that once belonged to his brother-in-law Gloucester, before he was killed at Bannockburn. The Despenser says they should pass to him. The king is slow about it. It is clearly an injustice and irks the Despenser to the point of apoplexy. In private Edward laughs about it.

"Let's make him stew a bit longer."

One wet night in May, she meets the Despenser coming out of the great hall at Westminster—an appalling place, Exchequer clerks bawling at each other over the massive marble chancery; the King's Bench and the Court of Common Pleas are in the same chamber, and the din is overwhelming.

It is sticky and warm, and she has long dispensed with her furs, but young Hugh still wears a heavy mantle and is blowing on his hands. The king says he is like a lizard and has to lie on a rock in the sun to get warm.

He is not like his father; he frequently forgets to be obsequious. He knows only one song, and that is that the world owes him more. *"Your grace, about these estates in Gloucester. Your grace, about this castle in Tonbridge."* He has the palest skin she has ever seen, and in a certain light he appears translucent. She thinks that if you were to cut him, his blood would be the palest blue.

"Shall you be appearing regularly at the king's councils, your grace?" he asks her, and she thinks he is about to make a complaint about having women in the chamber. Instead he takes her to task over the king's wavering in endowing him the Earl of Gloucester's former estates. Gloucester's wife has claimed that she was with child when Gloucester died, and an heir is on his way; but it's two years since Bannockburn, and unless the child emerges with a beard, it is unlikely now to be Gloucester's.

"I am sure the king will get to it in good time," she tells him and passes on.

As an earl, he would make a fine bailiff. Owe him a penny and before the year is out, he will have your castle, your horse, and your wife.

Mortimer nudges her one day as they gather in council with the king. The Despenser finds a seat, with a look that suggests he is unhappy not being placed at the king's shoulder.

Mortimer nods in his direction. "The ghost of Piers Gaveston has just walked into the room," he says. At the time she has no idea what he means by it.

———————

Warwick had not come to the council since spring. He no longer looked like Warwick then; he was thin and drawn, but not in the grim and poisoned way of the past. There were plum-colored shadows under his eyes, and he walked like an old man. It was the last time he was seen at court, for he did not live out the summer.

Edward, of course, is far from grief-stricken. When he is informed that Warwick has asked for a simple funeral, he chokes off a further guffaw of laughter. "I'll give him one. I'll throw him in a shit pile in Whitefriars, and the dogs can fight over his giblets. Would *that* be simple enough?"

There is a rumor, passed on by Eleanor and Lady de Vescy, that Warwick was poisoned. She asks Edward if he has heard this gossip. The king says no, but the king is lying. He adds the pious hope that Warwick died slowly and in pain.

Because his son is yet a child, all Warwick's estates pass to the Crown in trust. She doubts any in his family will ever see them returned.

Lancaster has meanwhile replaced all the sheriffs and bailiffs with his own men and issues pardons and grants petitions, while Edward sends embassies to Kenilworth to beg his leave should he wish to yawn or change his horse's saddle.

At night she listens to Edward rage and vow revenge, and keeps him from a war that he cannot win. She counsels patience. He listens to her, lets her hold him sometimes and stroke his head as one might calm a frightened horse.

Lancaster might have the power for the moment, but it is Isabella whom the barons love. She laughs, she charms. She is no longer thin and pretty; people tell her she is beautiful, and if they do not tell her, she asks them. The barons puff out their chests and try to look manly whenever she enters the great hall. There are other ways to play at politics, you see.

She transforms the court. She has found the English recalcitrant when it comes to fashion, and she has the royal dressmaker in Paris send her low-cut gowns that she insists her ladies wear. Lady de Vescy is scandalized and claims she is too old to display her bosoms—and is the first to wear one. Eleanor, even though she is youngest, is hardest to persuade. But eventually she brings them all to heel.

She receives from France a sideless surcoat trimmed with fur, and a *pelicon*, a fur-lined mantle with a cowled hood. Soon all the other ladies of the court are affecting them as well. She abandons the matronly chin-barbe for a diaphanous veil worn over her gold chaplet.

Edward watches and smiles and indulges her whims. He commissions a circlet of rubies, sapphires, emeralds, and pearls. He spends a staggering thirty-two pounds for a new chaplet and silk dress so that she might astound at the wedding of one of her demoiselles. It is studded with silver and encrusted with three hundred rubies and two thousand pearls. Let Lancaster set an ordinance against that.

She is elegant, she smiles, and she is beautiful. Edward basks in her reflected glory.

She announces a new son to be delivered at the end of the summer and withdraws to Eltham for her confinement. The castle is a gift from Edward, and he has refurbished her apartments there. From her window she can see the spires of Saint Paul's.

Eleanor, the Despenser's wife, is irregular in her attendance these days for she is frequently in confinement herself. She is ten years married and has six children of her own already. Her husband is not cold-blooded all the time, it appears, though she imagines he has the conjugal visits recorded in a ledger by a clerk and demands her to account for those that do not result in issue. Perhaps he has a system of fines.

"I see your husband wishes to be Lord of Glamorgan now?" Isabella asks her one day.

Eleanor bristles at this implied criticism. "Well, what man would not?"

"He is certainly impatient for it."

Eleanor flushes. She has a wicked little temper, and sometimes Isabella amuses herself by prodding her a bit, watching how it gripes her to hold her tongue. "He only ever asks for what is his, by right, your grace."

"And six children to prove it!"

Eleanor's cheeks burn red.

Jacques de Molay's curse still echoes in the royal palaces of France. Her brother Louis catches pneumonia from drinking iced wine after playing tennis. A king cannot have too many heirs, it seems.

So she is pleased to give Edward another son, John. Lancaster is informed of the birth but does not deign to remove himself from his estates to attend the christening.

There will be another war soon. There can only be one king in a country, and presently England has two. It is a state of affairs that cannot continue forever.

Chapter 24

Edward looks up, gives her a reassuring smile. Pembroke's expression is comforting, and Mortimer's is unreadable. Lancaster is there; she feels his enmity as she walks in, a mere woman. He does not want her on the king's council, even if she is queen. Let him issue an ordinance about it.

Old Hugh looks rattled. His son is here again today, perhaps Lancaster owes him money.

Even before she has taken her seat beside Edward on the dais, Lancaster is on his feet, blaming them both for the Bruce's latest ravages in the north.

"One wonders why the Bruce plunders everyone's lands but yours," Edward says, making no effort to appear conciliatory. It is true; only Lancaster's dominions remain untouched by the Scottish *hobelars*.

"Can we not discuss what we may do about it, rather than apportion blame?" Isabella asks them.

She earns a nod of approval from Pembroke. She has assumed his role of peacemaker, and he seems relieved to be rid of it. It is a thankless task when other men have no interest.

But Lancaster is not to be appeased. He moves on to his ever-green contention, recounting all of Edward's failings against the Scots, one by one.

"And yet, Uncle," she says when he is done, her voice so soft he has to strain to hear her, "you still have not explained to us why your own lands remain untouched in these raids."

"Because he fears me," Lancaster says.

"Some say that is not the reason!" Edward shouts.

"What other reason could there be?"

"Could it be you are plotting with the Bruce against the Crown?"

Lancaster looks from his niece to his king. He feigns outrage, but his eyes tell a different story and confirm the suspicions they both have of him. "To do such a thing is treason. Who accuses me?"

"You deny it, then?"

"Of course I deny it! Where is your proof?"

There is no proof. The other magnates fidget in their seats. They can all see England sliding again to civil war. Mortimer says something ferocious, and soon everyone in the chamber is on their feet and shouting at each other and nothing is achieved.

Lancaster hurls yet more insults at Edward, who cannot contain himself and rises red-faced to the challenge and hurls them right back. This is not about the Bruce. This is about Gaveston. Everyone knows it.

"Uncle." She speaks so softly that they all stop their yelling to listen to her. "Uncle, you say the king allows this Robert Bruce to raid our northern borders with impunity, but you are the one who prevents England from going to war to stop him. With these restrictions you have placed on the king, what is he supposed to do?"

Her voice is so sweetly reasonable, it calms him for a moment. He leaves off shouting to reflect.

But this is not what the king wants. "You are a whoreson dog," he growls at Lancaster, and the time for peace making is past. Lancaster storms from the Parliament. She doubts he will ever return.

After they disperse, she sees the Despenser with Edward. They withdraw to a window and converse in whispers, some private matter of the realm she supposes. But she does not like the way the Despenser looks at the king, as if he were something he would like for dinner.

But it is only a moment, and she thinks she must be mistaken.

A scandal, and one that brings Edward a great deal of merriment when he is not fretting about two more of his barons going to war. Lancaster's wife, Alice, tired of her husband's whoring, has absconded with one of Surrey's knights. Lancaster blames Surrey, musters an army, and marches south. He does not care about losing Alice as much as the damage to his pride.

By now Isabella is confined to Woodstock. She has two sons, and now there is a daughter, Eleanor. A healthy brood, and no Gaveston to come between them. Surely this is her moment of triumph?

Yet something is missing.

Lonely in her bed, she thinks of Marguerite and Blanche and their lovers; they paid dearly for their pleasures. They said her brother Louis had his wife strangled in the nunnery to stop the inconvenient breaths she continued to draw. It had allowed him to take a rather beautiful princess of Hungary as his new queen.

At the time, she had been shocked by Marguerite's behavior and had been glad of her punishment. Now she is no longer as sure of what is right, and there is no king of either France or England to remind her. A bed as large as this is cold in winter, and in summer with the sheets kicked back and the sweat trickling down her breastbone, she longs for a man's caresses and his kisses on her face.

It no longer seems important if that man is Edward.

Was this how it was for Marguerite? But when a woman is royal, she cannot think of what she wants for herself. Her silly sister-in-law did not understand that. *"You will love this man. Do you understand?"* She has a duty to France, and a duty to her husband.

Sometimes she thinks of Mortimer. Why Mortimer? She does not even find him pleasant. Perhaps it is the way he looks at her. Edward has never looked at her like that, with such hunger. How can she think this way, of being touched, of being taken? These are not proper thoughts. She is a mother now, and a queen.

Mortimer is back at court, restless and dark, prowling the corridors like a mastiff, on some errand or other, and every now and then, a look, a flash of the eyes, nothing that could attract any attention but hers. She wishes Edward would send him back to Ireland.

She hears her father's reprimand in the darkness. He looks disappointed, disgusted even. When she closes her eyes, she sees Marguerite, how she laughed and flirted with d'Aulnay. Empty-headed women do not anticipate the risk. She imagines her in a bare cell in her sackcloth, head shaved, how the shadow falls over her face when her assassins come for her. They say she was half-mad by then and didn't understand what was happening even when they put the pillow over her face.

She imagines them dragging her out by her feet, her head bumping down the stone stairs. This was a woman who might have been queen of France if she had kept her legs closed.

A lesson for us all.

Is that what you want, Isabella? Because you are a queen, and if you persist in this way of thinking, one day that could happen to you.

How can you entertain such monstrous daydreams when you have a new daughter in the nursery?

She is almost asleep when the door opens. When her ladies see who it is, they scamper from the room in their nightgowns. The king removes his robe and climbs into the bed. He is as cold as a marble statue, but she lets him warm himself on her, though she thinks she will scream at the touch of his cold hands.

The branches of trees move in the moonlight beyond the dull glass like ghosts—and there are enough of those. He shivers in her arms. It reminds her of those long nights after Bannockburn.

His hands creep beneath her nightgown. It is like being fondled by the dead, but she resists the urge to push him away and hopes that he warms soon. She has hungered for his touch, but in her dreams his hands were not so chill.

———

It is clear that something must be done about Lancaster, though he has lost much of the support he once enjoyed from his fellow earls. As the summer wears on, the king spends many afternoons closeted with Pembroke. One day he summons Isabella. "Pembroke says the only way forward is for you to go to Lancaster," he tells her.

"Go to Kenilworth? Should he not come here, your grace?"

"He should. He won't. Pembroke and Mortimer think it is important that we have the peace. Bruce has taken Berwick. He must be attended to, and for that we must have a truce of sorts. They think you are the one who can arrange it."

"Me, your grace?"

He takes her by the shoulders and kisses her cheek. "He is still your uncle. And these barons defer to your gentle words more than they will to the threat of my sword. If I cannot do this by force of arms, then I will do it by your sweetness."

She has waited a long time to hear these words from him. She has wanted him to long for her. Relying on her seems to do just as well.

———

Every journey the queen makes requires as much planning and marshaling—according to Edward—as it does to raise an army against the Scots. Her household and much of her furniture must go with her, all packed in boxes and stacked onto carts and covered with waxed canvas to keep the rain out. Sumpter horses carry the rest.

There are not cushions enough in the world to make the journey from London to Kenilworth any easier. It goes on for days, jarring her spine with every mile as they bump over roads better suited to goats. Finally she peers from the litter, sees flocks of sheep on wild moors, a burned and ransacked priory. Her uncle is a brutal landlord.

She craves rest, but her uncle is all business. He seems amused that Edward has sent his niece to negotiate with him. He slouches in a chair and asks her what favors she requires of him.

She does not let him see her fatigue. She is, after all, queen of England, and royalty may bend, but it does not break.

———

The daughter of France wins England her peace. One hot summer's day she watches from the banks while Edward and Lancaster meet on the bridge at Loughborough and once again share the kiss of peace.

A charade, for she knows her husband would rather run a sharp blade across his throat as kiss him. But it is politics, and it is necessary.

"But I still have to obey his ordinances. He can still tell me what I can do and whom I can take as advisers!" he shouts at her afterward, when they are alone.

"Not Lancaster. He has agreed to relinquish his place as an ordainer. He doesn't want it anyway. He is as bored with government as you are."

"You have bribed him?"

"We have compensated him for the loss of an important post."

"So who will be Ordainer in his place?"

"Pembroke."

Edward sucks his teeth. "That might work."

She takes his arm. "Pembroke has no great love for Lancaster. Nor does Mortimer. Surrey hates him heartily. You can play these barons one against the other until you get what you want."

A moment of reflection. "You've done well."

"I understand politics."

He wraps his arms around her and kisses her, taking her breath away. It is not passion, but it is enthusiasm, at least. It has all been worth it, to watch Lancaster ride away, outplayed if he but knew it. It was worth it to see her husband beam at her, the peace done.

"I am going to have his head," he says.

Two months later the rebellions in Ireland are over. Mortimer is recalled in triumph. There is just the small matter of the Scots, and then they can turn their attention to their real enemy, the Lord of Kenilworth Castle.

Chapter 25

Restless, she roams the palace. In the great hall, the Despenser's clerks snore in the chancery, other servants sleep where they can on the benches. She sees lights in the king's Painted Chamber, hears a man laughing.

She had forgotten what there is to learn from the common folk: stand at a door of a stable or a kitchen, and you may learn how a whole country is thinking. No one can speak their mind like a steward with his private opinion of the king of England: "They say he goes to it with every stable boy and every young buck at the court, and where will that get him when all know it is a sin in the eyes of the Lord, and one day the devil will stick a red-hot poker up his nether parts for all damnation."

The kitchen girls giggle and tell him to keep his voice down, but this only encourages him, and he tells them he has heard that Edward's twizzle is shaped like a pig's, all corkscrew shaped when it comes out, and it has seen more back entries than a Turk. The king, they reckon, has sucked more cocks than a Jerusalem whore when a new crusade comes to town.

Once she might have been shocked. Now she is merely curious. What is in Edward's heart?

───

She finds Mortimer idling in the hall. Her cheeks flush when she sees him. "Lord Mortimer," she says, as casually as she can. "What are you doing lurking in a drafty hallway?"

"I am waiting to see the king."

"Then do so. Announce yourself."

"I am afraid I have to see young Hugh first."

"The Despenser boy? Why?"

Mortimer looks surprised that she should ask the question. "No one sees the king without first seeing . . . the Despenser boy."

Really? Why does she not know of this? A few weeks away from court and everything changes. "You are well returned from Ireland? I have heard of your triumphs."

"I have heard of yours. You won England a great peace."

"I am glad you think so."

"They say your presence on the councils has made the barons more reasonable men. Edward is fortunate to have such a one as you. You are his greatest adviser."

She flushes to the roots of her hair at this compliment.

"You are to be congratulated on the birth of a daughter. She is well?"

"The rudest of health."

"And the princes?"

"They grow taller every day."

"And you, your grace. Look at you! You grow more beautiful with each passing year."

Now this last remark is unexpected. She blinks, wondering if she has actually heard him correctly. His eyes bore into her, and there is no mistaking the message in them.

He must be mad.

A secretary appears, his approach disguised by the carpets. "My Lord Despenser will see you now," he says to Mortimer, and the Scourge of Ireland bows meekly and follows him.

She stares after him, trying not to appear disconcerted in front of her ladies, who appear suddenly from one of the apartments. She grapples with the news. *My husband's general has just tried to seduce his queen, and now the king has a new favorite.*

These days it is difficult to keep up.

Chapter 26

June 1321

Mortimer has asked to see her. She hopes there are to be no more declarations about her beauty. She hardly feels beautiful now. She feels heavy and bloated with the new baby, and she is not long from her confinement.

He is ushered in by Lady de Vescy, who disapproves of him. Mortimer has eyes for one of her demoiselles, at least when his wife is not at court. But today he spares no glances for anyone; he appears to be a man in a hurry. He asks if they may speak in private.

She walks to the end of the passage and stands by the window overlooking the gardens.

"An unexpected pleasure. Should I be alarmed?"

"I wished to see you because it is easier than seeing the king. You do not have Lord Despenser standing guard over your every word."

"You make much of nothing."

"Do I, your grace? Your husband's new chamberlain leads Edward like a cat after straw. It is Gaveston all over again."

"You sound like my uncle Lancaster."

"What make you of young Hugh, your grace?"

"He is good with figures. The Exchequer is much healthier since he took over the role of chamberlain. I shall admit his greed outweighs his charm."

"You underestimate him."

"Lord Mortimer, you would say that about any man who has the king's ear over you."

"He uses Edward for his own ends. You know that he is building an empire in the west country by every means he can. He steals and cheats and uses the king's men and the king's name to do it. And Edward allows it."

"Why do you come to me with this?"

"Because you have Edward's ear. Tell him he must listen to his Marcher lords or there will be war."

Another rebellion, this time in the marches, on the border with Wales. It's becoming habitual with these mighty lords. *Will there never be peace in this blighted country? Yet Mortimer is not unjust in his accusations. Why does Edward continue to provoke them?*

"This sounds very much like a threat."

"He is not only a threat to me, but he is a threat to you also."

"Once perhaps, when I was young, but Edward needs me now."

The look on his face is twisted between jealousy and pity. "There are rumors told about the king."

"There are always rumors about the king. If he is wise, a man would not listen to them."

"The young Despenser has stolen d'Amory's inheritance, and the king let him to do it. Is this just?"

"They say that many years ago your grandfather killed Despenser's ancestor in some baronial feud. Is it true?"

"You think that is why I go against the king in this?"

"I think my husband has suffered enough at the hands of his magnates. He is the king, and his lords should obey him."

"He has confiscated Gower from John Mowbray and given it to his new favorite! It is against the law."

"On the contrary, as I understand it, Mowbray did not first ask for the king's license."

"That is mere form. It is commonly never done!"

"So you agree: my husband was within his rights to confiscate the lands. He is then at liberty to give them to whomever he pleases. Or is it rather you do not wish one of the Despensers for a neighbor?"

Her ladies are staring, startled by the sound of their raised voices. *How dare he!* But then there are many things that Mortimer might dare, if given the opportunity. She likes that about him.

He takes a breath and bows. "Your grace, I defer to your greater wisdom in the matter. I shall pray that all goes well with the birth of the royal child."

"Thank you, Lord Mortimer. Shall I announce you to the king?"

"Would that you could," he says and strides away through the ladies, several of whom eye him speculatively. Even Lady de Vescy.

The man is insufferable.

He had not told her she was beautiful this time.

———

"I heard that Mortimer paid you a visit today," Edward says to her that night as they dine in the great hall.

He chooses a morsel of chicken and places it on the silver plate in front of her. Occasionally he can be very charming. "He complains about your new chamberlain."

"His name is Hugh. You may call him by his name."

"Whatever I call him, he will not like him any better."

"No chamberlain I choose will be acceptable to the magnates. They are jealous of everyone."

"It is what I said to him. But he seems greatly upset. You should take him seriously."

"I did."

"He said that he cannot see you anymore without your chamberlain's permission."

"Well I cannot talk to everyone." He smiles. "Do you find him charming?"

"Not especially."

"Many of the ladies do. I don't know how Lady Mortimer suffers it."

"Will there be war, Edward?"

"That is not my decision."

"They should obey you. You are the king."

"That is what I would have them understand as well." He sighs. "I should have left Mortimer in Ireland. He was useful to me there. Now he has no one else to fight, he wants to fight me."

———

Whatever the true reason, Mortimer is surely spoiling for a war. He joins the Marcher lords who have formed a confederacy in the west. Hereford is among them, and together they have assembled a massive army. Newport, Cardiff, and Caerphilly fall; and then they burn half of Glamorgan and Gloucester, ransacking every Despenser castle in their way.

Edward leaves to confront them the day Isabella goes into confinement in the Tower. He orders them to disperse and they refuse. He cannot impose his will; the forces ranged against him are too great. Once again, Edward is powerless in his own lands.

Then Mortimer and Hereford march north and join with Lancaster.

———

It is raining the day he returns from the borderlands. Isabella is in labor, but no one has thought to make provision for her comfort. She is forgotten, except by her ladies, who do what they can for her. Water leaks through the ceilings and onto the bedclothes. When Edward sees this, he summons the constable and sends him sprawling down the stairs.

"What have they done to you?" he shouts and carries her out of the room.

She clings to him. Even defeated, he is still a man to be reckoned with.

"Whose drums are they?" she asks him, as he trails along the corridor looking to find her a bed that isn't soaked through.

"Mortimer's."

As they pass a window, he stops and shows her. They fly Edward's Plantagenet banners even while they lay siege to his castle. The fields beyond the suburbs are an armed camp.

"My barons are threatening to burn London from Charing Cross to Westminster. Lancaster leads them. It is just like old times."

Later that day she gives birth to a daughter. She is easier won than the others, gentle Joan. Isabella had thought little Edward would kill her; she had heard a lion roar in the king's menagerie when he was born. When Joan comes, there is just the warbling of doves in the apple trees below the tower.

Chapter 27

"My Lord Pembroke."

Pembroke has a new wife, and is just recently returned from France. He had hopes to spend the summer starting a new son and heir but instead here he is again, trying to mend fences between his king and his lords.

He bows, all grace and inexhaustible patience. No wonder Edward forgave him for Gaveston. "Your grace, I was overjoyed to hear the news that you were safely delivered of a daughter."

"Thank you, my Lord Pembroke. And I believe I should congratulate you also, on your new wife. You have chosen well." Indeed, her grandfather had been Henry III. "We are glad to see you safely returned."

"I wish we had come back to England at a more fortunate time."

"You have spoken to the Marchers? Perhaps you might ask them to remove themselves from London."

"Well, your grace, that is why I am here."

"They wish my husband to forego his new chamberlain. What does he say to that?"

"He does not seem well disposed to it."

"Would you, if you were king?"

"There is one who might bring him to see the sense in it."

"And who is that?"

Pembroke smiles. There is a wealth of meaning in his every expression, and she now understands what he is here for. She hands young Joan to Lady de Vescy and begs them all leave her in peace with Lord Pembroke.

"I cannot ask it of him," she says when they are alone.

"You must."

"He is king of England. No one ever asked my father to exile any of his advisers."

"Your father never allowed any one man to so dominate his affairs."

Isabella stares at Pembroke—a shrug here, a puff of the cheek there. Everything he does is an appeal for accommodation among reasonable men in a kingdom where such a man does not exist. And so he has come to her.

"He will hate me for it."

"On the contrary, it will help him save face. If you plead on behalf of England, he can acquiesce and not lose his honor."

"This is rebellion."

"They claim they march under the king's banner. They say it is Despenser they wish removed, not the king."

Isabella considers: If she does this, it will make her preeminent. Should he listen to her at such a time, it will prove to her, and to him, that she is indispensable. Isn't that what she wants?

Isn't this what he needs?

"It is the only way out of this for us all," he says.

She nods. He is right. She will try.

———

"No," Edward says. "I have made a vow. I shall never give in."

She sees the pleading in his eyes. He wants a way out of this, but he also wants to win. He has never won before, and he is so tired of losing: losing to the Bruce, losing to the barons, losing to his dead father.

She sees that Mortimer was wrong about the Despenser. It is not the same as it was with Gaveston. This time it is the principle of the thing.

He stamps from his throne and waves a document at her, at his entire court. Evidently it comes from Lancaster. "He says my chamberlain bars my magnates from my presence, that he alienates me from my people. To which people do you think he refers? This from a man who sets himself up at his castle like a foreign prince in my place!"

Edward is so angry he is frothing. He throws the document in the rushes, where a secretary hurries to retrieve it. *We cannot have the dogs sniffing at the correspondence.*

"Mortimer says he wants my chamberlain and his father and all their servants gone from my palace or he will relinquish his homage and set up another in my place. That is treason!"

He is wild-eyed. The Despenser moves to console him, places a hand on his arm, and begs forbearance, but the king brushes him away.

"You wish me to negotiate with traitors?"

There is a silence in the great hall. Even Pembroke is cowed by Edward's temper. But he manages: "Your grace, I beg you. He perishes on the rocks, he that loves another more than himself."

It is at this moment that Isabella rushes forward and falls to her knees in front of him, before Pembroke, before the king's bishops, before the king's court. "My Lord, they threaten to depose you and put Lancaster on the throne. I beg you, make this sacrifice for the sake of the people."

Edward sees her on her knees and is astonished. "The people?"

"It is the people of England who need this peace. Do not do it because of their army, do not do it for fear of their arrogance and their infidelity. Do it to spare us from tyrants. Do it for England."

Edward sees his salvation. He takes her gently by the arm and raises her to her feet. "You do not have to do this," he whispers.

"But you do."

She sees the Despenser glaring at her over her husband's shoulder.

"He does not love you like I do."

He knows whom she means. "What do you suggest?" he says.

"Play for time. If you will fight, you must fight on your own terms. That time is not here, and it is not now."

He leads his queen to the dais and sits her again on her throne. He bends his knee and kisses her hand. Pembroke raises an eyebrow, impressed. Even the bishops smile. Everyone seems relieved but the young Despenser, and he no longer matters to her now.

Edward summons Mortimer and Lancaster and Hereford and the rest to Westminster Hall. He sits stone-faced on the throne and tells them that the Despensers will be sent away within the month. Lancaster grins and claps Hereford on the back. He does not even have the grace to appear magnanimous. Only Mortimer betrays no expression; he catches Isabella's eye just once, and she looks away.

The earls all fall then on their knees, and the king pardons them for what they have done. His voice shakes. He sounds as if he is choking on a bone.

That night he comes to her bed, but he does not blow out all the candles, and he does not try to caress her. He lies quite still in the darkness and, when she reaches for him, he squeezes her hand and holds it to his chest.

"You must help me," he says.

"Anything. What is it you wish?"

"This cannot stand."

"You did what you must. There will be another day."

"You have said this to me before, but I am tired of waiting for the right moment. This time I must make the right moment."

"You have a plan?"

"Just say you will do it."

"My loyalty to you is absolute."

"Good," he says and rolls on his side and sleeps. She lies awake, staring into the darkness.

Chapter 28

There is a mist on the river, and the way is lit by torches. The clip of their horses' hooves are muted by the fog. Though it is summer, it is cold tonight, the landing chosen because so few eyes can see them.

The ship is pulled up at a long jetty, and she and Edward are escorted aboard. She wrinkles her nose at the reek of mud. There is planking laid across to the deck, and her ladies help her across it. She is wrapped in a long-hooded cloak. She sees rough-looking men without uniforms stare back at her.

The Despenser does not look as he did when he was the king's chamberlain. He has a thin beard now and rough clothes, and shouts orders as if he has been a privateer all his life. The king's chamberlain now makes his way in the world by running this pirate ship out of Bordeaux. He has recently plundered a Genoese vessel and helped himself to five thousand pounds in treasure. Whatever else they say about him, he knows how to make a living.

They go below to a cabin dimly lit with oil lamps and candles. He gets out the wine. She refuses, but the king doesn't.

He outlines his plan, and the king is enthusiastic. They look to her. She agrees, for she has given her word to the king that she will do it. She wants to see him win, and if she must use this silken ruffian to do it, then so be it.

———————

Isabella and Edward return to the Tower just before dawn. The fog has cleared, apparently at the king's command, and as they enter the water gate, the white tower shines in the moonlight. She hugs the cloak tighter around her shoulders.

"He is no threat to you, Isabella."

"I have your word?"

"You are my queen. No one can ever replace you."

His hand reaches for hers. She is reassured, and all doubts are cast aside.

Chapter 29

Leeds Castle

The wake made by a pair of white swans ripples the black lake around the castle. Helmeted men watch them from the crenulated towers. Isabella leans from her litter, her breath clouding on the damp evening air. Her sergeant races to attend her.

"You sent word ahead, requesting lodging?"

"Yes, your grace."

"Then why are the gates not open to us?"

"Lord Badlesmere is not inside, your grace." She knows this: he is with Mortimer and Lancaster, having joined the conspiracy against the king, though he hardly had choice in the matter as his daughter is married to Mortimer's son. His absence is the reason Edward sent her here, though the rest of the world thinks she is on a pilgrimage to Canterbury.

"Lady Badlesmere has told the escort that her husband left her firm orders to permit entrance to no one."

"The queen of England is hardly 'no one.'"

This intransigence is just what Edward has hoped for; how could Lady Badlesmere be sure that Isabella is not here to take possession of the castle in the king's name? Despenser is an astute man, when all was said and done, as well as a passably adept pirate.

"Go back to the gate. Tell her the queen requires lodging for the night."

Her sergeant hesitates. "If she refuses?"

"Tell her."

He leads two dozen of the royal escort across the isthmus and up to the castle gates. He shouts her request to the guard on the tower of the gatehouse. She cannot hear the reply, but it must be a refusal for her sergeant shouts the request a second time.

A moment later, he pitches back in his saddle, an arrow through his throat. He tumbles to the ground, and his horse rears up. More arrows arc through the mist, and two more men go down. Trapped on this narrow neck of land, the rest cannot avoid a second volley, and in moments a dozen of her men lie dead or groaning in front of the gates of Leeds Castle.

The survivors gallop back. The blood drains from her cheeks. It is one thing to plan a provocation, another to see good men die because of it.

She lets the curtain drop. Several of her ladies are squealing in fright.

I have done my duty to my husband.

She imagines her father smiling and nodding; this is how he would have done it. He would be proud.

Two days later Pembroke's banner appears outside the priory where she has retired with her surviving escort. Mounted on war-horses, the earl's men clatter over the stone bridge.

She comes out to the cloister to meet him. He sweeps his mail coif from his head and tosses it to his man. He kneels.

She counts fifty men at his back. "Is that all you have to take Leeds Castle?"

"Your grace, there are thirty thousand men over that hill. Lend your ears closely, and you will hear them."

He is right. She hears drums on the wind and the tramp of feet, though faint. But thirty thousand?

"You exaggerate, my Lord Pembroke. That is not like you."

"It is the truth. The whole country is outraged at the way you have been mistreated. They have risen to your cause as they never have risen to Edward's. All of London is with me, and Norfolk, Kent, Surrey, Arundel. And how many are there inside the castle? They will sh— They will be terrified when they see us."

"What of Lancaster and my Lord Mortimer?"

"I have parlayed with them, and they know their cause is lost. They are running back to Shrewsbury. But there is no place for them to hide now. Shall we to Leeds?"

Chapter 30

Tonbridge Castle

Edward's face shines as if he has experienced divine revelation. He has endured their humiliation for ten years. Now he has his moment, and he is going to draw from it in full measure.

"Isabella!" He takes her in his arms when he sees her. She is the key now. While his earls would not go to war for their king over the many insults thrown at him, it takes just one against the queen, and the whole country is on his side.

"It worked," she whispers.

"Thanks to you," he beams at her. "See how they fear their king now!"

He cannot stop moving. He sits, he stands, he goes to the window, and then sits again. He has been so long bowed by defeats that it is as if he has been unchained.

"What of Mortimer and Lancaster?"

"Running like rabbits back to their rats' nests in the Welsh slop lands. This time they shall not escape. Now I have an army to pursue them."

This is more like a king. Now she may truly be a queen again.

Soon he is out of the tent, organizing the siege of Leeds Castle and congratulating Pembroke and Surrey, though they have done nothing yet.

———————

The swans have gone and there is ice on the lake. Lady Badlesmere's soldiers watch the king's vast army take up position around the walls. She can imagine what they must be feeling.

On a crisp October morning soon afterward, Lady Badlesmere surrenders the castle to the king. It is Edward's first victory. He finally knows what it is like to win.

The constable of the castle and a dozen of his men are led out in chains, and Edward supervises their execution. When the last is finished jerking on his rope, Lady Badlesmere and her children are brought out in chains and hustled into a carriage.

Isabella is there and sees it all. For a moment their eyes meet. Lady Badlesmere looks frightened and confused. She has done her duty by her husband, and her reward is to be imprisoned in the Tower at the king's pleasure.

In later years, Isabella will look back on this moment and curse it. This is when the king changes. From this very moment everyone in England will pay for what happened to the only one he had ever loved.

"You did this for me," he says to her.

"I did as you asked me. I am always your dutiful queen." She cannot banish the image of Lady Badlesmere being dragged from her castle in chains. It terrifies her.

"I am bringing Perro back from exile."

"Lord Despenser, you mean?"

"Yes, Hugh, that's what I said. He will soon be back here at my command. They will never dictate my friends to me again." He grins but his eyes are cold. "There shall be more kisses of peace.

They have put my face to the dirt enough times, now they shall all taste the earth."

———————

Pembroke looks frail; the hard roads of England have taken a toll on him, and he looks more ready for a place by the fire and a blanket than riding after Edward's enemies. He bows stiffly. He is tired of it all.

"How are my husband's fortunes?"

"He has taken Mortimer," he says.

"He surrendered?"

"There was nowhere left to run. I tried to make terms for him as best I could. I told him that if he came freely to the king, he would be pardoned and his life would be spared."

"Why should you offer such a thing?"

"He never rose against Edward, only against Despenser."

"It's the same thing."

"I gave my word."

As he had given it to Gaveston. This old man never learns a thing from his own history. She cannot imagine how he has survived so long in the hurly-burly of English politics. "Where is Mortimer now?"

"Edward has had Mortimer and his father put in chains and thrown in prison. They are to be tried for treason. The king has confiscated Mortimer's lands and arrested his wife and children, his daughters are all sent to nunneries. It is a harsh fate."

"Taking an army against your king is a harsh decision."

"He felt he had no choice."

Isabella steps closer. "You sound as if you have sympathy for him."

"I understand his reasons even if I do not agree with them, your grace."

"What of my uncle Lancaster?"

"Fled north. He now calls himself King Arthur, and says that he champions the common man of England against a king gone mad. Some say he is hoping the Bruce will provide protection."

"Then he is the one who is mad."

"The king asks that you send to your brother in France to seek assistance in his travails against Lancaster."

"That is not possible. My brother Philippe is dead. Charles is the new heir but not yet crowned."

"Dead?" Pembroke looks shocked. She knows what he is thinking; since the Templar Grand Master shouted his curse at his execution, her father and two of her brothers have died. It is a black and savage magic, this.

"I shall send messages to the sheriff at Westmoreland and have him assemble his army, ensure Lancaster cannot reach Scotland. Lancaster must not escape my husband's displeasure."

Pembroke is about to speak but thinks better of it.

"What is it, my lord?"

"What shall I do?" Pembroke says. "I gave my word to Mortimer."

Ah, Mortimer. Just the name makes her shiver, unreasonably so. "He knew what he was about when he started this."

"He has been a faithful servant to the king for many years."

"So faithful that he brought his soldiers to London and besieged us in the Tower."

"The king is not the man he was. I had never suspected to see such venom in him."

Really? Isabella thinks. *Then what did you expect after all they had done to him?*

"Mortimer is to be tried as a traitor. It is a harsh fate for a man who served the king so."

Isabella sighs. Pembroke the peacemaker is fast becoming Pembroke the dreamer. He is not much longer for this game, she suspects, or this life. He overlooks that a ruthless streak behooves all great kings. Look what her own father had done to Marguerite and Blanche.

"My lord, Edward does what he must. When you stir the anger of a king, you cannot expect him to shrug his shoulders and walk away."

Pembroke admits defeat. He bows and takes his leave. The queen calls for her secretary and starts dictating letters, galvanizing support for Edward. He relies on her now, and she will not let him down.

Yet will he let me down? She has had these fourteen years to grow acquainted with Edward, and she knows him to be unreliable at best. Now he is vicious as well. *"You will love this man. Do you understand?"*

"I will not disappoint you."

But I was a girl then. I am a woman now, and I think I deserve better than this. I wonder if I will get it.

Chapter 31

Pontefract Castle,
Former Seat of the Earl of Lancaster

Her carriage bounces over the cobblestones outside Pontefract Castle. Isabella dares a peek through the curtains; blackened and rotted bodies, or parts of them, hang on pikes outside the gates. Edward has not only embraced vengeance, he is now completely enamored of it.

Anyone who supported Lancaster is now either dead or rotting in a prison. Many have been butchered and their quarters sent to the corners of Lancaster's estates as signs of the king's intent.

He trapped Lancaster at Boroughbridge. As Pembroke had predicted, he intended to treat with the Scots. So much for England's great champion, all his carping about Edward's failure to tame the Scots, and there at the end he was groveling to the Bruce for his own neck.

They had brought her the news at Langley: Lancaster had been tried as a traitor. The most Edward would do for him was commute his sentence of drawing and quartering to a cleaner, more merciful death.

Edward's soldiers are everywhere. The bailey is a sea of gray steel and grim faces. When she is brought into his chamber, he cannot wait to tell her what he has done.

"He was trembling like a woman! We put him on some sorry nag and took him to this little hill, a col like the one where they slaughtered my Perro. I let the mob have some fun with him, throw snow and offal at him and such. This for his pride! So much for the man who sent for me at Kenilworth as if I were his vassal. I let him know a little of what Perro felt when they dragged him from his dungeon in the middle of the night and slaughtered him!"

"How was it done?"

"A splendid touch! He was made to kneel in the direction of Scotland—to remind everyone that it was from there he had sought his salvation. It took three strokes of a blunt sword to get his head off, the stiff-necked bastard."

"What did he have to say in his defense?"

"I did not permit him to speak. He did not allow Perro to do so, so why should I grant him such privilege?"

"Did you kill him for treason or for killing Gaveston?"

A moment's silence. "Does it matter?"

An usher announces that the Despenser is here to see the king. He saunters into the room as if he is coregent. Instead of a bow, he kisses the king's cheek, smiling over Edward's shoulder at the queen.

"My Lord Despenser, how pleasant to see you returned from abroad."

The sleek privateer she had met on the Thames is now replaced by an overfed cat, one that purrs as Edward strokes him, and glares at anyone who would shift him from his lap.

Edward seems likewise indulgent. She remembers what Mortimer had told her. "*The ghost of Piers Gaveston has just walked into the room.*"

"So it is done then, your grace?" she says.

"Done?"

"Lancaster is dead and Mortimer arrested. They cannot challenge you now."

"Of course it is not done," the Despenser says.

What did he just say? His insolence is beyond bounds. She waits for Edward to rebuke him, but instead he just sits there and lets Despenser stroke his arm.

"There are heads and shanks from Pontefract to Kenilworth. You have made your point."

Edward shakes his head. "While there is one man who supported Lancaster against me, I shall not rest. I will weed them all out."

"Have you not done enough? You executed a nobleman of England, something not done since the time of the Conqueror. You have terrified all of England's magnates. None will stand against you now."

"We feel they are not nearly terrified enough," the Despenser says.

She stares at him. This is a different Despenser; the pirate is off to plunder different treasures, and she suspects the king will be the first prize he goes after.

"You forget, he was my uncle, and royal. A blood relative. I hardly think it is *not enough*."

The Despenser is defiant. "He didn't act like a blood relative when he confiscated your estates and besieged you in the Tower."

She turns back to Edward. "I would urge a lighter hand, your grace. You did enough with this one act to give everyone due warning that Edward may not be trifled with."

"You wish him to be soft with the rest of the traitors and ingrates?"

Really, she should not be addressed by a chamberlain like this. Perhaps it would be better to speak to Edward alone tonight, in their bed.

She smiles at the Despenser; the Despenser smiles back. Edward looks dreamy. "You know we hanged Badlesmere?"

"At Canterbury. Yes, I was informed."

"I will not stop until I have the very last ingrate on the gibbet."

The Despenser looks as if he longs for her to contend the point.

"Whatever you wish, your grace." She bobs her head and leaves the room. She feels the Despenser's eyes burning into her back.

Well, Mortimer you were right after all. Much good it has done you.

———

Edward does not come to her bed that night, or the next. When he finally draws back her cover, almost a week later, he is sulky, as if he expects she might demand something unreasonable from him. Tenderness perhaps. Affection.

He slips into bed. There is a cold windswept moor between them. He snuffs the candle. He would rather be in his own rooms, clearly.

"What has happened to you?" she says.

"I can tell by your sulky looks that you do not like me to be king. You rather I was still downtrodden and in your thrall?"

These sound like someone else's words, not his.

"I have done all you have asked of me. I do not deserve your reproach."

"I do not deserve yours. Why should you think that Lancaster did not warrant his fate?"

"I did not say that, only that there has been enough bloodletting. People respect a merciful hand in equal measure to a stern one. Hereford is dead and Lancaster and Badlesmere. Mortimer will be, soon enough. Is that not enough blood?"

"I shall not abide sleeping here if all you do is chide me!"

She rolls toward him, stretches a hand across the vast divide of the bed. She finds his hand, squeezes it. He does not respond.

"I have to ask you something."

Still nothing.

"Is Despenser sharing your pillow?"

He throws himself out of bed. She hears him raging down the passage, calling for his steward. Two of her maids whisper outside the door, unsure what to do.

One of them peeks in, holding a candle. After she snaps at her maid, the door closes again, leaving her alone in the dark.

Chapter 32

Her steward informs her that a lady has come to see her, someone sent from Skipton Castle by the Lady Mortimer. Isabella recognizes her. She is the wife of one of Mortimer's retainers.

She looks pale and nervous. The blackening torsos and hindquarters that decorate the outside of the castle leave many feeling faint. Nothing like a severed head to sober the mood, especially after the crows have been at it.

Isabella receives the woman in her chambers, has her sit, and then sends a servant to fetch spiced wine to revive her. It is a long journey from Skipton.

The woman is clearly awed by her surroundings, being here in the lair of the man who imprisoned her mistress and her mistress's husband. How quickly Edward has advanced from being a jest to a monster.

"My mistress, the Lady Mortimer, sent me, your grace." She hands her a letter. Isabella breaks the seal and reads it quickly. She is asking for her help, wishes someone to argue for her husband when he is brought to trial.

She hands the letter to Rosseletti and returns her attention to the girl. "How is my Lady Mortimer?"

"She is bereft. She fears the king will put her husband to the gallows."

It is all but certain, Isabella thinks. "The Lord Mortimer took up arms against the king. It is hard for me to argue his position."

The girl chances a glance at Rosseletti, and bites her lip.

"You may speak freely here. He is my servant, not the king's."

"The Lady Mortimer asks me to remind you that even though he was wrong to go against the king, he was right in his purpose."

"How so?"

"She says the king is yet not the real king. It is the Lord Despenser that rules us all, and not well."

"He is merely his chamberlain."

The girl hangs her head, looking utterly miserable. She has said what she had been coached to say, and now she fears she will be whipped for it.

"Thank you for bringing me the letter," Isabella tells her. "Tell your lady I shall do all I can for your lord and her husband."

"Thank you, your grace."

After she has gone, Isabella looks at Rosseletti.

"She is right," he says. "The king gives him everything he wants. He takes land from other lords and names his own price. The chamberlain is the most powerful man in England next to Edward. The king does nothing to curb him."

"Mortimer is a dead man."

"You still have the king's ear."

"Do I? It seems he forgot his queen as soon as the Despenser returned to England." She had worked tirelessly to give Edward dominion over his barons, but now that he has what he wanted, he has turned his back on her again. "You know, in the end, I think I liked Gaveston better. If he had to have a friend, I would rather it be one who dresses in purple than one who has a dagger hidden in his tunic."

"It cannot last."

She shakes her head. "You do not know Edward."

———————

"No!" Edward shouts when she puts the proposition to him. "He is a traitor and he will die a traitor's death!"

She could badger him with any number of mitigating circumstances, but she knows that he will demolish them all. Instead she falls to her knees. "Your grace, I ask this as a favor, to me."

"Oh, don't. Not again."

"Then don't shout at me."

He pulls her to her feet. "They cannot see me weak ever again!"

"This one act of mercy will cost you nothing in public esteem. It may gain you admirers. Being unpredictable is just as feared as tyranny."

"Who told you that?" He lets her go and regards her with some suspicion. "What is he to you anyway?"

"He is nothing to me. But his wife I count as one of my dearest friends. I would do her this one favor for all that she has done for me. Let him live his life in prison. At least she might see him now and then."

"He deserves to die."

"I do not doubt it. But I ask this for me. I did as you asked at Leeds Castle, did I not? I gave you your victory. Now give me this one small grace as the price of it."

Edward can be conciliatory when the Despenser is not there. "I will think on it," he says.

And he does.

Mortimer is tried and sentenced to death; the next day Edward commutes his penalty to life in prison.

The Despenser is not amused.

"Who persuaded you to this, your grace?" he says, his voice rising impertinently in the presence of the king. He glares at Isabella. *Soon he will shout at me, too.*

Edward looks sulky. "I wish to appear unpredictable."

"You appear weak."

"Hardly that," Isabella tells him, "when all you have to do is step outside the castle and smell the reek of decaying flesh. He has put half of Yorkshire to the gallows."

He clearly resents her, this Despenser. He knows she has Edward's ear in the marriage bed, the one place he does not have a voice, or his spies. It's written on his face; he believes she is meddling with his king.

He turns back to Edward. "Then at least ensure his stay is not too comfortable."

"What do you suggest?"

"The Lanthorn Tower, and no more than three pence a day for his keep. It is still more than he deserves."

"That seems harsh," Isabella says.

"Not as harsh as losing his head, surely?"

"The Lanthorn Tower it is," Edward says. He smiles. There, he has pleased them both. Or so he thinks.

Another victory won.

Chapter 33

Tynemouth Priory, August 1322

The king sets out on his quest; defeating the Bruce has become his Holy Grail. He wants greatness, he wants to be admired and feared as his father was. Isabella urges caution, but he will not listen.

It is a morning late in summer, warm for the north country, and for a rare moment the king is unattended by the Despenser and his clerks and money counters. She catches him out on the walls, walking alone. He stops and turns his face to the sun. His hair shines, his face is beatific.

He is talking to someone. She comes closer to listen, but there is no one there. Then she hears a name: he is talking to Gaveston, and for a moment he looks happy.

She feels guilty for interrupting this reverie, as if she had caught the two of them abed. He turns and sees her. He is not at all abashed, does not realize he was speaking his thoughts aloud.

"Ah, Isabella. A fine morning."

"It's always good to see the sun shining. Where is the Lord Despenser?"

A hollow laugh. "You don't like him much, do you?"

"It is not for me to have an opinion in the matter."

"I wish you would get on. He is a great help to me, you know. The Treasury is full at last, and he is fond of those details that I am not good with."

"It seems so. You spend all your time cloistered with him."

"There is much to discuss in the running of a kingdom." She bridles at this. He speaks to her as if she is some twittering maiden who has spent all her youth with ponies and sewing. But she lets it pass.

"What of Scotland?"

"We leave within the week."

Isabella is astounded. No word of this has reached her. "Would you not make me party to these plans?"

"This is war, not politics. It is men's business."

"Was Lancaster men's business? Was it men's business when they fired arrows at me at Leeds Castle?"

He laughs. At her. "You were in no danger. You did not ride up to the gate."

"Once, you would have consulted me on such matters. You said, when you asked for my help in the matter of his exile, that if he came back, he would never usurp me, that he was no threat to me. You promised me this."

"And I have kept my word. He is no threat to you." The sunshine has gone from his face. "Do not give me cause to rebuke you, Isabella. You are becoming tiresome."

"I beg your leave, your grace," she murmurs and turns away, before her face betrays her.

———————

The days up here drag by like centuries. There is only so much piety one can take, kneeling before the moldy bones of Saint Oswin, here in a place as far from God as one can go and still freeze. The sun has made its brief appearance and has now fled south once more.

Outside, the sea batters on the rocks, and even the light that seeps through the high lancet windows appears gray.

The velvet cushion under her knees cannot keep the chill from settling in Isabella's bones. Tynemouth priory may be one of the best-defended priories in the country, but it is so bleak it makes death seem attractive. She had never been so cold, even in Scotland.

The monastery has stout walls but is unlikely to keep out the Scots should they wish to get inside. They have taken better-defended castles than this. The Black Douglas once scaled Berwick's walls with rope ladders in the face of a hail of arrows. If they ever discover she is here, they will do anything to take her. They could ransom the throne of Scotland for England's queen.

She tries to concentrate on her rosary.

When the king appears, her lady helps her rise to greet him. His breath freezes on the air.

The king smiles at his queen; his queen smiles at him. Such a beautiful man, and so dazzling on this forbidding day in his red tunic and cloak. He towers over her, all booted and ready to ride. She craves his touch. Hers is a constant state of longing.

His voice is imperious. "I must leave."

"So soon?"

"I take our army against the Bruce tomorrow. This time I will rid our northern marches of him forever."

"And your queen?"

"You will stay here at the priory until I return. You are safe here."

Isabella thinks back to when Lancaster declared his Ordinances, how Edward lay with his head in her lap, weeping. It seems so long ago. She was indispensable to him then; now she is baggage, slowing his advance on destiny.

"I beg you do not leave me here. I shall go mad."

"I will not be away long."

"I should be with you, that is my place."

"It would not be wise."

The Despenser is standing by the door of the chapel, wearing a soft and golden smile. She pretends not to notice him. She has never been jealous of any of her maids around Edward, but when she sees the Despenser, she aches.

She watches him leave in the bitter dark just before dawn, followed by his knights on snorting warhorses and accompanied by footmen carrying flambeaux. The air is filled with the clatter of hooves, the clash of harness and weapons.

When he is gone, she goes back to the chapel and falls again to her knees. She finds herself praying, not for some dreary saint, but for her own life and that the Despenser would disappear from it. *Let him be struck by lightning or be taken in his bed by apoplexy. Better yet, let the Scots get at him. The Bruce is good at killing Englishman, why not this one?*

But she knows now it is pointless. There will always be a Despenser. She will never be the king's favorite, no matter how hard she deals with God.

Chapter 34

If happiness were a buffeting gale with occasional flurries of sleet, then she should be overjoyed. She stands on the battlements, letting the wind burn her cheeks for the sheer exhilaration of it. Anything but another moment in these dark, drafty halls, listening to the chanting of the monks. Out here is a world of sea-battered rocks and forbidding cliffs.

She leans on the parapet, watches the gulls blown about like leaves on the wind. Foam piles on the rocks.

She has heard reports from Scotland that Bruce has laid the land to waste, and Edward's army is starving. She imagines Bruce's hobelars swooping down on them, Edward caught once more in a trap like Bannockburn, and no cool head to advise him. He does not have the head for war, and Despenser's cunning for figures does not translate to the battlefield, or so they say.

Eleanor appears, wrapped in thick furs. "Riders," she says, and then mutters under her breath: "Pray God, they're ours."

The guards at the priory gates shout a welcome, and there are sighs of relief all around. A troop of a dozen riders clatters through the gates. The captain throws himself from his mount. Whatever news he has, he is in a hurry to bring it. He looks grim and is covered in mud. Isabella steels herself.

She hurries down the tower's narrow steps, almost tripping in her haste. There is a meagre fire burning in the hearth in the great hall, the monks do not believe in comforts. Her messenger huddles by it, shivering. She has a servant fetch hot mead.

It is one of Despenser's men. Well, she will not hate him for that.

"Is the king safe?" she asks him.

"He is, your grace. He asked me to bring you this letter."

She hesitates to read it. She hands it to Eleanor to break the seal.

Isabella turns to the captain. "Did you find the Bruce?"

"We did," he says, but it is what he does not say that alarms her. She reads the letter:

Our Dear Consort, I write to you in haste. The Scots fled into the valleys, laying waste the land behind them. Our army has been much reduced by the flux and by starvation. Our losses necessitated the need for a hasty withdrawal, and we have taken what remains of our gallant army by way of Bridlington and are now at York, where we await you. The Bruce has pursued us, so I am sending my lords Richmond and Athol to convey you to safety. My councillors advise that the Scots may be aware of your location and will ride on Tynemouth so you should prepare to leave posthaste.

May the Holy Spirit bless and keep you.

Edwardus Rex

This 16th day of October, 1322

Her hands shake.

"Ma'am?" Eleanor murmurs.

"He is safe," she says, and remembers that Eleanor is concerned more for her own husband. "They are both safe."

"They are on their way to us?"

"They are in York."

"York?"

"They would like us to meet them there."

Edward, what have you done? You have allowed this Bruce to outwit you again.

The letter slips from her fingers, her ladies and her squires stare at it but none dare pick it up. Her hands dip back into the sleeves of her surcoat.

"So Captain, as a soldier and a veteran of these marches, give me your opinion: What are the chances that Richmond might reach us here before the Bruce or his raiders?"

He fidgets, never a good sign. "I would say we should do well to look to the priory fortifications."

"We cannot hold this place against the Scots."

"We may have no choice."

"We will have to find one," she says and sweeps from the hall.

———

"The king had no choice," Eleanor declares when they are alone in her rooms, and Isabella looks up at her in surprise. She did not think the girl owned a tongue.

"I am sure he took good counsel before he made his decision," Isabella says.

"He could not risk his army or the reputation of the English Crown by returning here and exposing himself to capture."

She does not believe she asked her maid's opinion, but she is intrigued anyway. "You do not mind that your husband and your uncle both abandoned you?"

"I should hardly say 'abandoned.' What would the Scots do to me, even if they caught me here? I should be ransomed, as you would be. They will not harm us. But my husband and the king risk their lives and the Crown itself to come back here. It was the prudent thing."

Ah, that was it: he has fled south and left me here on this damned rock because he is being prudent.

She does not wish him to be prudent. She wants him to put everything at stake for her, as he had for Gaveston. She wants him to sweep in and save her, or show at least that she is as important to him as he had been.

But this is not queenly, this is a woman's petty jealousy, and it is not worthy of a daughter of France.

Eleanor is flushed. It has taken much for her to speak so boldly. Perhaps what she says is true, or perhaps it is only what she needs to believe.

"That will be all," Isabella says to her and draws herself straight.

"Is there anything else, your grace?"

"Ask the servants to fetch me some spiced wine."

Eleanor bobs her head and leaves. Isabella turns back to the window. The sea heaves in the wind, black clouds sweep in. Not yet vespers and it is already dark. Should she wait for her husband's knights, or risk a boat? She cannot let herself be taken, for the ransom will bankrupt England, and Edward will no doubt be forced to give up all claim to Scotland. She will not have England's humiliation laid at her feet, and neither will she have her squires die defending these walls when they cannot in any way repel a determined assault. The result is foregone. If she is to prevent disaster, then she must act like a queen.

————

The next morning she meets the bailiff in the gatehouse. He looks a worried man; he doesn't fancy much having to protect the queen of England with just a handful of men. This could turn out badly for him.

There are dark clouds out there beyond the horizon. Not a good day for sailing. Where are the Scots? She has to make her choice. Can she risk delaying one more day?

"Load the ship with provisions. We leave today."

He is about to object but then thinks better of it. He goes about his business, pleased to be rid of the onerous responsibility of being the queen's protector. She feels a slap of rain. Even down here on the river, the waves are rising.

The sky is ominous. She hopes she has not miscalculated, but it is too late to change her mind. As they come out of the gate, they are almost blown over by the wind. Their ship does not inspire confidence; it was damaged in a recent storm, has just now been repaired and refitted at Newcastle.

Edward should be with her, he should not have abandoned her to this.

Chapter 35

York

York is not quite the same as she remembers it—without the heads and the hacked off limbs stuck on poles. She is not nostalgic for them. But Lancaster's ghost seems to prowl here. She doubts they will ever be rid of his haunting now.

She steps out of her carriage under the shadow of her uncle's bailey, and curses him for what he led them all to. Their civil war allowed the Bruce to grow more powerful. Lancaster should have put his energies into fighting him, not Gaveston.

She had sent messages ahead, but her husband is not waiting for her when she steps out onto the cobbles. The Despenser waits for her in the great hall. He is unusually solicitous. A servant takes her cloak, the fire is built up. She declines the offers of spiced wine and food, though she is in dire need of both.

The Despenser has a silver smile on his lips. He wears furs, and gathers them about his smug, smooth person as if waiting to be petted.

He delivers his king's message with silky grace. She listens, unbelieving.

"The king refuses to see me?"

"He is indisposed, your grace."

"My Lord Despenser, do you know who you are addressing?"

"I mean no disrespect. These are the king's orders, I merely pass them on."

Isabella is exhausted. She has not been warm since Tynemouth, and was never much warm there anyway. She has spent three days vomiting on a pitching ship, one of her ladies lost over the side in a gale.

Her clothes are foul, her hair crusted with salt; she is in dire need of a bath, a wardrobe, hot broth, and spiced wine. But most of all she needs to speak her mind to the king, and she does not care if the daughter of France sounds like a fishwife.

"Do you realize what I have been through?"

"We have all suffered much. The king has watched his army starve by degrees, and he has lost his treasures and personal possessions—all left behind in Northumberland."

"I am told that Bruce has defeated what remains of his army and has captured the Earl of Richmond. Is this true?"

He nods.

"How could he let this happen? Is he always to be out-thought and outmaneuvered?"

"Robert the Bruce is a cunning and treacherous adversary."

"And Edward is hardly the Hammer of the Scots," she snaps and immediately regrets it, for this remark will certainly find its way back to Edward. *She made unfavorable comparison between yourself and your father, he will say. She mocked you.*

"Tell Edward I wish to see him," she says to one of the stewards, but he looks instead to the Despenser. It is clear who has the authority here. "You will not stand between me and the king!"

"I do not. They are his orders; I am merely his servant."

He says this without the whole court bursting into disbelieving laughter. He has them well trained.

"Why did he not come to me at Tynemouth?"

"You think this was my doing?"

"They are your words, not mine."

"You may accuse me of many things, your grace, but in this I am blameless. My own wife was there with you."

Yes, his wife, who is standing here in the shadows of the great hall, awaiting her husband's passionate embrace. She should not keep her from it.

This is twice now she has lost her patience in front of these Despensers. From now on she must conduct herself with more care.

"Have a servant prepare a bath. My rooms are ready?"

"Of course."

"I await the king's pleasure," she says and sweeps from the room, with as much dignity as a queen can, in a salt-stained dress and hair stiff as hay. Let Edward hide from her, he cannot hide forever. She is still his wife, and his queen.

She has saved him from humiliation. A word of thanks is all she wants.

That, and his adviser's head steaming on a spit.

Chapter 36

Her counsel is no longer important to him. He spends much of his time cloistered with the Despenser and his crowd. His chamberlain only has to ask and he receives. There is hardly a castle in the western marches he has not taken possession of. The king waves a hand airily to his every request.

"*Oh, what,*" the young earl sighs, "*not another castle!*" He will make him the Baron of Britain if that is what he wants. He tosses out earldoms and castles as if they were sweetmeats.

There is a flush to the king's cheeks, his eyes shine. There is much whispering when they are together, private looks and secret smiles shared with no one else. If Despenser should grab the king by the crutch and satisfy him on the throne, it would not appear as lewd as the looks they give each other.

What are these moments they share? It is very like lust, but that is not quite it. It is like Gaveston but it is not. There is a puzzle here, and she is resolute to solve it.

And now they are to winter, the king and Isabella. A gray sky, gray fields, even the sun would be gray if it should come out, which seems unlikely. It shall be gray and cold like this till the end of days.

How dull her spy looks. Rosseletti never draws attention to himself wherever he is. He sits in corners and blends with the tapestries, the carpets, the walls. If it is not for the scratching of his quill, you might forget he is there altogether.

"It should be announced that I am to go on a pilgrimage," she tells him.

"Where will that be, your grace?"

"Anywhere but where the king is."

"Until when?"

"Until Forevermas," she says. "He is heartily tired of me it seems, and for my part I am weary of him. Just to see him makes me feel that I should like to be holding a horse whip and a branding iron."

"I thought that was the way of all matrimonies," Rosseletti says. She is startled; she thinks he has just made a joke.

"I wish my brother could help me."

"It seems unlikely there is much he can do. He cannot interfere in affairs between a husband and a wife."

"I am his sister."

"With respect, you are Edward's wife, your grace."

She fights an urge to stamp her foot.

"Is there no hope of conciliation?"

"What might I do, Rosseletti? Forget that my king has a mistress?"

She wishes she could bite off this sharp tongue. She must take care to guard it better when others less trusted are around. There is an awkward silence.

"It is not unknown for men to have . . . consorts, other than wives. Kings most of all."

"I know that."

"If Lord Despenser were a woman, do you think you could bear it better?"

She ponders the question. The answer, she supposes, would be yes. The king would never talk politics with any woman aside from her. It would be just a fleshly thing, and she supposes she would not fear that as much as a rival who shares her husband's bed as well as his plans and his royal seal.

So what might she do? The king can snub his nose at the Church and even the fires of purgatory for his private lusts, but the queen of England can only dream of other lovers. She thinks of Marguerite, strangled by hired ruffians in a tower. Of Blanche, head shorn and shuffling along a cloister in her penitent's habit, spending the rest of her days with a missal and prayer book.

Her ladies say she is beautiful, and men of the court flatter her in obsequious ways while their eyes burn. What good does beauty do her? She might as well be a dried out hag praying rosaries in a nunnery.

Rosseletti tells her: "You know he still pays eighty pence a day to the Dominican friars to pray for Gaveston, over a hundred pounds a year just on offertory candles for his soul?"

"Still? It has been ten years."

"A long time to keep milk, but they say that certain loves can stay fresh an eternity."

She stares at him. Who would have thought the Rosselettis of this world harbored such romantic opinions? He will not meet her eyes.

He is right, she thinks. *Edward still loves his Perro.*

———

Eleanor casts baleful, sidelong glances as if she wishes to say something but is constrained by either fear or good manners. If she is now Edward's spy—as Rosseletti believes—then she has little enthusiasm for it. Perhaps she too thinks that the Despenser is spending too much time in the company of the king. Eleanor's attitude toward her seems to have softened. She sometimes hurries to fetch her cushions when she sits and volunteers to water her wine on hot days.

Isabella receives another messenger from Lady Mortimer. She resolves to help her, but the king pays little heed to his wife anymore. She will need one of her ladies to run the errand for her.

It has always seemed to her that if you wish someone to carry your load, then it is best to do nothing but stumble. So she spends the day sighing and pricking her finger with the needle at her sewing and weeping silently when her ladies pretend not to be watching her.

Finally it is too much for even a mouse like Eleanor. "Your grace, something troubles you?"

"It is nothing."

Eleanor stares with her huge, liquid eyes.

Finally, as if it is too much to bear: "My friend is in trouble."

"Your friend? Then I am sure the king—"

"I scarce think so; it is the king who is the cause of it. Never mind this, Eleanor, it is not something that need trouble you."

"You mean Lady Mortimer?" Eleanor says, for she is a bright young woman and needs little coaching in such conversations.

"A little while ago she sent me a letter. She suffers terribly. She has not enough to feed her children, let alone herself. She is granted just one mark per day for her necessities, and out of this sum she must feed her servants as well. The place they have locked her is drafty and leaks when it rains. Lock up her husband, yes, but what guilt does the wife bear? She was nothing but a good friend to me while she was my lady-in-waiting. Think on it, Eleanor, should your husband ever rise against the king, would that be a fault of yours?"

Isabella watches a squirrel on a branch attack a hazelnut. *You just need patience and knowledge of the weakest spot in the nut. Oh, and sharp teeth.*

"Have you spoken to the king, your grace?"

"The king will not see me. You know this, Eleanor."

"Perhaps then I should do so."

Ah, so I may not see the king, but one of my ladies has his ear. Should I be offended? "The Lady Mortimer is my friend, not yours. I should not have you trouble yourself unduly on my account or hers."

"Perhaps then I shall do it because we are both wives and mothers, and it is the right and charitable thing."

"Well do not tell the king that I sent you. Or your husband. They will refuse any request if they know it is from me."

The Lady Eleanor dares put a hand on Isabella by way of comfort. Then she withdraws. Isabella thinks she will do it. She hopes this will help Lady Mortimer, for she very much likes her as a friend, and it will also show the Despenser that she is not quite toothless, not yet.

———————

The king, she has heard, has gone to Langley, as he does on this day every year, the anniversary of Gaveston's death. He has masses said, and takes rich, golden cloths to embroider his tomb. He has established a chantry there, and prayers are made for Perro in perpetuity.

The Despenser is a rare visitor, but she supposes he has nothing better to do now that his king is elsewhere, on his knees with his hands cupped for another man, albeit this one dead. Still, the Despenser would not be human if he did not feel a pang of jealousy.

He smiles, appears relaxed, though he prowls the carpets like a bear looking for its lunch.

He is not an unhandsome man. Fine living has made him a little soft, paunchy even, but he still wears many of the marks of youth. He is dressed not in velvets but in plain linens, purples and some scarlet silk to denote his rank and position. It is land he lusts after, not ostentation.

He appears bookish, but she remembers he was at Bannockburn and has some reputation as a warrior and pirate. His wrists are so narrow and delicate, she would not think him burly enough to wield a broadsword. She supposes his greatest asset is that others misjudge him until he is inside their guard, and then it is too late.

His eyes glitter, the fleshy lips part. He smiles, or employs an expression that he has learned is very much like one. He says in a silky voice: "So, how is Lady Mortimer?"

"She suffers."

"Much?"

"Intolerably."

He would not be here if she had not perturbed him with her plea to the king. He must still be afraid of her, then. Well, that is something. She supposes Edward may have relented in the face of the entreaties by his favorite niece—who is also the Despenser's wife!—and she can only imagine what this has done to the Despenser's equilibrium.

He leans in. "The king does not yet realize how clever you are," he says with a smile.

"I do not know what you mean."

"You cannot win this game."

"I am sure you must be speaking in riddles. I was never good at riddles."

"Your eyes are so wide and blue, and the king is so narrow and trusting."

She holds his gaze. His smile is so like a grimace, he can no longer hold it. "Do not think for a moment you can best me."

"My Lord Despenser, I do not know what it is you think I have done. Despite our recent misunderstanding, I remain his loyal servant, and wish only to do what is best for him and for the Crown."

He simmers. He withdraws. The Lady Mortimer remains at Skipton.

———————

She has decisions to make. Is it enough to be the cosseted wife of a king, a shadow gliding around the anterooms of one of his palaces? She will go mad. She was raised by France to be a queen. She was made by God to be a woman.

She cannot abide it, but railing against Edward will do her no good, and showing her intent to the Despenser will only forewarn him. From now on she must be more circumspect.

She has a servant fetch Rosseletti. She sits him down with his seals and parchments and shows him the letter she has just received from the Lady Mortimer. He reads it, shakes his head, and holds it to the candle flame. "You must have nothing to do with this," he tells her.

"You will write to my brother."

"Your grace, I will not."

"You will do as I say. You will write to my brother and tell him that should Roger Mortimer ever one day appear at his court, he is to give him all possible assistance."

"That is treason."

"Rosseletti, you are my clerk, not my keeper."

What was it her father had said to her? "*You will obey your husband in all things.*" But he could not have imagined a situation such as this. *Would they shave my head and shut me away in a tower?* The king of France might, but should Edward dare such a thing, he would risk war with France.

She sees her father's ghost in the room, glaring at her. *Well, hector me all you want from your grave, I shall not submit like a pretty little lamb and let them make the rest of my life sewing and walking in the garden.*

I am a queen. I want my place at the council and at the king's side, and if he will not give it to me, I will force his hand. He will see that I am no coward. If he will call for rain, then I will give him a tempest.

Chapter 37

The Tower of London, July 1323

She resides for a time in London, at the great Tower, with the young Prince Edward, now ten years old and growing tall and fair like his father. It is a grim fortress, with its green-slimed, reeking moats, its cavernous gateways and iron-tipped portcullis. But her apartments are luxurious enough: jet-black beams on the roof and thick glass on the windows.

Occasionally she spares a glance at the Lanthorn Tower. Mortimer is up there, cooped in his little cell.

Tonight she walks the battlements, restless. There is a wisp of mist on the river, lights on the Surrey side, riders out there in the dark. All evening she has heard the sound of carousing from the guardroom downstairs, but it has died down now. Lord Mortimer has bought his guards wine and a feast so they might help him celebrate the Feast of Peter ad Vincula.

She hears a noise from the chimney, mice in the bricks she supposes, but then as it gets louder, she realizes there are men up here, and she is alone and defenseless. She freezes in alarm.

She watches, astonished, as two silhouettes emerge from a small door that opens onto the constable's private walk on the Hall

Tower. She takes one careful step back into the shadows, holds her breath, terrified they might see her.

The two men leap on the leads of the adjoining tower and scramble away across the roof. It takes only moments. Then they are gone.

It is a moonlit night, and she cannot make out their faces, but she is certain from his voice and from his size that she knows at least one of those men.

She hears the splash of oars as a boat pulls away from the wharf, sees them row across the river toward the Surrey bank. A torch flares; there are men waiting over there in the dark.

She lets out her breath.

She might now safely raise the alarm, but instead she stumbles back down the stone stairs to her apartments and takes herself to her bed. Her two ladies are already fast asleep in the trundles.

She gets under the sheets and lies there, listening to the lapping of the water around the pilings at the water gate and the lonely cry of a water bird. She recalls impudent looks, smoldering eyes. Lord Mortimer will be far away by the time she wakes. She wonders what Edward and the Despenser will say when they find out he has escaped from the Tower. Perhaps that will make them a little less cocksure.

It should.

———

Young Edward has grown into a fine boy, and he has his father's looks. His eyes are so serious, he watches her with such intensity it is frightening. He has strong opinions and tells her loudly which servants he trusts and those he does not. He is already very sure of himself.

"Did you really help that man Mortimer escape from the Tower?" he asks her.

The escape is all that anyone talks about. Mortimer is the first prisoner to escape from here in a hundred years. She is told he had the connivance of the constable, d'Alspaye, who smuggled him an iron to take out a stone in the wall of his cell. He then climbed a chimney, with a rope, and escaped through the Hall Tower. He and d'Alspaye then scaled down the outer bailey to the wharf with rope ladders. There were boats waiting. It is supposed he has fled back to the marches or to Ireland, where he has friends.

"Helped Lord Mortimer? Of course not. Where did you hear someone say such a thing about me?"

"Father says Lord Despenser told him about you, that you had planned it with Mortimer's friends."

"That is a vile thing to say. I would never plot against your father."

"Well, that's what he said. A lot of people are saying it."

"A lot of people?"

"People talk in front of me like I'm not there. It annoys me."

"What else do they say about me?"

"The king or Uncle Hugh?"

"*Uncle* Hugh? Is that what you call him?"

"Father says he is my uncle. Almost."

She has a rejoinder for that, but she bites her tongue. If the young prince is telling her all the scandal about the king, then he would just as surely carry everything she says back to him.

"What else does . . . Uncle Hugh . . . say about me?"

"He says that you had an uncle too, called Lancaster, and that you sent him secret messages to help him in his war against Father. Is that true?"

She shakes her head and forces a smile. It makes her jaw ache to appear pleasant in the face of such outrageous calumnies. *Not only has he exiled me, but he wants me tried for treason! It is clear now what the Despenser wants.*

He wants to become queen in my place.

Chapter 38

She is invited to Hanley as the guest of the Despenser. She has not seen the king for many months, and when she walks into his chamber, she is shocked at how careworn he looks. It is clear he does not want to see her. He will not meet her eyes.

"Oh, what have they done to you, Edward?" she murmurs.

She remembers when she first saw him at Boulogne. She was unscarred then, and he still had Gaveston. They were both innocent in their own way. They both had hopes that love could come to something.

"Hugh said you wished to see me," he mumbles and sits by the fire, still without looking at her.

"I wished to ask you about the children."

"They are all healthy and well cared for. What else do you wish to know? I should like to keep our interview short. I have much to do."

She blinks at him. She suspects he has been coached. "I do not understand what I have done to offend you."

He taps a finger on the arm of the chair. He does not answer.

"Can you not see what he is doing?"

"Can you not see what *you* are doing?"

She slumps to her knees. He ignores her. Once it would have melted him, no matter how hard his heart. Has it come to this? "What has he said to you about me?"

"He does not need to tell me, the facts speak for themselves."

"What facts are these, your grace?"

"My enemy finds succor with your brother. How do you explain this?"

"Ah, you mean Lord Mortimer?"

"Yes, I mean Lord Mortimer. You know he has appeared in France? He has offered his sword to your brother, the king, to go against our fellow Englishmen in Gascony."

"Does that surprise you?"

He is suddenly on his feet. "Should he betray his country so?"

"I think you have rather forced his hand, don't you?"

"Did I force his hand when he took his armies and marched against me? Did I force his hand when he surrounded us in London, his army around the walls?"

"I rather think the Lord Despenser is his enemy, not you."

"You argue like a lawyer."

"You say that as if it is a bad thing."

A rare smile from him despite himself. "Oh, get up," he says. He lends out a hand and helps her stand. He guides her to the seat by the fire.

"You know your brother blames me for what happened in the Agenais."

"The insurrection, you mean?"

"Well, if he would not build a *bastide* on my lands, then the locals should not feel the need to attack it. No harm was done."

"A sergeant was killed."

"Only a French one." He is immediately sorry for that remark. His cheeks flush. She lets it go.

"This could lead to war between us," Edward says. "The very thing our marriage was meant to prevent!"

"Not the only reason, surely?"

He ignores this remark. "Did you know Mortimer had signed on with your brother Charles?"

"Why should I know this?"

"You are in constant communication with your brother through that little spy of yours, Rosseletti. He would have told you all this. Was it you who asked your brother in France to protect the gallant Lord Mortimer when he ran away?"

"Of course not!"

"You have to deny it. To do otherwise would be to admit treason, wouldn't it?" He stares into the fire. "I should have executed Mortimer when I had the opportunity, but you persuaded me to mercy. Perhaps even then you were plotting against me."

"Is this the Lord Despenser speaking or my lord and husband?"

"How is it Mortimer has found succor with your brother?"

"My brother does not consult me on matters of policy. I am neither his prime minister nor his queen, and I have not his ear in the council chamber or the bedchamber, so I cannot answer that question for you."

"Have I not treated you with all decency and gentleness as becoming your rank in this world and your place in my household? You have wanted for nothing, and I have never insulted you publicly or caused you or your servants physical harm. Have I? Yet you insist it is not enough. What is it you want from me?"

"I want you to want me."

"What you ask is impossible!"

"You are a man. Am I not pleasing to you?"

"You are indeed a very beautiful woman."

"Then what?"

"You would not understand!"

There is color in his cheeks, and his fists open and close at his sides as he struggles to pacify her. She wants to shake him, like she would a child.

"I have been loyal to you and helped you in all that I am able."

"Indeed you have, and I have acknowledged that in all things."

"I want to be your queen!"

"You are my queen!"

She hears a servant scurry down the stairs. Just as well, for if she found any hall boy sneaking behind drapes to listen, she would thrash him to Michaelmas.

Edward goes to the window and stares at a dove on a tree branch outside. By the look on his face he should like to hurl a stone at it for its pretty cooing. "They sent an assassin from France to murder Hugh, do you know that?"

Yes, she knows. "You credit me with much more information than a lady living in exile might reasonably acquire."

He sighs, his hands behind his back. "Look."

She joins him at the window. There is a monk at the gate collecting alms. He is a jolly fellow with a stave, and he is laughing at some frippery with the guard at the gatehouse. "He looks happy, that man," states the king.

"He looks cold. He has sandals. In this weather! His feet must be blue."

"But he has time to pass the day with a soldier and a laundry maid. What must his life be like?"

She puts put a hand on his arm. For once he does not try to shrug it away.

"I sometimes think it would be better as a foundling than a prince," he says. "Let me have a day working in the field, some mead at night, and a few prayers. I think it should not be such a bad life."

"You should miss the company of women," she says, and he looks thunderous, but just for a moment, and then he laughs.

She strokes his beard. He rests his cheek against her hand and closes his eyes. "Sometimes I think you know me better than anyone."

"Come to my chamber tonight. I have missed you. Husbands and wives should share a marriage bed. You don't have to do anything, just keep me warm."

There are tears in his eyes—for his situation, for hers. He nods. When she leaves the chamber, he is still at the window, watching the friar go about his day.

———

The candles gutter in a draft and their shadows dance on the wall like demons. The wind is howling around the tower, the Despenser's animus prowling the night, free from its anchoring body, peering in at the windows and howling in jealousy.

Edward takes a breathy gulp and his hand slides along her thigh. "Don't ever leave me, Isabella."

"But my king, it is you who sends me away."

"You know I don't mean it."

"I think that you do."

He caresses her breasts, places his hand enthusiastically between her thighs and kisses her with as much passion as he can. She pities him in his efforts. For all his writhing, he remains incapable of anything with her besides tenderness.

"You should be my touchstone."

"But I'm not." She cannot see his face in the darkness.

"Just hold me," he says, and she does. They keep each other warm. It is enough. She wakes with him still in her arms, his hair warm and musty.

She wishes the light would not creep up the sky, that she could not hear the servants clattering pans in the kitchen. Let this moment stay.

Later that morning the Lord Despenser marches into her chambers unannounced. It may be his castle, but there are still common forms to be observed. Her ladies-in-waiting look up, alarmed. "A word in private," he says.

She considers refusing, but that would appear churlish. She nods, and her ladies flee the room.

The Despenser smiles. "You passed a restful night?"

"I slept very little," she tells him, and his eyes blaze. *Does he love Edward,* she wonders, *or is it that he thinks that lust is the only way he can control him? If he thinks that, then he should study himself more carefully in a reflective surface.*

"You told the king he was ill-advised."

"I said to be careful whom he listens to. There are those who would counsel him to their own advantage."

"You refer to me?"

"I refer to no one in particular."

He walks around the room, examines a little of his wife Eleanor's embroidery, some of her French ladies' handiwork as well. It appears that his hold on Edward is not absolute after all.

She remembers this morning, the damp sheets, holding Edward in her arms as his breathing slowed. *Does he think of me when he loves me, or of someone else?* She doesn't care. She will take him as he is, she will even share him with a ghost, but not with flesh and blood.

The Despenser is looking worn of late. His youth is creeping away from him.

He steps toward her, still smiling. She is unnerved by how close he stands. Suddenly he spins her around, clamps one hand across her mouth, and pins her arms with the other.

"Do not try to interfere with my plans, you fucking French whore," he whispers.

She struggles, but he is surprisingly strong. She cannot breathe. He pinches her nostrils with his thumb and index finger, and she thinks she is going to pass out.

"I may do what I wish with you, and the king would never believe you for a moment."

His hand squeezes between her legs and, even through her dress, it is painful. She tries to push his hand away, but she cannot. There are black spots in front of her eyes; her knees will not hold her. Even as she goes down, he is calling out for help.

She blacks out. When her ladies rush in, he is leaning over her, cradling her head, and telling them that she fainted and that he fears she may have hit her head as she went down. Isabella wants to ask them for help, but for the moment she cannot speak. Her ladies crowd in, and then the Despenser is gone.

Was it real? Did she just imagine this? He surely would not have dared to lay hands on his queen.

Her ladies help her to a bed. They bring water and spiced wine and wave towels over her. They whisper among themselves that it might be the sweats.

"He choked me," she murmurs, but her voice is so hoarse none of them can hear her. As her breath returns so does her rage.

As soon as she is recovered, she goes to see the king.

———

"Whatever is the matter?" he asks her.

"Your beast has shown his colors."

"Meaning?"

"He assaulted me."

"Who?"

"Your Lord Despenser. He was incensed that we spent the night together, it seems. He tried to choke me and he put his hands . . . where no man should touch me but you."

There is a smile on his lips. This is not the reaction she was looking for. "Where did this happen?"

"In my chambers."

"There were witnesses to this?"

She shakes her head.

"Where were your ladies?"

"I had sent them out of the room at Lord Despenser's request."

An eyebrow is raised.

"So there are no witnesses to this . . . assault?"

"He said that he could do what he wanted with me, and you would never believe me."

The smile is replaced with cold fury. "This is what he said you would do."

"Your grace?"

"This is so like you. You have to have it all, don't you? Anyone who competes with you, you have to destroy them."

"I am telling you the truth!"

"Hugh would never do something like that."

"Why would I lie?"

"To drive a wedge between us!"

"But that is what he has done with us!"

"And now you wish your revenge?"

She realizes her mistake, but it is too late. The Despenser is far cleverer than she gave him credit for. He has outwitted her again. Why did he assault her? From jealousy or because he knew the king would never believe him capable of such a thing, that women were not his true passion?

He did this to entrap me, and he has succeeded.

"I thought we could yet be friends, you and I, Isabella."

"Your grace, I do not lie to you."

He turns his back on her. There is nothing left to say, so she bends her knee and leaves the chamber. The Despenser waits outside. He smiles at her.

She smiles back.

She would rather cut out his liver, but she will not give him the satisfaction of letting him see her rage.

Chapter 39

The summer is returning just when she thought it wouldn't. There are bumblebees in the garden, and she does not have to huddle by the fires in the morning to get warm. She is summoned back to the king's presence at Windsor. What is it now? Perhaps the Despenser has convinced him that she murdered Gaveston, dressed as a Welsh soldier. Or that she crucified Christ.

She walks into the chamber, and the king jumps to his feet, smiling broadly. "Your grace, we have missed your presence here at court. Welcome back."

Ah, he wants something.

She refuses food and drink, though this time Edward appears solicitous. A real king would not have taken no for an answer, he would have made her sit and forced lampreys and spiced wine on her.

The Despenser stands in the shadows. His smile pains him; they might as well be drawing him on the rack. He looks mild, but his eyes glitter like rubies. Pembroke is there too, though he has aged. She can hear his bones creak every time he moves, and there are lines on his face as if they'd been furrowed with a plough.

Perhaps the new wife has worn him out, or more likely he is tired of kings.

They sit, and Edward fusses around her. He asks if she has brought Rosseletti with her, and the moment he asks her that question, she knows what the favor is.

It is the Despenser who is first to get down to business.

"It is about this affair in the Agenais," he tells her. "Your brother, the king of France, has threatened to seize Gascony. The very reason for your marriage to Edward was to assure the peace. Now it seems we are to have war anyway."

"Are you saying that our marriage has failed?"

Edward breaks in cheerily. "He is saying nothing of the kind, just that your brother should be reminded of our union and how we might use it to create concord between us."

I feel like a court jester, she thinks. *They only bring me out when they need a riddle or a good laugh.*

"This has nothing to do with me."

"Once, you would have had suggestions to help us through this crisis, your grace," Lord Pembroke says.

"That was back in the days when I was invited to the council. But I have retired from affairs, Lord Pembroke."

"Then we should like you to renounce your retirement," the king says.

"To what purpose?"

"Write to your brother. Remind him of the great affection England has for France, as evidenced that his sister is queen of England."

"Am I? I thought *he* was," she says and nods at the Despenser.

"Come, Isabella, don't be difficult about this. England needs you. I need you."

"My brother knows the regard the people of England have for this man." She nods at the Despenser. "He knows how you treat me."

Pembroke leans forward. "Men make war," he tells her. "It is the woman's role to make the peace. And you are the greatest woman I have ever met."

This declaration disarms her. Lord Pembroke is a kind man who has given too much of himself away in the service of his country. He forestalls her anger for the moment.

Edward holds out his arm. She takes it, and he leads her to the end of the hall, out of earshot. The Despenser cannot bear private conversation. He looks as if his head will burst.

"Help me, Isabella," Edward says. "Things can be as they were between us before. I will have you back with us on the council."

"Your grace, you know that is a lie. You have broken your word to me on this so many times."

"This time I mean it."

"No you don't."

"Please, Isabella."

"Tell me what you want me to write. I'll do it."

"Thank you."

She gives him a withering look. "Don't thank me, thank my father. I'm just doing what he taught me to do."

She returns to the table, lets him follow behind. She is disgusted. She came here a queen, she will leave a pawn.

———

When Eleanor walks into the room, she looks careworn. It is unlike her, for she is by habit unbearably cheerful. Isabella is playing a game of tables with the other ladies, but Eleanor does not come to join them. Isabella is distracted by her mood. Eleanor sits in the corner, as gloomy as death itself.

"Whatever is wrong?" she asks her finally, unable to contain herself.

"It is the Lord Pembroke."

It is not hard to imagine what has happened. The last time she saw him, the angels were already warming a spot by the hearth for him.

"What happened?"

"He died of apoplexy, they say."

One of her girls bursts into tears; some of them will cry if one of the cats dies. She feels old and jaded at twenty-nine.

But sad just the same. She liked old Pembroke. There, another ally gone at court. He probably died of fright; the Despenser knows a thing or two about frightening old men.

The news depresses her. She leaves the game and decides to walk in the garden. Her ladies try to follow her, but she sends them away.

It is summer and the garden is alive with bees and fat flies, hovering sonorous over the windfall. A fat and lazy time to be doing your dying. She imagines Pembroke in heaven trying to make conciliation between God and the Devil. *Now come gentlemen, there is no need for this unpleasantness between you . . .*

And where does his death leave Isabella?

It is months since she has seen any of her children. She spends her whole life at her embroidery, listening to the silly talk of the younger women, or sitting in the garden looking for entertainment in watching butterflies flit among the honeysuckle. She cannot bear this; this is a life fit for a nun, not for a queen and a mother and a woman.

Last night she dreamed she was back in France. She was in a lawyer's chamber with her father and the pope and her brother. The judge was de Molay, the Templar her father had roasted over a fire for his heresy. He sat in his scarlet robes with the blackened flesh peeling off him in strips, and pointed at each of them in turn.

"You shall die of the apoplexy," he said to her father. "You shall drown in your own bed," he said to her brother. He completes a circuit of them all, delivering his curse, and finally the blackened finger fell on her.

"And you, daughter of France, you shall die of boredom and grief."

Well, I won't. She tears a daisy by its roots from the lawn. *He loves me, he loves me not. Well it's clear he loves me not, not anymore. I must force his hand. Dear Pembroke will not have died in vain.*

She goes to find Rosseletti.

"What news do you have for me?" she asks him.

He has rheumy eyes like a bloodhound. Did he even know what good news was? "Your brother has invaded Gascony, your grace."

"Well, he no doubt thinks he has had provocation enough."

"It does not augur well for you."

"No, I imagine it does not. How did this come about?"

"Edward delayed handing over the men who killed the sergeant at Saint-Sardos. Your brother lost patience with him and has sent an army to regain the castle."

"What is the problem with my husband, do you think? Is he incapable of reason? Can he not see any side of an argument but his own? Of course this is what my brother would do. If he wished deliberately to provoke him, I should understand it, but Edward cannot afford a war right now, neither financially nor politically. I do not understand him."

"I believe it is the Lord Despenser who makes the decisions on these matters."

"No, we cannot blame this on the Despenser. This is typical of Edward. This is what he does. He courts disaster like a lovesick boy."

"Your position may become . . . difficult."

"You should take a letter."

"Another missive to your brother?"

"No, this to the pope at Avignon. He will not wish to see two Christian kings at war over this. Suggest to him that he might find another peace broker now that the good Lord Pembroke is with our merciful God in heaven."

"Who did you have in mind?"

"You are looking at her."

For the first time in all the years she has known him, Rosseletti smiles. The poor man has bad teeth and he quickly covers his mouth with his hand, as if to cover a cough. "You are thinking ahead of everyone here."

"It is not so difficult, even for a woman."

He has the grace not to laugh at this last remark. She means it only in jest, and he knows it.

Chapter 40

It is wet for September and unusually cold. The winter will set in early this year. Bishop Stapledon is dressed in black furs, and the rain glistens on them. He looks like a mole just burrowing his way out of the moist ground. He is a mean man with thin lips and small eyes. Never trust a man with small eyes. If he were not a bishop, she would swear he was a man sent to strangle her. He would make the public executioner look homespun.

The bishop is the king's man, and if he is here, then it is to impart some news that Edward does not venture to share himself. It can only be bad. She sits by the hearth and has a servant fetch spiced wine. She lets the bishop stand and drip. Her father would not have approved of her manners, but her father is not here.

Edward has made this creature his Lord High Treasurer. It is his job to tie knots in the strings of the public purse. All that is sure is she will be the poorer when he leaves.

He looks cold standing there. She smiles and waits for him to begin.

"The king sends his wishes for your continued good health."

She bites her tongue on a slick rejoinder and returns the warm wishes.

"You have heard of the unfortunate events in France."

"If I am able to assist the king in his troubles, I am at his service."

The bishop of Exeter blinks. He has doubtless been briefed to anticipate a she-wolf. But this woman is just a lamb. "We are now at war with France, and it has become necessary to sequester your estates."

She has expected this, though it is still a bitter draft to swallow. But she forces a smile. "Really? What makes it so necessary?"

"Cornwall for instance. It has valuable tin mines and is susceptible to attack. It cannot be left outside of the king's control."

He thinks I am his enemy? Not yet. But he is making one of me. He and the Despenser.

"Is that all?"

"The constraints of war have made it necessary to reduce the allowance the Crown provides for your expenses."

Her fingers tighten around the arms of the throne. "Oh? By what degree?"

"We have allowed one thousand marks for the coming year, should it please your grace."

One thousand marks, down from eleven thousand. She feels the blood drain from her cheeks. "If that is the king's pleasure." She sips her wine. She would rather dash it in this creature's face.

"We thank you for your service," she says. "My servants will now show you the kitchen if you need provisions for the journey back."

He dithers.

Surely not . . .

"There is another direction I am required to pass on to you."

Another one? Surely this is enough humiliation for one day. Perhaps he requires her to dress in sackcloth and service the king's infantry.

"The Parliament has declared that all French subjects must leave the realm, for the safety of the kingdom."

"You are asking me to remove my closest friends and servants?"

"With great regret." But Stapledon does not look like a man who harbors great regret; he looks like a man who is enjoying himself hugely despite his wet clothes.

"We understand the king's concerns. All in my household are all loyal servants of the king, but it shall be as you say."

He looks disappointed. He would rather she threw the chamber pot at him, she supposes. But it seems he is done with his dressing down of the queen of England. For a man who was once just the bishop of Exeter, this must be a day to remember. His family and friends will hear this recounted word for word for years to come.

After he leaves, she sends everyone out of the chamber and hurls an expensive glass goblet at the wall for the pleasure of watching its contents run like blood down the wall. She does not scream for fear that someone will hear her.

She is a daughter of France, the king's royal blood. *How dare they!*

But it is not all.

When the Despenser's good wife returns to the household, Isabella's son John is given to her care. This is intolerable. When he shirks his lessons, she does not scold him, and she gives him sweetmeats whenever he asks for them. The queen is not even allowed to teach her own son his manners now.

Eleanor is much changed from the woman that sailed with her from Tynemouth, whom she held when she thought she would die in the tempest.

She was persuaded to follow her conscience once, and go against her husband's wishes in the service of Lady Mortimer; it is clear she is of a mind never to make the same mistake again. She resents the situation Isabella brought her to. The queen imagines that the Despenser made it clear to her with the flat of his hand that he did not much like his wife having a mind of her own.

Isabella supposes he has turned Eleanor's mind against her as well. *She is a French spy, watch her well: any letters she writes, you must open; any word she utters, you must report to me. Provoke her if possible. We must know what is on the traitor's mind.*

"Do you love him, your husband?" Isabella asks her one day, outright.

Eleanor looks as if she has been caught secretly taking a chess piece from the board. "He is a fine husband and much misunderstood."

"I think you are like me, Eleanor. We both see ourselves as a Guinevere looking for her Lancelot. And look what we married! I have a Greek and you have a banker."

"I am nothing like you, your grace," she says sniffily, managing somehow to be subservient and condescending at once.

"Oh, I think we are very like. I wonder what it is with your husband, do you think? Where did such greed come from? I suspect it a surfeit of pride. All his life he has passed unnoticed, and now he wishes to make the world pay."

"You do not know him as I do," Eleanor says, and feels so secure in the Despenser's primacy that she turns her back and leaves the room without asking leave.

———

It has become a lonely vigil. Many of the servants she has had since she first saw Dover as a child-bride flee back to France; she sends Théophania home, Rosseletti too, for his own safety. Just a handful remain, in defiance of the new regulations.

As the winter nights draw in, Isabella stares at the logs crumbling in the grate and sees her life come to nothing. She was once one of the greatest landowners in the realm; now she is a pensioner.

Her two daughters are removed from her household and are taken into the care of Edward's brother-in-law at Marlborough. She is virtually a prisoner now. She has lost her lands, her income, her children, her husband, her influence, and her friends. She supposes the Despenser will not be truly content until she is dead, and she wonders if he is planning that too.

———

She is finally summoned to the king's presence.

She is taken by barge up the Thames. A little more than sixteen years ago, when she first came to London, there were not so many houses. Now the Exchequer has moved from Winchester, and the spaces between Westminster and London are filling up. The archbishop of York has his house on the Strand, there are big houses for the bishops of Norwich and Durham. Soon there will be no empty land at all between London and the palace. Where shall it all end?

When she arrives in the great hall, it feels as if she has been hauled before the saints for final judgment. A vast crowd is there, like crows sitting on a fence, waiting to pick at her eyes. The Despenser is there, and Stapledon of course. Old Hugh as well; he has seen the chance of quick money and been led by his son into this devil's bargain.

But there are some friendly faces, at least: the archbishop of Vienne and the bishop of Orange, the pope's men in England; and the bishops of Norwich and Winchester, as well as the Earl of Richmond, just returned from their embassy in France, where they have tried to repair the king's diplomatic missteps.

Edward is slouched on his throne, bored and resentful. He meets her eyes briefly, then looks away. It is like that first time in Boulogne Cathedral. She knows what that look is now. He is embarrassed.

She cannot believe his malice. She had expected it of the Despenser, but not Edward. Why would he do this to her? All her servants, those who did not abandon her, are now detained and shut up in religious houses. She is quite alone.

He had never been deliberately cruel to her before; he had been guilty of neglect, but only of her affections. But what he has done in these last six months is venomous. Has the Despenser really taken his mind so much?

"Dearest consort," he manages.

"Your grace."

"We trust we find you well."

"May I first inquire about my children?"

He flushes with anger that she should have the temerity to raise the subject of their offspring in front of these others. "They are well."

"I have not seen my daughters for three months. And Edward, he prospers?"

Old Hugh cuts in. "May we to the business at hand?"

Richmond tells them all in bald terms their situation. It has been suggested that she travel to France to negotiate a peace for England with her brother, the king of France. Charles has promised that he will make Prince Edward the Duke of Aquitaine if he comes to France and pays homage to him there. This arrangement has been ratified by the French council.

"This is the general principle. But he will only confirm this arrangement in the presence of either the king or queen."

"Impossible," Despenser shouts. "If we let her out of the country, she will foment unrest in the French court against us."

"Should I go, then?" Edward asks him, but the Despenser balks at this too. Without the king, who will protect him from the barons and earls he has robbed? And he dare not accompany him and set foot in France himself; her brother would have him hanged from the nearest tree before his boots were dry.

"She is sister to the king of France, and has already proved her worth in such negotiations," Richmond points out. "It was she who had the Earl of Lancaster make peace with the king when a civil war seemed inevitable."

Heads nod in agreement. The Despenser scowls.

"How do we know we can trust our wife?" Edward says to her.

"I have been a good and faithful wife to you, your grace. As these gentlemen recount, I have helped you with the Earl of Lancaster, and many times before and after. I understand your suspicions, for I am of France, but you must know that it is my duty and my heartfelt desire to serve you, and only you, and has been from the day we were married at Boulogne, a day I carry in my heart always."

The pope's nuncios, the bishops of Orange and Vienne, nod and smile, well pleased with this speech. Stapledon looks as if he has bitten down on a lemon. The Despenser can see the debate rushing away from him. But what is he to do? Someone must go, the king of France has made it plain, or else the king loses Gascony. It is he or the queen.

Old Hugh speaks over the top of all of them. "May I remind you all that as we speak, Mortimer is in Hainaut raising troops for an invasion? The duke has given him levies, and he is using his wife's money to get more soldiers from Germany. We cannot afford a war with France at this moment. Anything is preferable."

"You know about this?" the king asks her.

She wants to say: I am virtually a prisoner, how would I know what goes on in the world? But this is not entirely true, nor is it the answer the king is seeking. She shakes her head and looks resigned.

"This is madness to let her go," the Despenser says. "She will only hatch more mischief."

"My lord, I understand your apprehension," she says, "and I acknowledge there has been bad blood between us in the past. But in this matter we are in agreement. We both want peace for

England and for Edward, and this war serves neither my brother nor my husband. I only wish for there to be peace again between us so our lives can be as they were before."

This little speech astonishes the Despenser. Richmond smiles and nods approvingly. The nuncios turn to the king.

Her poor tortured Edward. He looks as if he would rather be mending thatch than sitting here weighing such dilemmas. His hands grip the edge of his throne, and he looks at the ceiling. "I will think on it," he says, and finally he gets up and leaves the chamber.

———————

It is a Sunday, and she is at her prayers when Eleanor disturbs her there. She prepares herself for the news. Eleanor's face is a study in equivocation. She is unsure if she is witnessing the queen's rise or her downfall.

"You are going to France," she says.

Isabella smiles and thanks her for the news and returns to her prayers. She would call her friends for a celebration, but there are none left—not in England.

Chapter 41

March 1325

The wind is cold, and there are whitecaps on the narrow sea. They say that on a clear day you can see all the way to France, but she has never been in Dover on a clear day. Servants bring spiced wine and bread. She refuses it all. She will not keep it down long, once she is aboard the ship.

Her retinue is thirty strong, mostly spies masquerading as servants; Joan of Bar and the Countess of Warwick are her chief attendants. She feels as if she is about to be released from prison and is terrified that her jailers will change their minds at the last moment. Her hands are shaking, and she tries to conceal them beneath her cloak.

"The king of France has offered to make the prince the Duke of Aquitaine," the king reminds her. "In return Edward will pay homage to your brother in person. For this you will demand that he withdraw his army from Gascony and cede the province to our control."

"This last he did not promise," Isabella reminds him.

"It is up to you to negotiate the details," the Despenser says. "Your children are here in England, ransom to your good conduct and intentions."

Edward puts a restraining hand on his arm. "No need to talk of ransom. She knows where her duty lies," he says, and it is the first time she has seen this gentleness from him in many months. She nods her head in acknowledgment, but directs her reply to the chamberlain.

"You want what is best for England," she says, "and so I understand your concerns. But I shall do all in my power to bring this matter to a peaceful resolve."

"Once it is done, young Edward will join you in France to conclude the matter. Not before."

She looks at Edward. "I will give you reason to trust me again, your grace. On this I give my word. I am sorry for our differences in the past."

The Despenser has the grace to blush at this. He sits back, having failed to provoke her. Edward looks rueful. Perhaps he wonders if he has misjudged her.

He is right; he has.

———

The king joins her at the dock, while the Despenser stands a little way off. She makes her obeisance, and he kisses her chastely on the cheek. She lingers, though she is eager to be aboard. Even the churning sea is welcome after so long wandering like a specter in the towers and gardens at Windsor.

"Help me, Isabella," he murmurs.

"I will do all I can."

"Do this for me, and all will be as it was between us. You have nothing to fear from the Lord Despenser. You will always be my queen."

She watches him from the rails of the ship as it leaves the harbor. He stands at the dock's edge until she is out of sight, the loneliest king she has ever seen.

Chapter 42

Boulogne depresses her; she has bad memories of the town. Her household is soon overblown: the thirty bodyguards and servants who accompany her from England swells to a retinue of hundreds as supporters come to welcome her, among them a good many knights sent at her brother's command to ensure her safety.

Her retainers from England stick close. She will not believe she is free of England and Despenser until she sees her brother again.

The crossing was rough, and her nervous energy is exhausted. The countryside beyond the town is rutted, and badly made roads plough through ice-bound pastures and soaring hedgerows. Finally, late one afternoon, they arrive at Charles's camp, a sprawl of fine pavilions flying banners bearing the golden fleur-de-lis of France.

Isabella emerges from her litter in a somber black gown, carefully trimmed with Bruges lace at the cuff and neck. One needs to look dowdy but not *too* dowdy. She is greeted by boisterous shouting from the French side.

Charles is reclined in a cushioned chair in his pavilion, his slippered feet resting on a stool. A clutch of tittering women watch her from behind his throne, and courtiers in velvets and silks whisper about her behind their hands.

She sinks to her knees. He looks like her father; the resemblance is uncanny. It is like seeing him again, in a younger time. Charles is the last one left, the rest of her family are dead.

He does not let her stay on her knees long. He jumps up and takes her hands, helping her back to her feet, preserving her dignity. He smiles and brings her close. "Sister, do not be downhearted. We will find some remedy for your condition."

She rediscovers her resolve. It has been so long, she has almost forgotten who she is and where she is from.

———————

The negotiations are a public spectacle. The pope's nuncios are there, as well as Stratford—the bishop of Winchester—and Richmond, Edward's envoys; Sully; and all the French ministers. She bargains hard for Edward, but even if she had not a prior understanding with her brother, she doubts if she would have had much sway. Certainly no more than she would have had with her father. The Capets did not become royal by being soft at the bargaining table.

It is one thing to give assistance to your family, another to sell the birthright.

Eventually a treaty is agreed: if Edward comes to France to pay homage before the end of summer, then Charles will return Ponthieu and Montreuil, Isabella's own dower lands recently lost to French royalists. But he will not give up the Agenais; its fate he leaves to a court of French judges "at some future time."

She knows the vagueness of this last resolution will set Edward's teeth on edge. And at the last moment, Charles feigns to argue over the terms of the *existing* truce. He is playing for time. His intransigence is reassuring.

The nuncios, Norwich and Vienne, are charged with taking the resolution to Edward. She does not envy them their task. He will erupt when he hears it.

She says she will stay in France until it is all settled.

After all the diplomats and professional dilettantes have gone and she is alone once more, she walks out onto the terrace with her cloak wrapped around her shoulders and watches the moon rise over Poissy.

For all that she is grateful to her brother for giving her refuge, it is hard to love him. The pope has annulled his marriage to Blanche, and she will see the end of her days in a nunnery. His second wife has died in childbirth, and now there is talk of him marrying Evreux's daughter, Jeanne.

She thinks often these days about Blanche and the looks her sister-in-law gave the knight that day in the church. It was she who told her father about the rumors. She told herself she did it from duty, but now she wonders: *Was I jealous?*

Was I bitter that my stupid sisters-in-law knew something that I never would?

All of life's certainties are replaced with doubt. She thought she knew Isabella of France. *Sweet, gentle, and amiable.*

She does not know her at all.

———

April finds her in Paris, in the king's salon, among friends again. Life here is simple, the king is the king, and the magnates do not stamp about with threatening looks. The women, though, are empty-headed. She thinks of Marguerite and Blanche—that is where an empty head gets a woman. There should be a law.

"It is a terrible position you are in," Charles tells her. "What are you going to do?"

"I cannot go back to England, not while Despenser is there."

"You think if you threaten to stay here, then your husband will send him away?"

"If he does, he will only invite him back again, and I shall be worse off than before. He has already done so twice. He will do it again."

"Then what will you do?"

"I don't know."

"A wife is a husband's property, and his honor is invested in her no matter how wronged she may be. This is true if he is a king or a carpenter."

He speaks from bitter experience, of course.

———

Stratford returns from England. He is supposed to be Edward's man, but she sometimes catches him regarding her with a quizzical expression, as if he is imagining what life might be like if she were his employer and not the king of England.

He looks ecclesiastical and businesslike. The king is not happy that the Agenais is not returned. He is blaming the pope's legates for holding out false hope of success. They had suggested her mission, and now it seems to him, the queen may as well have stayed home.

But he has agreed to the terms she has negotiated; he will come to France and do what must be done. Now he should like his queen to return at once to England and be done with it. Such is the gist of the message.

Isabella looks at Richmond, and Richmond looks at Stratford. "Does the king say when he shall make his journey to France?"

"He says he will do it by the end of August."

"And the Lord Despenser will let him go?"

Stratford shrugs. "He is not well pleased by it, as can be imagined. He fears being left alone in England, like a child fears being left in the dark without a candle. But with much better reason."

"I hear," Isabella says, "that the chamberlain has cheated Pembroke's widow out of twenty thousand acres of her estate."

"Your grace, he has cheated everyone at some time or other. But while the king protects him, who is there to gainsay him? The only men who can stand up to him are in France."

Richmond leans back, sighs, and looks at the ceiling. "I once had a dog," he says. "I used to toss it morsels from my plate. And every time, my wife's cat would jump on the tidbit first, take it from between his very paws. And he would just lie there and watch her do it. Sometimes she would eat it, right under his nose. And he was a fearsome dog. I used him for hunting. But never once did he chase the cat away, no matter he was twice her size."

"Perhaps the dog loved the cat," Stratford suggests.

"Perhaps. But to truly know the answer for his behavior, you would have to be the dog."

"Why did you not stop tossing him the meat," Isabella asks Richmond, "if you knew the cat would always steal it?"

"Because I hoped one day he would learn. But he never did."

"And neither has Edward," she says.

He smiles. "No. Neither has he."

———

The king is in the *chambre à parer*, receiving ambassadors, dealing with affairs of state. This is the center of court life, containing the great ceremonial state bed, everyone of importance in France. All Charles's princes and nobles are here for the ceremonials.

Isabella is here, dressed conspicuously in widow's weeds. She makes no embassy and speaks to no one. But simply by her presence and her black veil, she makes it clear to the nuncios and to all of France that she has been supplanted in her husband's affections by another, and so she has therefore retired to live as a nun. Her mourning clothes make this clear to everyone. Some are very affected by the position she has taken. There is much disgust about how Edward has treated her.

News of this will reach England. Edward's blood will boil.

———————

It's a windy night. Summer has still not found France, and there is rain on her visitors' cloaks. The king of England has said he wants Isabella back in England. Charles refuses to expel her.

Her guests in the palace tonight need no persuasion to her cause. They are England's disaffected, those who have fled or been expelled by the king's favorite. They are all men who are guests here but would find themselves in chains in their own country, desperate men living as landless exiles.

Treason is not spoken but is implied in every whispered conversation. They are there to pledge their loyalty to the queen, who is now the focal point for their disaffection.

They listen as she grieves her lost estates, her lost position; she grieves the loss of her children; she grieves the loss of her income and her lands; she grieves most of all the loss of her husband to another who has supplanted her in the king's affections.

And when they have gone, she lets the candle burn down and thinks about the one man who has not yet appeared. France's most celebrated exile is raising an army in Hainaut. They say he is the one man who can turn England's fortune.

She wonders if he is all they say he is or just another greedy baron like the rest. She thinks about the shadow she saw on the roof of the tower that night. Why did she not give him up? Perhaps even then she imagined how he might be useful to her one day.

Every night more shadowed figures pass in and out of the gates to whisper over candlelit suppers and plot over the wine. They are careful in what they say, and she is careful about who listens. There is yet a part of her that hopes Edward will change his mind.

He sends letter after letter, insisting that she return, but there is always a reason to delay. Let him come to her. If she can get him away from the Despenser, things might be different. In England he is never alone. He is constantly surrounded by that toad and his people. Before summer is out he has promised to come to France, and even if he is not vulnerable to her sex, surely he will listen to reason and to friendship. At heart he is a good man, and she will not let him destroy himself this way. It seems impossible to her that he might not finally see the danger and save his throne.

Chapter 43

Edward changes his mind. She can imagine the scene: the Despenser almost on his knees, begging him not to leave him at the mercy of his enemies—almost everyone in England aside from his father, his wife, and his dog. He will have reminded him what happened to Gaveston without his king's protection. He will have whispered endearments or pleas in his ear, probably both.

But invoking Gaveston's name will touch the king. He will remember that day in June when his barons dragged his lover up a hill and gutted and beheaded him. He is never far from it, even in his dreams.

Stratford and Richmond look abashed when they bring the news. The king was at Dover, ready to board the ship. "He was taken ill," Stratford says.

Richmond shakes his head. "No, he wasn't," he mouths to her.

"What shall you do now?" Charles asks her. They walk along a wide gallery, out of earshot of his courtiers, of her spies.

"I must do something. I am unable to meet my expenses. He has cut off my funds."

"Can you blame him?"

"This was his last chance. He has showed his hand now."

"He has shown his hand many times, dear sister. It is just that those who love him persist in ignoring it."

"He cannot love the Despenser more than me, more than his country. More than the Crown."

The king of France considers this proposition. Finally, he asks her: "Why not?"

Why not indeed.

———

She meets with Richmond and Stratford yet again. Charles's proposal is this: he will yet make the young Prince Edward the Duke of Aquitaine, if he comes to France and pays homage to the king in person.

"Is this your idea?" Stratford asks her.

She ignores the question: "It has been ratified by the council."

"He will never do it," Stratford says.

"Oh, he might," Richmond says.

He might, because if Edward wants Gascony, someone must come and bend the knee before Charles, and the Despenser will not let it be the king. Stratford's eyes widen. Either the queen of England or the king of France is more clever than all of them. By his smile he seems to think it is Isabella.

In the end, Stratford goes back to England alone. By now he has become a seasoned seafarer, and Richmond has taken to calling him Captain Stratford in jest. Richmond does not accompany him, feigning illness. If it is good enough for the king . . .

Richmond stays in France, he has made his choice. Stratford may be the one best acquainted with the Channel, but it is Richmond who already sees which way the wind blows.

Chapter 44

The young prince is stiff in her arms. It is not that he does not love her, but when a young boy has his mother and father compete for his affections, it makes him guarded with the entire world. He will be a fine man one day, but for now his chestnut bangs and soft cheeks only make him look vulnerable. He is precise and measured in all he does. His eyes watch everything.

He is the age I was when I married Edward, she realizes. *Was I this callow?*

Stratford catches her eye. *I cannot believe you managed this.*

The prince is introduced to the French court. She watches what he watches. He is just a boy, but even a boy's lowered eyes will turn toward a well-shaped ankle, a plump bosom, if they are offered for view. She has to know if Edward's curse has carried to the son. Life would have been different if her husband had longed for a woman, any woman really.

It would not have been an entirely happy life, but she might have managed.

———

The king is dressed in a blue robe emblazoned with golden lilies, and there is a relic of Saint Louis hanging on a chain around his neck. His hair is freshly oiled, his beard trimmed. There is a bejeweled ring on every finger. His ministers stand either side, dressed in black, crows looking for easy pickings. Behind the king is a great tapestry of Saint Louis at Damietta, his knights on snorting warhorses charging from a blue sea, the white dove of the Holy Spirit watching from a pure sky. Its wings are edged with gold.

It is like being in the presence of God. A *French* god.

Knights in royal livery flank the king, their hands resting on their broadswords.

The court is in their silks, and the women in their velvets, all burgundy and gold. Edward, her beautiful son, bends his knee, and after his homage he is pronounced the Duke of Aquitaine.

There, it is done.

Charles is buoyant. He announces that he thinks he will retain the Agenais as indemnity for losses suffered in the war. The nuncios appear stricken. Isabella keeps a straight face. When Edward learns of this, he will cough up his liver. This was not what he supposed would happen.

Later, in the gardens, Stratford trails after her across the wet grass. It has been raining, and her skirts soak up the dew and are heavy to drag across the lawns of the palace. "The king has ordered you home," he tells her.

"Is that what he charged you to tell me?"

"He sends this safe conduct," Stratford says, holding a scroll toward her. She ignores it. Instead she turns to Richmond. "And what is your advice?"

"Should you go, you put yourself at the mercy of the Despensers, and you know what I think of the Despensers."

"No, I do not."

"Did you know he kidnapped Elizabeth de Comyn and kept her imprisoned until she signed over her estates to him? The man's greed has no bounds. For myself, I think he is half-mad. At least as mad as the king, who cannot see any side of an argument but his own. Should you go back to England, I should think you mad as well, for you place yourself in his purview, and this time he will brick you in, and you will never see sunlight again."

"My Lord Richmond, can you keep your voice down." Stratford looks around as if there might be spies hiding in the hedges.

"You don't like your king either, do you?" she asks him.

His face is blank. He is a bishop and a statesman to the bone. "It is not my position to say," he answers.

As soon as news of Charles's equivocation on the Agenais reaches England, a new envoy is sent back to France. This time it is Stapledon, the bishop of Exeter. He is in France for a month, and Isabella avoids seeing him or receiving his letters, which are returned with their seals intact. She stalls this meeting as long as possible. But finally she relents. Charles is becoming restless over her expenses, and she must talk finances with Stapledon.

From the moment the king's envoy appears in her company, he berates her. He tells her he does not like the company she has been keeping. He says she is consorting with disaffected exiles and traitors who plot against the king. *Really, who does this impudent crow think he is?* She would not tolerate such interference in her affairs from her own husband.

Who is this man again? A mere bishop?

She would gape at him in astonishment, but she remembers herself.

"My Lord Stapledon, you were commanded by your king to help with my finances during my embassy here in Paris, which is at my husband's command. So far you have done nothing to assist me. Let us discuss that first."

He draws himself up to his full height, which is not very far. "I have been unable to do so. It is not for the want of effort."

"I do not care much for your efforts—it is funds I need. I remind you, I am here at the king's service."

"In the opinion of the king, your service to him is finished. He requires that you return at once to England."

"I am unable to do so at the present time."

"What prevents you, your grace?"

"What prevents me is my husband the king's disposition. Should I return, what life does he warrant me? My estates have been sequestered, and my income should scarce fill the needs of a peat cropper. I require his guarantees that should I return, I shall again be treated in the manner that a royal daughter of France requires and deserves. The first of my conditions is that the Lord Despenser is told that his presence in England is contrary to our wishes."

"Your condition for your return?"

"I want an agreement from the king confirming my position in the realm and the income he has set aside for me as his queen. The Despensers are to leave England, and it is to be set in the statutes of England—by the king's law—that they are forbidden to return. They have placed themselves between my husband and me, and by God's law, I cannot abide it any longer. Nothing less than his agreement to these terms is acceptable to me. I would be obliged if you would convey this message to him immediately."

"I do not know that he will care for your conditions. It has come to my attention that you have met with individuals who the king regards as traitors to the Crown and enemies of England."

They regard each other.

"Perhaps you did not hear what I said," she says, finally.

"Very well. I shall convey your exact words to him in person."

"I should rather you send a messenger to convey my wishes. You should remain here to assist me with my finances. Do I make myself clear?"

His eyes are pinpoints. "Perfectly."

No sooner has she ordered him not to leave the country than he is back in England.

"He will tell the king all he has seen and heard here," Richmond says to her when he hears the news.

"Well it is too late to go back now. The die is cast."

"It always was, I think. You just didn't want to think it. None of us did."

"You know, if you took a gravedigger or a tailor—a simple man—and put him on the throne of England, I believe the result would be the same. Edward is not a bad man. He is just not royal. My father was royal and ruthless by design. Edward is ruthless through exasperation."

Richmond sighs and looks over the roofs of Paris. If things go badly, this will be his only view for the rest of his life. The windows of her apartments frame the Sainte-Chapelle on the Île de la Cité, which Saint Louis had built to house the Crown of Thorns.

We know about such crowns, Edward and I.

A steward brings wine and Richmond sips at it daintily, toying with a garnet ring. "The king has ordered me home."

"Again?"

"I think only so that he might be aggrieved at my refusal."

"I shall not forget your loyalty to me."

"I never thought I should be disloyal to my king. But Lord Despenser makes it impossible for me to be otherwise. The man is a lout. I should rather be ruled by the Irish. Why does Edward allow this?"

"I don't know."

"Gaveston—well I didn't condone it, but I understood it. The man had a certain roguish charm. I enjoyed those jokes he made about Lincoln. But Despenser has no humor. He's a lawyer with a mean streak."

"You'd go mad trying to work it out. I did."

"Well I trust I shall never fall into his clutches, or the king's, not now. Or it's the traitor's death for me." The wine glistens on his beard, like blood. "You know that the king has sent the pope a bribe?"

"How much?"

"Five thousand florins."

"Has the pope accepted it?"

"With alacrity."

"What does Edward want for his money?"

"He wants him to declare you excommunicate."

"Will he do it?"

Richmond shakes his head. "He pretends it was a gift, like it was a ham, or a new carpet. All he has done is send a letter to Despenser telling him to be more pleasant and make his peace with you."

"It is Christian of him."

"Well, he is the pope."

"Still, I think we are well past the point of reconciliation."

"Do not let the nuncios hear you say that. Did you know that he wants you stripped of your title and exiled?"

"Despenser suggested that?"

"He believes he has found some precedence in law, a ruling on some old Saxon queen. It is so long ago it might be a folktale. He would enshrine an ugly rumor as the eleventh commandment if it suited his purposes."

"I cannot ask you to throw in your lot with me, Lord Richmond. It is too dangerous. But whatever happens, you have been a good friend to me in France, and I shall never forget it."

"I threw in my lot a long time ago. The Lord Despenser made the choice an easy one."

"You know, before I came here, I spent my days sitting in a garden. Watching two robins chase a crow from their nest was the most excitement I ever had in one day. Now I have the future king of England in my care, he is heir to the throne and the most eligible prince for all the royal families of Europe. Why should I give this up for two birds in a hedge?"

"Yet, your grace, if you continue to defy Edward's orders you risk the reproof of the entire Church as well as the people of England. This is not how a wife commonly behaves."

"And this is not how a wife is commonly treated, not when she is a princess of France and a queen of England. Neither is a queen considered common, at least not in France—I can no longer speak for England. So I will run the risk of approbation, my Lord Richmond, because to do otherwise is to put my neck under the Lord Despenser's boot. And I shall never do that again."

———

Young Edward has a haunted look about him. Everyone here treats him with such deference that he cannot help but suspect some subterfuge. He sits at her table as stiffly as if he were the head stable boy invited to say grace at the king's coronation feast.

He wants to know when they will go back to England; he wants to know why he had to pay homage to the king of France. Is it true that that man is his uncle? Then why does his father dislike him so?

And why do the people here say such horrid things about his uncle Hugh?

The servants hover around him; he is a lad and he needs feeding up. There are roast meats and goose, duck, capons, eels. He stabs at the food, examines it, eats hardly any. He takes a sip of the watered wine, and his lips gleam scarlet in the candlelight.

"I should like to go home," he tells her.

"What is it you miss?"

"My father."

She tells herself he is too young to understand. Besides, no damage can come to him. In the end he will be king, no matter what others decide.

But whose king will he be? Hers? Or Edward's?

———

When her uncle Valois dies, the noble and powerful converge on Paris to pay their respects. Jeanne, the wife of the Count of Hainaut, is there. Also in her retinue is a man she last saw as a shadow in the moonlight, newly emerged from a chimney on the Hall Tower. In the cold vault of the church, she can feel his eyes boring into her. She will not chance a glance over her shoulder for fear that it will encourage him.

Just once then, a glimpse.

Such naked lust on his face. She smiles, despite herself, but with care that he does not see it.

Charles takes her aside later. "Jeanne has an offer to make to you."

"To me?"

"She wishes an alliance." Charles has been growing impatient of late; keeping his sister has proved expensive. He was prepared to be expansive at first, but now he wants a resolution to this problem. He cannot host another man's queen forever, even if they are related. "Mortimer has been their guest since he escaped England. Her husband and Edward are not friends. You know this. He would rather someone better disposed to his interests on the throne of England."

"What is she likely to propose?"

"A marriage."

"I do not think the countess and I would produce many heirs."

He frowns. He does not understand humor and simply finds her remark tasteless. "Your son, Edward, is a priceless asset to you, and to any family into which he marries. You know this, Isabella."

"Whom would he marry?"

"The count has several daughters. I can never remember their names. One of them should suit your purpose."

She finds herself praying for her son, that this slip of a boy should love the role of kingship as much as her father did. Let him be uncomplicated by desires, let his ambition be simple, and let him be ruthless in the getting of it. No darling favorites, no headstrong queens. She wishes him a pliant wife, mistresses as he needs them, and barons who will find no weakness in him.

"It is only the Despensers I oppose," she says.

Charles says nothing. The silence grows uneasy.

"You don't believe that."

"I do not believe you can separate Edward from the Despensers or the Gavestons of this world, chérie. There will always be someone between you and the king. It is up to you now, Isabella. You must act as you see fit. Mortimer is raising an army in Hainaut. There are many whose argument is not only with the Despensers."

"Will you give me an army, Charles?"

He laughs. "You think you will win over the English with an army of Frenchmen? We are the ancient enemy, the only people they perhaps despise more than the king's favorites. Talk to Jeanne. Listen to what she offers."

And what she offers is exactly what her brother has promised: a marriage and an army. As they talk, Mortimer hovers in the background, and she finds it hard to concentrate. The terms of the contract between Hainaut and her are left for her to consider.

But what of Mortimer? If she is to do this, she will need a champion, a man with a good sword arm and a decisive nature;

a man who is not afraid to take risks. And these are terrible risks indeed.

If she is no longer Philippe's daughter, then she supposes she is free to be whomever she chooses; the demon that the Despenser has painted her, perhaps.

When she takes a rest from the negotiations to walk in the garden, Mortimer is there beside her. "I did not expect to see you again," she says.

"It seems fate has brought us together again for a purpose."

No man has ever looked at her like this. To Edward she was an obligation; to everyone else she was a queen and out of reach. Only Mortimer had the impudence to suppose she was not beyond him. He looked at her like Gaveston had looked at Edward. She was beginning to understand why Edward risked so much for him.

"I will need a general."

"That is why I am here."

"What do you wish in return?"

A slow and lazy smile. "What are you offering me?"

"A position of eminence when I am queen in my own right."

"Shall I be your Despenser?"

"My trusted adviser and counselor, yes. And you will be ceded all of Despenser's lands."

He steps closer, too close for a loyal subject. "I told you they misjudged you. You are a rare woman indeed."

He is intimidating, this close. This terror is a singular feeling. "You are good at climbing roofs I am told," she whispers.

"Passingly fair."

"Can you climb mine?"

"If necessary."

"Make sure you are not seen. My nurse will be waiting after matins. She will show you the way."

His eyes widen in surprise and pleasure. For her part, she can-not believe what she has just done. Her hands are shaking. It is one thing to depose your king, another to bring down God's law.

Wherever he is in heaven, she hopes her father cannot see her now.

Chapter 45

Her ladies are puzzled when she sends them out of the room and says that she wishes to sleep alone tonight. She tells them that they snore and keep her awake.

Theophania is the only one trusted with her secret, and it is midnight when Isabella hears a soft tapping at her door. It opens a fraction, and he slips inside, stealthy as an assassin.

She has been awake, praying to whatever god listens to a woman asking for good fortune on the eve of her adultery. He strides toward her, all ardor and purpose, and she puts out a hand to stop him coming closer. It is as if he wants to crush her into his arms immediately.

"A moment, my lord. This is not an invasion."

"I have hungered for you since the moment I first saw you."

This is exactly the right thing to say, words she has longed to hear from Edward and never has. She ventures a hand to his chest, strokes it. She likes the feel of the velvet and the hard muscle underneath. *He's a brute, your Mortimer,* she thinks. It will be like lying with a force of nature.

There is a vein pulsing in his temple. He presses her against the wall. He is ready for her. She ventures to test him out, something she would never have done with Edward. It is like an iron bar. This is impressive and surprising.

She had always thought a lady must be prepared to wait and work for something as pleasing and as substantial as this.

He takes her curiosity as invitation to kiss her roughly—her lips, her neck, and her breasts. She has wondered if she would disappoint with her lack of skills and artistry when they came to it, but it is soon apparent that all she is required to do is cling on for her very life and occasionally gulp for breath.

It is like being washed overboard.

While Edward is tentative in his lovemaking, almost apologetic, Mortimer is about ravishment and assault. He wants her naked and spread, and he wants it now. A battering ram is brought to the gates; she is pinned and violated. No prisoners are taken.

This is more like it. At one stage she laughs with delight, and he perhaps takes this as criticism of his performance, for he only sets to harder. Her nightgown catches underneath her and is torn in his enthusiasm for the task. She is rolled onto her belly, then her back. Her beauty is at last much admired, and from every possible view.

This is what she has hungered for. There is nothing genteel about it. When it is almost done, he withdraws, and she is impressed and horrified by the warm splash of his seed on her body. There is so much of it. He groans so loudly, she is forced to put a hand over his mouth for fear he will wake the servants.

He bites her palm.

And there it is done. At last she has become the object of a man's desire and fulfilled every sinful wish. She feels bruised, pleasantly so. He has crushed bones in her groin. Her breasts are sore where he has bitten her. This is altogether a novel experience.

He rolls onto his back, a beast of a man with scars and a pelt of black hair. It is as if she has been ravished by a bear.

And it is not enough. It is not nearly enough to make up for the years of frustration. She kisses his beard, his chest, tries to stir him, but he is having none of it. Roger Mortimer has won his great victory; now he needs time to regroup. At tender moments such as this, Edward would hold her and talk about inconsequential things. But this is not Edward, and this is not his bed.

She remembers the first time with Edward, lying under damp sheets, embarrassed, the sheets pulled up to her chin. He had not looked at her; she wonders now if he was thinking about someone else. A woman needs only lie there; it is the man who must seek inspiration. Edward was never as urgent as this, not as desperate for fulfillment as Mortimer clearly is.

He sleeps briefly, and wakes, startled, and reaches for his weapons, then remembers where he is.

"You must be proud of yourself," she murmurs.

"How so?"

"You have not only bulled the queen of England, but you have made a cuckold of the king. A fine revenge for what he put you through in the Tower."

"That was not my intention."

"But it was the consequence. Do not tell me you do not lie there thinking about it."

"And what of you? Have you not struck a blow at your husband tonight for all his negligence?"

"Perhaps." The sweat has barely cooled on their bodies, and they are at each other's throats. She supposes it can hardly be helped when there are a wife and a king betrayed. Perhaps he has less cause than her to feel such a burden of guilt. They say adultery in a man is a necessary evil; in a woman it is a mortal sin and unforgivable.

"I thought this day would never come," he whispers.

"What of the Lady Mortimer?"

"Must we speak of her?"

"She is your wife."

"And you have a husband."

"It is different for me: my husband wants another. Lady Mortimer dotes on you."

"I do not wish to speak about my wife."

"She is my friend."

"If she is your friend, what are you doing here with me?"

Isabella leaps to her feet, goes to the door, opens it, peers outside. There is no one. "You should leave now."

"Very well, your grace." He dresses. She watches by the light of the candle, a fur wrapped around her shoulders. The guilt is crushing. She should never have done this. What was she thinking?

He hesitates at the door, bows stiffly, and wishes her a good night.

After he has gone, she promises herself this can never happen again. She will make a long pilgrimage and find relief for her sin. She will never see Mortimer again.

———

Her resolution weakens the next night as she lies alone in the vast bed and thinks about being taken. Each time she closes her eyes, she remembers the delicious violence of it and wants to rake her nails along his brute back again. It is like any hunger; it is easy to disavow it when the belly is full, but even the heartiest of feasts will only keep us until the next day.

And like a hunger it is mild as it begins, but after three days she is weak from it, and after a week she can think of nothing else but to satisfy it.

She meets with Jeanne and they discuss suitable matches for her son, but all the while her eyes are on Mortimer, and his on hers. It is agreed that she and the prince will come to Hainaut to meet Count William's daughters.

That night there is a gentle tapping at the door, and Théophania escorts him to her bedchamber, and the shame and the wanting starts all over again.

In the days that follow, they are discreet in public, just glances, nothing more. Does one of her stewards see Mortimer one night as he passes down the stairs, hooded and cloaked? He thinks he saw a shadow watching him, but he cannot be sure.

Her brother is nobody's fool, and he has spies everywhere. Every scullery maid knows it is worth a few coins to report anything she sees or hears. Soon Isabella catches her brother looking at her with a frown, nothing in it perhaps except he has been told something he cannot prove, or wishes not to believe.

He invites her to dine with him. The king of France eats well, and there is always music and entertainment. It is only when all the entertainers have been paid and the servants sent to their beds that he calls for the best wine and settles in and asks her what she thinks of this fellow Mortimer. The question is posed in such a casual manner that she is immediately on her guard.

She does not fall into the trap of indifference. "He is a fine fellow. He served Edward faithfully and well and is much maligned by him in my opinion. His wife was one of my ladies, and I count her a good friend."

The king, perhaps expecting evasion, considers carefully. "There are rumors. That you are amorously inclined toward him."

She frowns, then laughs. "Any royal court is full of gossip, especially when a married woman is unescorted."

"Because it would be unthinkable, Isabella. You realize this? While the king has wronged you, society is prepared to forgive your actions in seeking my protection. But you are still the man's wife. You cannot just do as you please."

"I have no interest in Lord Mortimer."

"Do not lie to me, sister. I have seen the way you look at him. The whole world has seen the way you look at him!"

She can no longer hide her blushes. They spent their child-hood together; he knows her stratagems better than anyone.

"He is a married man, and you are still Edward's wife. Should your feelings become known, whatever advantage you hold over Edward will be lost in an instant. Be prudent."

"I will take heed," she answers, careful neither to admit her affair nor deny it.

When Mortimer next comes to see her, she is careful to speak with him in full view of her ladies, and there is no coy laughter or fluttering of the eyes. They make desultory conversation: the weather, the gossip from England. He drops his voice and casually suggests that should she ever return to England, certain barons would use her name as a rallying cry.

She is alarmed that he might speak so openly of it. She looks around for spies. "It is the Despenser I am against, not my husband."

"The king has ruined England. If we were to take off the Despenser's head tomorrow, another would grow in its place. You know this better than any of us."

She laughs as if he has made some jesting remark. Joan of Bar looks up from her needlework and frowns.

"You think it can be done?"

"It should have been done after Gaveston."

"You supported the king then."

"He hadn't locked me up in the Tower then. It is up to you, Isabella. You have only two choices: One is to put your son on the throne of England; it is his to claim one day anyway. The other is to go back meekly to England like a lamb, and you know what will happen to you if you do."

He is right. She knows he is right. "I saw you that night," she says to him. "When you escaped from the Tower. I was on the roof."

"You saw me? Why did you not sound the alarm?"

"I did, but the guards would not wake."

He laughs. "No, you didn't. You wanted me to escape. I wonder why. Was it because you wished one day to employ my sword arm?"

"I could not have known it would come to this."

"Something in you did."

There is snow in the bare fields. The nights are cold and lonely, and soon the hunger matters more to her than good sense. She does not sleep with Mortimer to make good use of his sword arm. For now, it is another part of his equipment that matters more to her.

She has been too long starved for this. Good sense tells her to delay, that there will be a time to satisfy this craving. But good sense has been left behind, in England.

———

The air is frigid, the coals in the brazier are out as Isabella, dressed in nothing but a thin shift, carries a candle into her private chapel. She stretches out on the bitter cold flagstones, and edges forward like a penitent to the rood screen and, face down and arms outstretched, begs God for forgiveness and to take this longing away from her.

But that night, again, she rests a long finger on the velvet tunic of her lover, breathing hard, and kisses his fingertips and touches them to her lips.

All things seem possible. "They will destroy us if we do not stop," she whispers.

"We will stop tomorrow."

"I mean it."

"They will not do anything while we are still of use to them. You have Prince Edward, Isabella. All can be forgiven."

"But will God forgive me?"

"Given time," he says, and then he pins her on the bed again, and the time for strategy and wisdom is gone.

Later, lying in his arms, she whispers: "I do not want harm to befall Edward. I still love him. It is the Despenser I want to be rid of."

"Those are just words. From the moment you came here, you knew there could be only way out. You make your son king or you go back and spend the rest of your life shut up in a monastery like your sisters-in-law."

Her destiny gathers pace. She sees the way her servants and her son look at her, but she cannot help herself. Soon she is notorious.

Chapter 46

There are candles burning in the chapel, and the air is sweet with incense. Isabella prays to the Virgin, but what good is a virgin for problems like these? She cannot possibly understand the need to be adored, to be desired. A woman should not want these things, her confessor once told her. It is wanton.

When she sees her son, he is cold to her. He is sullen when she asks him about his day; the Lord Mortimer has been hunting with him, they caught two hares with the falcon, it rained, the dogs cornered a boar, and Roger killed it with a well-aimed arrow.

"A good day," she says, hopefully.

He shrugs. He does not like Paris, he says. It is dirty and it is too cold. It is, of course, just like London, but he does not complain when they stay at Westminster or in the White Tower.

"I should like to go home and see my father," he says.

"Soon."

"I am a prisoner here, aren't I?"

She laughs. Her laughter is too loud, and it startles them both. "Of course not, how can you be a prisoner when you are with your mother?" She knows where this idea is from. His father has been writing him letters again. She asks him what else he wrote.

"Nothing," he says, and his cheeks flush with the lie. After a pause: "Is Lord Mortimer your new friend?"

Now it is her turn to lie. "He has helped me much since I have been in France."

"Father says he is a traitor."

"Bad men have lied to your father about him. He is a loyal Englishman. Did you know it was Roger who subdued the rebellion in Ireland?"

Edward does not care about the rebellion in Ireland. He wants only to know which bad men have been lying to his father. She sees the trap and says only that Mortimer has enemies who wish to see him destroyed, and in time all will be clear.

She squeezes his hand. He lowers his eyes. He does not smile back.

This boy is all that stands between her and her exile. He must become her creation and not his father's. She must build here a prince that all men could be proud of. It must be done for England's sake, not just for her own.

This she believes.

"I promised my father before I left England that I would not contract a marriage without his knowledge and consent."

"Who talks of marriage?"

"Lord Mortimer tells me I shall marry one of the Count of Hainaut's daughters. He says it is all arranged, that there are four daughters, and I am fortunate because I can choose from any one of them."

"Nothing is decided yet."

"Father says in his letter that he can annul the marriage and disinherit me. He says a disobedient son will suffer the wrath of God."

"Yes, well, he would say that, Edward."

"Can he disinherit me?"

"On what basis?"

"I gave him my word that I should not marry without his consent."

She remembers her father's face bent to hers when she was his age. *"You will make him love you."* She reaches out and strokes his cheek, offers bright laughter instead of the truth. "Nothing is decided," she tells him again and goes in search of the Lord Mortimer.

———————

"You told him that he was going to marry one of the Hainaut women?" She is livid, controls her temper only with difficulty.

"What of it, Bella?"

Bella. She remembers last night, the sheets still damp, he put an arm around her, called her Bella la Belle. A pun, an endearment she had allowed in the moment. But she does not wish him to make a habit of it, certainly not when they are away from the bedchamber.

"He should have heard this only from me. It is my decision alone."

The lip curls. It might be a smile . . . it could be something else. "But what else can you do in your position? I am trying to negotiate a way for us to bring young Edward to the Crown. You must give me leave to enable this as best I can."

"By promising my son in marriage to the Count of Hainaut's daughter?"

"I promised nothing. I have explored the possibility of it with Count William and with your son. We are in a parlous position, what else would you have me do?"

It is a pertinent question. Wasn't this what she had always wanted, a strong and decisive man like her father? "I am the only one who will negotiate the prince's future."

Mortimer slams his hand on the table. "We need him. He is all that keeps us from disaster, do you not realize that?"

He is not accustomed to being questioned about the way things should be done. As a lover it is an admirable quality, but this is not the bedchamber, and she is not reclining.

He sees the look on her face, and his expression softens. He takes her hand and leans in, smiling. "I have received secret communication from Norfolk," he whispers. "He says that should you return to England, even with just a thousand men, all England will rally to you and place your son on the throne. Where will we find ships and a thousand men, Bella?"

She stiffens. There, he has used that name again. Even as he whispers hope of redemption, he curdles it. "It is for me to decide whom he marries."

The smile fades. His arsenal is exhausted. He has tried bullying and wheedling, now he is disarmed, and he crosses his arms and sulks. "We need William of Hainaut."

"I need no one anymore."

He raises an eyebrow at that.

Finally, he bows and leaves. In the chansons of the troubadours, love was always sweet and gentle. But that is not Mortimer; and Mortimer is not love.

The next day she meets with Charles at the Palais de la Cîté, along with Mortimer and her cousin Jeanne, and it is agreed that the young prince will contract a marriage to William's daughter Philippa. In return, William will provide Mortimer with troops and ships for the invasion.

They all look at her.

"This is what you want, isn't it?" Charles asks her.

Her throat feels tight. She wonders if she might feel better about this if she were not sleeping with the man who would depose her husband from his throne. After all Edward has done, or has failed to do, it is hard for her to sleep at night. She has gone through this over and over in her head. If she does not do this, then she must resign herself to Blanche's fate and spend the rest of her days in a convent somewhere. If she agrees to this, then she is guilty of the unthinkable.

She hesitates.

Finally she nods her head, not trusting her voice.

There, it is decided.

Mortimer smiles. Charles looks resigned, Jeanne relieved.

There is no going back.

Mortimer goes to it the same way as always. He hoists the flag and makes his charge. Once is novelty and twice is breathtaking. But now she is accustomed and looks for more. She remembers his tenderness in the garden with his wife and children. Why does she never see this in him? She feels at times that he is angry with her for making him a scoundrel.

He lies on top of her, breathless, his face flushed, muscles corded in his chest and arms. His seed pools on her belly and thighs. Tonight she had to struggle with him—he almost forgot himself and did not withdraw. Or does he wish to father an heir himself? The thought has occurred to her.

Later, as he lies beside her, he says: "My mother has been forced into hiding."

"By Edward? But she is an old lady!"

"She is apparently a threat to the state. He has ordered her arrest. It is just spite."

"Edward has not done this. It is Despenser."

Mortimer sits up in bed and frowns at her. She runs her hand down his back. She used to leave scratches there, but it seems her passion is fading already. "Must you always defend him? They are his orders, under his seal. He allows it to happen, it is the same thing."

"I think the problem with Edward is Gaveston."

"Gaveston? He has been moldering in his grave for almost fifteen years."

"And Edward still pays the friars at Langley to say a mass for him every day. He prays at his tomb on his birthday and the anniversary of his death."

"It is unnatural."

"It is love."

"It was sodomy and against all God's laws."

"I only wish he loved me as much. He could have put it where he wanted."

She cannot believe the words have come out of her mouth. He turns and stares at her. They are both shocked. What is he supposed to say to that?

She cannot meet his eyes.

"We have made a fool of him, Roger. All Christendom will laugh at him because I cuckolded him with his greatest enemy."

He is grateful to be talking of something else. "Only if he knows about us," he says.

"The whole world knows about us. Almost the entire retinue sent here with me from England has deserted and gone back to England. They will regale Edward with stories of my disloyalty with all England's traitors as well as my dalliance with you."

"Well, it will soon be too late."

"I hope so. Every day we delay means another day that he is ready. He has set up watches all along the south coast. He is prepared for invasion."

"He thinks it will come from your brother, not from Hainaut."

"It will not matter where it comes from if England does not love us."

"How can they not? They despise the Despensers, they will greet us as saviors." He rolls toward her, puts a hand on her breast—the royal breast, his possession now, to fondle as he pleases. "I cannot get enough of you," he murmurs, and finally he has said the right thing.

"Be gentle," she murmurs. "I am sore."

"I am always gentle," he whispers, but of course he is not. He batters away again as if he were trying to break down the gate of a castle. Sometimes she is nostalgic for Edward. He had such gentle hands for such a big man.

———

The king of France smiles, no more than a curl of the lip, the eyes glittering like steel points. The effect is unnerving. He has a pretty face for such a ruthless man. He may be her brother, but Charles is only concerned about Charles, she knows this. She would expect nothing less of a son of France.

"You slept well?" he asks her, and as he rarely inquires after her sleep, she knows the question means something else entirely.

"I am well rested."

He seems to struggle with himself. How indelicate can he allow himself to be? "I had the nuncio in here this morning," he says. "He was roaring against you."

"The nuncio? He has said nothing to me."

"He is a man of God. He cannot say aloud to a queen and sister to the king of France what he might say to a common sinner."

"A sinner?" she inquires, as sweetly as she can.

"You may flash your eyes like that at my Lord Mortimer and find it has some effect, but Isabella, do not attempt these same stratagems with me. Remember who I am." He gets up and stalks the carpets. Expensive, brought all the way from Damascus or Aegypt.

"Why Mortimer?"

She considers a denial, but that would just insult his intelligence. She chooses silence. She supposes he will not wish to know too much of his sister's earthly longings.

But he presses her. She finally mutters something about strategy.

"This is not strategic! Mortimer and the rest were yours to command anyway." He looks out of the window, hands on his hips. "You had all Christendom on your side, and now you have thrown Edward a lifeline."

"He has let the Despenser reduce England to tyranny. He has dishonored me."

"And now you have dishonored *him* and set confusion in people's minds! What were you thinking? You are his wife, Isabella. While you were wandering the palace in your widow's weeds, they felt sorry for you. Even the pope! But now . . ."

"But now?"

"Now Edward knows you are lying to him. He has written to the pope asking that he disallow any marriage between the prince and Philippa of Hainaut. He has also made it known to the English Parliament that you are consorting with a convicted traitor. You have played into his hands."

"What will the pope do?"

"It is adultery and a sin before God. He must do as popes do. Oh, Isabella, what have you done?"

She hears herself say: "I could not help it."

"That, I do not wish to hear."

"You will not send me back?"

"You must stop this affair."

"I cannot."

He shakes his head. "You are willful."

"Sometimes it is counted as a virtue."

"Not in my eyes, and not at this moment."

"You will not desert me?"

It seems he has considered it. Finally he shakes his head. Is it an answer or is it despair? "You must delay. You need William's support and you cannot have that without a contract of marriage between his daughter and the prince. For that you need the pope's support. I thought you were better than this, Isabella."

He looks so like her father when he says this. Even his expression is the same, or the same as she imagines it would be. She had never given him cause for disappointment, and if he were alive today, there would be no Mortimer. She cannot blame this on de Molay's curse. This is the natural consequence of sin, she supposes, but she feels she has been dutiful long enough. Even now, she will not back down.

Chapter 47

Thomas Randolph, Earl of Moray, is mantled in velvet, and speaks French and English as well as she does. He is the Bruce's most trusted ambassador, some say he is his nephew. It is the first time she has met with the savage enemy, and she is surprised at his eloquence and his manners. He seems on friendly terms with Mortimer. They fought against each other once, he says, when he was in Ireland with the Bruce's brother. It is as if it makes them family. Soon they will be exchanging stories of common acquaintances they have butchered and gutted.

This meeting seems as deadly a sin as her carnal embraces with Mortimer. She is talking to Edward's deadliest enemy. His father was the Hammer of the Scots; now his wife is offering them lasting peace. Enough that she should make him a cuckold, now she will put him in his father's shadow forever. She might as well sleep with Robert Bruce and be done with it.

But this must be done. When they cross the Channel, they cannot have the Scots decimate England the moment they are in command of it. She consoles herself with the thought that you cannot tame these Scots anyway; you beat down one, and another two come whooping down out of the bogs, screaming bloody murder at you.

"So I may take your word on this to my king?" Randolph says.

Mortimer tells him it is so, but Moray hesitates and looks at Isabella. Mortimer is not king of England, nor even his mother.

"You may tell him," Isabella hears herself say, her voice choked.

"Only I have heard that the pope may oppose you. You know these rumors?"

Mortimer rushes to assure him that it is not so.

"Prince Edward is here in France, not in England. What does that tell you?"

"It tells me you have the advantage for now. But if the pope will not countenance this marriage, it makes any agreement we may reach moot."

"The king of France supports us."

"The king of France wants to be the next Holy Roman Emperor. He will not want a conflict with the pope."

Edward had called the Scots savages. This man is not savage, he knows what he is about. If the rest of the Scots are as canny, it is small wonder they trounced Edward thoroughly every time he marched north of Berwick.

She cannot believe that the Bruce is finally offered everything he has fought for, and here is his ambassador questioning it as counterfeit.

"There will be a new king of England before the year is out," Mortimer tells him. He gives himself away in that moment. She sees his ambition naked as a newborn.

Moray sees it too and smiles. He has the measure of them now. "I'll tell my king all that you have said."

A month ago, he would have danced a jig out of the door. Now he takes solemn leave. How all their fortunes have changed.

———

The nuncios look grim, as well they might. One king blames them for losing half his land in France, the other resents them for coming here to upbraid his own sister for her morals. They finger their crucifixes as if they are warding off bad spirits. They are aware that everyone sniffs and scowls wherever they appear in the palace, as if they were a bad smell that cannot be removed from the drapes.

A steward pours water in their wine. They refuse sustenance. Orange looks righteous; Vienne looks ill.

"The Holy Father is most concerned to hear of your situation," Orange says.

"None of it is my doing. I have been a dutiful wife and an obedient queen. Another has come between my husband and me."

Vienne sucks in his breath and leaves the bishop of Orange to the heavy lifting. "Yet wherever the fault may lie, it is in forgiveness and reconciliation—not blame—that we find the goodness of God."

"I have offered conciliation, Father, and been rebuffed again and again."

"It is never too late."

Finally Vienne finds his voice. "On what conditions might this disagreement between you be resolved?"

She knows where he is going with this and she is ready. "One, that he puts aside he who has come between himself and his lawful wife."

"You mean the Lord Despenser?"

"He is to leave England and never return. Two, I should require assurances—written assurances—as to my status as queen, and my lands and privileges. Three, I should further require a guarantee for the future safety of my Lord Richmond, who fears for his life should he return to England for the simple fact of doing me good service while I was in France. Should he fulfill these three conditions, then there shall be nothing standing in the way of God's holy union."

They look at each other. They are imagining stepping into Edward's court, with the Despenser standing behind him, and repeating these terms. Is it legal to have a nuncio drawn and quartered? Possibly not, but she still would not like to be in their holy shoes.

"The Lord Despenser says that he has done nothing to cause this enmity between you, and that before you left, you had nothing but sweet words for him."

She leans forward. "Excellency, if you are cornered by a mad dog, do you shout at it or do you talk softly while you look for the nearest stout stick?"

"There must be a way we can mend this misunderstanding."

"There is no need to do so for I am not married to Lord Despenser. But you should ask my husband if *he* is."

Vienne coughs to hide his embarrassment. Orange sighs. She supposes he foresees an uncomfortable voyage to England ahead of him and an even more difficult homecoming. No doubt he had never imagined that giving service to the Lord would prove to be so difficult.

At this moment Mortimer bursts in, choked with rage.

"What do you think you're doing, woman?" he shouts at her. *Woman?* He starts to upbraid her in front of the nuncios and within earshot of her servants. This will not do.

"You will not address me this way," she says, rising to her feet, a tremor in her voice.

"You are making terms behind my back with the pope's lackeys?"

"I have made no terms."

"You told them you would go back to Edward if he exiles Despenser!"

She looks around the chamber. *Is nowhere private?* They might as well discuss the future of England in the marketplace with the jugglers and piemen. "Lower your voice, Lord Mortimer, you are in the presence of a queen."

His eyes bulge. For a moment she thinks he will slap her like a common wife. He storms out.

———

From her room she can see the Tour de Nesle, the place where her brothers' wives had begun their infamous liaisons. A stark reminder, if she needed one, of what men thought of royal women who put their own pleasures before their duty to their husbands and the state.

She watches him dress. A bull of a man, with hair on his back and a soldier's scars on his arms. His sheer brutishness had pleased her once, but something is changing, in him, or in her. What had once excited her now fills her with disgust.

"The whole world knows about us."

Mortimer stares at her, as if she is to blame.

"My brother has seen fit to reprimand me for my loose morals."

He shrugs. "Let them say what they want."

"You do not understand, do you? There will be consequences."

The look in his eyes. He doesn't like having a woman explain politics to him. His thoughts have moved quickly from admiration to resentment. She turns back to the window, watching the moonlight ripple on the river far below, her back to him. "Have you heard from Lady Mortimer?"

"Lady Mortimer?"

"Yes. You remember. Your wife."

"I thought we understood each other in this."

"It is not only Edward who will be hurt when news of this comes to England."

"You still care what Edward thinks of you?" he says.

"And you no longer care what your wife thinks of you?"

He does not answer her.

"Don't hurt her. She has given you children and been a good wife. She has suffered much in your exile."

"It is a little late for conscience, isn't it?"

"I don't know that it is ever too late."

She looks back at him over her shoulder. He is dressed now, standing by the candle, running his hand backward and forward through the flame.

"Are you frightened you will offend the pope?" he asks her.

She sighs. "Sometimes I wonder how you have survived so long in public affairs."

"What do you mean by that?"

"Today. The papal nuncios."

"Ah, at last. I have been waiting for your explanation with some eagerness."

"Firstly, I do not owe you an explanation. Secondly—do you not understand this?—they are the papal nuncios. I must be seen to try and conciliate if we are to win the pope's support. You do remember the pope? He is the most powerful man in Christendom, and without his tacit agreement for our endeavors you will spend the rest of your life in exile."

He steps closer. His voice is no more than a growl. "Would you betray me, Isabella?"

"Because you bed a queen does not make you a king. Remember yourself. I think you should leave now and return to your own chambers."

His hand rests on his sword, the knuckles white. He hesitates. "Very well. We will discuss this another time."

"There is nothing to discuss," she tells him. He bows his head—no more than a nod really—and leaves.

He had told her once that the people around her had underestimated her, and now it seems to her that he will make the same mistake. Her hands ball into fists at her side, and her fingernails bite into the flesh of her palms.

She really has had enough of men in her life who cannot control their rages.

———

By nightfall of the next day, the news of their quarrel is all over the palace. Even the young prince has heard about it.

"You are exchanging one yoke for another," he tells her.

She is astonished; he has never spoken to her this way before. "You will not speak to me this way," she tells him. First Mortimer, now her son. She wonders whom else she must remind about their manners.

"They said he struck you," he says.

"He would not dare."

There are tears in the prince's eyes. He is ashamed of them and runs from the room. Richmond is there and is witness to it. "He is a prince, but he is still a boy," he says, trying to reassure her. "He does not know what to believe."

"This is not what I wanted."

"No one wanted this. I never thought to exile myself from England, neither did you. And neither did Mortimer."

"Little Edward asked me the other day if he was my prisoner."

"It is hard for him to understand."

"Tell me this will come out all right."

"I hope so."

"You hope so? I asked you to reassure me!"

"The future depends much upon your brother. He already has what he wants. Further conflict wins him nothing. What do you think he will do, Isabella?"

She looks at him bleakly. She really does not know.

"I also heard that Mortimer raised his voice to you."

"Is there anyone does not know the story?"

"The king of Norway perhaps. But everyone in France has heard it at least twice. The man overreaches himself, your grace."

"It was right there in front of the nuncios, and no doubt they will tell all to Edward when next they see him."

"Step carefully. Mortimer is not your equal."

"He may be trained. He is useful to us. We like him."

Richmond considers. "I had a dog once. He was loyal, too. One day he bit me."

"What did you do?"

"I threw him in the moat with a rock tied to his leg. A dog might be trained from a pup, but only when they are grown do you truly know their nature." He finishes the wine, and bows and takes his leave of her.

For some reason she thinks about Gaveston. For all his fripperies and sharp tongue, she remembers him now as a sweet man. In all the five years she knew him, she never heard him shout at Edward.

———

The summer passes with meetings held behind bolted doors, whispered conversations in long corridors, letters read and quickly burned in the fire. The exiles say that all she has to do is sail to England, and the whole country will rise up. The other possibility is that the king will arrest her immediately and send her to molder in a tower in Wales, without enough food, without enough clothes, without enough logs for the fire.

Young Edward withdraws further into himself. She supposes this is normal for someone in his circumstance. He was never one over-inclined to talk, but she sees that now it costs him to keep silent.

Finally he breaks: "My father has written to me," he says.

She knows this. She has read the letter.

"He is displeased with me."

"Oh?"

"He says that I should return to England, and that keeping the Lord Mortimer as my counselor is a dereliction of my duty."

"All Lord Mortimer has done is take you hunting and given you some instruction with arms and with chess. Would your father have me ignore your education?"

"Am I your hostage?"

"What a thing to say."

"Father says if I were not your prisoner, I would have returned to England by now."

"I would gladly return with you to England if I could. But the Lord Despenser has done all in his power to dishonor me. If I were to return to England, I should be disinherited of my estates, and in fear of my life."

He looks right through her. "Father says Uncle Hugh is just an excuse, that you're doing all this because of Mortimer."

"Most others say I do what is best for England."

"I do not care much for Uncle Hugh. But Father is king."

"Is he? Then why does he take away my lands and my children?"

He lowers his eyes. He knows she is right about this—he has eyes and ears.

"I love your father, Edward, but he has shown little love for me of late, and he has allowed Lord Despenser to make all the kingly decisions for him. That is why I do what I do."

It is pleasant out here in the garden. There is a warm breeze, scents of flowers. She regards her son: a fine boy, his dark hair is the color of chestnuts. He is all that stands between her and despair.

I will tell you why Edward should not be king, she thinks. *It is because he let you come to France. He has no strategy; unlike Mortimer, he cannot play chess. A king who cannot play chess is*

fated always to find himself with nowhere to move, trapped between
a knight and a queen.

She remembers Edward with his court cronies, bent over the
table, playing at dice. That is Edward's game: boisterous, compan-
ionable, risking everything on chance. It requires no thought, just
a little money and recklessness.

Chess is the king's game. Her father knew that.

So does his daughter.

———

"A woman, though she is a queen, is meant by God to be instructed
by her husband."

It is the bishop of Orange who says this, and she smiles and
imagines cleaving him with a sword, right through his skull to his
breastbone, as the Bruce had done to Henry de Bohun at the battle
of Bannockburn.

"Yet what is a wife to do when her holy union is divided by
another?"

Vienne and Orange exchange ghastly smiles. "The Lord
Despenser is merely the king's adviser."

She leans forward, and they mimic her. There is a pregnant
moment when all grimace, knowing what she is about to say. "His
advice is sought everywhere. *Everywhere.*"

It is as daintily as she will ever say it. Vienne has not the stomach for such hard negotiation. He finds something of great interest
in the tapestries. It is left to Orange to continue the battle.

"The Holy Father is most unhappy at the discord between
you. Will you not return to England with us so that you may meet
Edward face-to-face?"

"You know my terms, sirs. There is nothing else to be said."

Chapter 48

The summer has been long and golden. The waiting has passed to the accompaniment of bees and birdsong. There is stubble in the fields, and soon the nights will draw in.

The nuncios have returned from England. Their journey has been fruitless. Edward will not abide her terms. It is clear to everyone but Edward and the pope that the marriage is irretrievable. She has made all possible efforts, for conscience's sake and for the sake of public opinion, but no more may be done.

It is a drab morning, the air close and uncomfortably warm, a day when the clouds are the color of pewter and seem too close to the earth. She is sweating even before she is in her brother's presence.

There are guards at the door, Brabantine mercenaries in the blue and gold of the royal household, the nose guards of their helmets hiding their faces. They stand at the foot of a polished staircase, their swords drawn.

The king of France is troubled, his features are set. Her smile of greeting is met with a scowl. He paces the room. "The pope has written to me," he says. "He knows of your indiscretions with

Mortimer. He says that sheltering you like this reflects badly on my honor.

"I warned you of this! I told you to be chaste, and if you could not be chaste, then to be discreet!"

He has told her no such thing. There have been frowns and shrugs, but he has been complicit in all she has done. But now he is remaking his own history for his own purpose.

"How could you do this? Have you forgotten Marguerite and Blanche?" He brushes aside a servant's offer of wine. He stalks toward her across the fine carpets, his eyes like points. "I think you goad me with this."

"Your grace, I would not."

"You may think our father cruel, but I thought he was mild with them. If I were Edward, I should do at least the same to you."

"He has estranged me."

"And you have cuckolded him before the whole world! I have protected you because you are my sister!"

"I am sorry if my importunate actions have allowed Edward to seem a wounded husband."

"There is no *seems* to it, sister. He is wounded. His pride if nothing else." She has never seen Charles like this, and it scares her. "You have made my position impossible."

A feeling of dread settles in her stomach, like cold goose fat.

"You know Edward sent a letter to the pope, telling him that you now share lodgings with Mortimer?"

"It is a lie."

"A lie that is true enough. It is something the whole world knows anyway. Now, see, we are at war with England. This is why you were sent to Edward and to England, sister, so that such conflict might be avoided."

"This situation was not of my choosing."

He sits down, then stands again. "I cannot fight a war with England on two fronts."

"You said you would give me whatever support that I needed."

"That was before you made yourself notorious with Mortimer!"

His eyes are blazing. She can feel her own heartbeat, her legs will not hold her, and she fumbles for a chair. There is a sheen of sweat on her forehead; it is too hot in here.

"The pope threatens me with excommunication should I continue to shelter adulterers."

"Adulterers!"

"It is what you are, is it not?"

She listens, numb, as he tells her that it is over, she has lost her support in France over this man, that he must now send her back. She has left him no choice.

It knocks the breath out of her. She is determined not to be womanly, not to cry or to faint. He is still shouting, but she hears him at a distance instead of right there, an arm's length from her face.

"What will I do?" she hears herself say when he is finished.

"There is nothing else to do. Go back to your husband, Isabella."

She thinks of Marguerite, as Charles bid her to do. She thinks of shivering in rags and a threadbare blanket, her hair cut with blunt scissors. Did the guards abuse her as well? She does not imagine that Edward will be kind, not with the Despenser standing at his shoulder, urging him to a proper settlement of debts.

She takes her leave of the king and totters along the corridor to her rooms. Her ladies hover, but she sends them away. She drops into a seat by the window.

Outside is a man digging a ditch. Edward loved to dig ditches; he is a beautiful man with his shirt off, laughing and slick with sweat.

There is a candle that has yet to be extinguished, and she puts her hand into the flame, for no other purpose than to feel something. Afterward she nurses her scalded fingers in her lap. What shall she do?

There is not enough air in here. She runs into the garden, runs for the sake of running, past startled servants and gardeners. She runs until she is breathless and then sinks to her knees among the strawberries and, to the astonishment of a red-faced gardener, she retches painfully among the sweet and ripening fruit.

Chapter 49

Mortimer's man is dressed for riding. "A good fur cloak for your shoulders, your grace," he says, handing it to her. There is a chill in the air tonight. When you are in the employ of Roger Mortimer, perhaps you grow accustomed to fleeing a house in the dark of night. For the queen of England, it is a novel experience.

Oh, there was Tynemouth, I suppose.

He leads her and her ladies through the garden to a door in the wall. She hears the jingle of coins changing hands, and the watchman hurries them through. Mud squelches underfoot as they hurry along a path beside a sheep meadow. Here the queen of England must scramble through briars. Her hair snags on a thorn. *So now we have come to a fine pass.*

Mortimer's man—she never finds out his name—helps her down a steep and muddy bank. One of her ladies falls and slithers in the mud, she lets out a yelp, and is hushed to silence.

Isabella proceeds on tiptoe, but after a while she is exhausted and so lets her skirts trail in the muck as they will. She smells manure. They are in a pasture. A crescent moon darts in and out of the scudding clouds, and everything is shadow.

———

She concentrates her will on the next step, reminding herself not to stumble. She will at least retain some dignity. She prays for deliverance, its shape and form unknowable in this darkness. *Let me not be remembered for my exodus tonight, but rather for the triumph that lies at the end of it; and if my father is watching, let him guide me and help me so that I do not spend the rest of my life reading gospels and staring listlessly out of a convent window.*

She sees the silhouettes of farmhouses and the flare of a torch, then hears Mortimer's voice. He is waiting in a cobbled courtyard with a dozen men and horses. He leads her to a barn. There, in the straw, the queen of England is ordered to change into humbler clothes so that she may more easily play the part of a merchant's wife. She was stripped of her lands and titles in plain view; now she gives up her finest velvet gown and her jewels in the dark.

The wimple and the fustian itching her skin bother her more than the mud squelching between her toes. It is the final indignity.

She leaves the barn and rejoins Mortimer in the yard. Without a word he helps her up onto a cart. Not even a cushion.

"We are merchants traveling north," Mortimer says, jumping onto the running board beside her. "If we are challenged, stay silent."

"Where are we going?"

"The only place we can go."

There are packhorses, a dozen men, and her ladies. Behind her, on the cart, are barrels of Gascon wine and salt beef. The prince sits hunched between them. He endures it all in silence. She wonders what she will do if he rebels. But it never comes to that; she is his mother, after all, and he feels he has no choice but to help her.

———

"William is not royal, but he is disgustingly rich, in both lands and money. You are a queen but landless and penniless. You will appear patronizing; he will incline toward impudence. Bear it best you can. We all need each other."

This is Mortimer's advice to her as they are received in the galleried hall of the Hotel d'Hollande. It is impressive; there are high Gothic windows and expensive Turkish hangings on the walls. The man has done well for himself. It seems it is not only in England that noblemen live better than kings.

He has his four daughters decorously arranged beside him so that the prince might more easily view the wares on offer, like gloves at a country market: Margaret, Jeanne, Philippa, and Isabella. She hears her son draw breath and repeat the names over to himself, trying to remember them all. She once again hopes he has more appetite for the game than his father.

William has a gift for him, a silver plate from Byzantium, with a relief of David slaying Goliath. Is there meaning couched in this? The prince dutifully hands over the gifts he has brought in return: some silks and a gilt mirror. He then subsides to an uncomfortable silence.

Mortimer and William seem on good terms, though. They know what they are about.

She never warms to William. He is like every baron she has ever known, the manners of a grandee and the heart of a banker. Behind the grand gesture it is all business. He reminds her of the Despenser, for he has no conversation if he is not talking politics or money. He has amassed a vast fortune, and this is why he can now buy his daughter the next king of England. She imagines it is like getting her an Arabian pony, only he is the one that will get the joy out of it.

She endures his hospitality with bitter smiles, the prince a ghastly presence beside her, fidgeting and scowling.

The mansion house windows look out over windswept fields where herds of fat cows bend to the grass, and cold biting winds sweep from the narrow sea. They eat from gold plates, their crystal goblets clinking and breaking the long and difficult silences. The prince picks at his food without appetite. She wonders if this is the face his own father wore when Longshanks told him he was to marry Isabella of France.

Chapter 50

Mortimer is restless. He wanted to make a start on this business in the spring, now it is close to autumn. He does not want to delay another year. The fruit is ripe for the picking; the harvest must come in now.

He harangues her about the prince. When will he choose? "It's only a wife," he says, damning himself further without even knowing it. If there were a coin with four sides, he could try his luck that way, he says, it's as good a way as any other. He passes the days riding with William, until gout forces the count to sit by the hearth, shrieking as if he were being drawn and quartered. The young prince spends time with the one called Philippa. She is a stout girl and not very pretty, but they both like horses. In Mortimer's mind that settles things.

"How many soldiers can William provide?" she asks him.

"Perhaps a thousand."

"A thousand?"

"He is not Lancaster."

"But so few? With a thousand men, we might not take Bury St Edmunds, let alone all England."

"We do not have to defeat England. Think of these men as a bodyguard, that is all. Once we are there, the country will rise to support you against the Despensers."

"And the ships?"

"A hundred and forty. Enough to transport our army—"

"Bodyguard—"

"—horses and supplies."

How did it ever come this far? She has never imagined taking arms against Edward. She wonders what her father would say about it.

"We await the prince's pleasure," Mortimer says.

"I shall talk to him."

"The money and the ships are being gathered. Once the marriage contract is signed, William will underwrite the entire expedition."

"What of the pope?"

"He will not approve the marriage while we are in Hainaut, but he will sing a very different tune when your son is on the throne of England. God is on the side of the victorious."

"What if we drown in the narrow sea? What if my son is taken prisoner? William undertakes huge risk here."

"Not so much. Charles is backing him."

"My brother? But he abandoned me! He threw me out!"

Mortimer shrugs his shoulders. "It was all a shadow play, no more. He had no choice. The pope put him in an impossible position. Do not believe for a moment that he abandoned you. You are French, remember. He plays a subtle game, your brother."

"He is convincing enough when he wants to be."

"As we all must be."

Another look between them, lovers considering their next move at chess.

A wind from the narrow sea rattles the shutters. *Is it never summer here?*

She thinks of that last night in Dover. Even then the Despenser wished to stop her leaving. Could Edward not see what must happen? When a king cannot leave his own borders for fear that his countrymen will rise up and slaughter his prime minister—for that is what Despenser has become—then it is time to appoint a new minister. If a king is not practical, he cannot long be a king. This is not her fault.

"I am sorry for my ill temper," Mortimer murmurs. "I have just had news. My uncle is dead."

"When did you hear this?"

"A messenger came this morning. It was starvation, they say. Edward let him die by inches in the Tower. I could understand it if he had gone against Gaveston, but it was done simply because of his relation to me. The king revenges himself on everyone now. I shall not forget this barbarity."

"I am sorry, Roger."

"Tell your son to choose one of William's brood, and let's be done with this. Remind him that he is not expected to be faithful to her when he is of age. What man is?"

"No one in this room," Isabella says. She cannot look at him these days without thinking of Lady Mortimer living in disgrace in a drafty castle in Yorkshire, a woman who yet thought her a friend.

"You are hardly a paragon yourself," he bites back.

"At last something you and the king agree on." They sit in silence, listening to the wind howling from England.

———

But when she sees the young prince, he is of no mind to be hurried.

"Must I marry?"

"It is a good union, Edward. You surely understand the importance of it?"

"But Father said I mustn't."

"Then I shall put you on a ship for England, and we must part. For you know very well that I cannot ever return with things as they are."

"What would you do?"

She holds her breath. The question is asked in earnest. Would he yet contemplate leaving her? Would she allow him to do it, or is she bluffing? "I don't know. All I know is that I fear for my life if I return to England."

"Father would never harm you."

"There are other men who would, and your father has a habit of looking the other way."

"Uncle Hugh," he says. *Uncle*—the name grates with her as much as *Bella*. She wants to shake him: *He is not your uncle!* Instead, she watches him make calculation.

How royal he has become. He holds out a hand for a cup, and a steward brings it. He lets him pour a little wine and add water to it. The future king of England does not even look at the man, just taps his foot with impatience when he is slow about it.

The prince says: "You're right, I believe he might do it."

The Despenser has surely considered it: a little poison in a cup would do the trick. Edward may not sanction it, but he would be relieved to be rid of her if someone else would do it for him and bear the guilt. There would not be the need for rough men with knives or ropes. She would feel unwell one day and then take to her bed, complaining of cramps in her belly.

Just as Warwick did.

"Philippa," the prince says.

He says it so softly, she misses it. He has to repeat himself. Philippa, he will marry Philippa. There, it is decided. They may move to contracts, they can load the ships.

God grant them a fair wind.

Chapter 51

By the end of summer the contract is signed, and the dowry—troops, ships, horses, money—is paid in advance. That night Mortimer takes her with breathtaking ferocity. Afterward she eases herself from beneath him while he snores. She gets out of the bed, wraps a fur around her shoulders, and pours water from the silver ewer on the nightstand. Mortimer stirs. He groans and snakes out an arm, stroking her thigh.

"You are a hellcat," he murmurs.

"And you, sir, make me purr like a kitten."

"I live to serve my queen." He raises himself on one elbow, and she shares her cup with him. He grimaces. He does not want water, he would rather wine. "This time next month we shall be lying in the keep at Windsor."

"Or dead in a field."

"I perhaps, but not you. I shall not let them take me alive, for I know what they will do to me. But he will not harm you. The worst for you is you will be divorced and sent back to France."

"Where Charles will have no choice but to put me in a nunnery."

"Better than your head on a pike above London Bridge."

The prospect makes him thirsty. He gets up and goes to the table by the fire and gets a jug of wine. So much muscle and hair; he is a bear to Edward's sleek, smooth stallion. "But it will not come to that," he says. "When the country knows their queen has returned, they will flock to you. They all pray for deliverance from the Despensers."

"I have pledged no harm to my son's father."

"Once the Despensers are taken care of and you are regent for your son, then Edward may retire to some country manor and take his pleasure in as many favorites as he wishes, and none shall come to harm."

It all sounds so simple.

There have been days since she has come to Hainaut when she wakes in the morning and wonders if her children will curse her for what she is about to do. She has angered the pope and is about to overthrow a king. This is not what her father had raised his daughter to do. *"You will obey him in all things."*

"England will mob you," Mortimer says, as if reading her mind. "The only men that will decry what you are about to do are the Despensers."

"And my husband."

"Oh, Edward," he says airily, waving a hand in the air. "Edward will be all right. We'll set him off to making thatches. He will be happier on a roof than on a throne."

Mercenaries arrive at Dordrecht from all over Europe; there are Flemings, Germans, and Bohemians. Including Hainaut's men, she counts a little more than a thousand, but not much more; not an army, just as Mortimer had said—a bodyguard. They have more on a night watch on a Welsh castle.

There are fewer than a hundred ships, not the hundred and forty that Mortimer had claimed. The soldiers, baggage, and high Flemish horses are all loaded on board.

There is wine and salted beef, enough to last them the journey over the narrow sea, and a little longer if they have to fight. But with a thousand men, they are unlikely to settle in for a long campaign. They will eat English beef and drink English wine or they will not be eating at all.

It is a blustery morning in autumn when they pull up anchors and slip out of Flanders. Dark clouds choke the horizon, and there are whitecaps on the gray sea. The wind whips the yards, and sailors mutter under their breath.

Spray crashes over the bows. Somewhere out there, through the storms and the churning waves, is England. Soon she will know what her fate holds. Edward and his lover are waiting.

Chapter 52

The mist lifts; she hears a gull cry overhead. A shoreline comes into view. Mortimer comes to stand beside her. She is so weak from seasickness that she has to support herself on the aft rail to keep from falling. Her knees shake.

"Where are we?"

"I don't know, your grace."

"There is an estuary to the north of us. Could that be the Stour?"

"I doubt that very much. If it was, there should be land on our starboard side."

For three days they have been battered by storms, which have come early this year. Has God pronounced judgment on her plans? They are supposed to meet Edmund of Kent at Thanet. Instead they could be in Norway for all the captain knows. They have lost two ships; they count themselves fortunate to make landfall at all.

Mortimer orders them ashore. He is first with the men and supplies that head for the beach in small rowing boats. She shivers in her cloak, watching them. The first bite of autumn is in the air.

Finally she can stand the rocking of the ship no longer and demands to be let ashore. She has changed into her widow's weeds.

If there is to be a welcome, she wants England to know she comes as a wronged wife, not as conqueror.

Mortimer comes out to meet her, wading through the gray and cold sea to carry her ashore. She could never imagine Edward doing that, though he might have done it for Gaveston. She smells cooking fires, her stomach growls. None of them has eaten for days. They are all so weak, if Edward finds them now, he could slaughter them all with an army of laundrywomen.

They have pitched her a tent, laid carpets on the sand beneath it. She stands within, out of the wind, watching the waves rush up the shore and suck at the shingle stones. Plovers dip and cry.

Mortimer stands, hands on hips, barking orders. She summons him. "How do we fare?" she asks him.

There is fire in his eyes, he has waited three years for this moment and the campaigner in him is warming to the task. "We have the last of the horses to bring ashore. Then the fleet will be ready to sail."

They want the ships away from here, so the mercenaries are not tempted to turn back if the business goes hard. It is probably already too late to work the element of surprise. Edward has posted watches all along the coast, and someone will have spotted them.

"Riders," the prince says, pointing along the beach to the north where horsemen approach, their armor glinting in the sun.

They come armed. A sergeant rousts the men from their huddles around the fires and forms a defensive line of pikemen, but before it is even half done a sentry shouts: "It's Norfolk's men!"

Mortimer grins. "We're saved then."

Isabella gathers her skirts and is about to head down the strand to meet them, but Mortimer puts a restraining hand on her arm. "Let them come to you," he murmurs. "You are still queen of England."

The young prince comes to stand beside her, and she puts her arm around his shoulders.

Norfolk has an escort of a dozen knights. When they reach her, he throws himself from his mount, beaming, as if he has just beaten all comers in a jousting tournament. He marches up the sand and kneels in front of Isabella and the prince. "Your grace," he says. "I came as soon as I heard the news. We were not expecting you so far north."

"We were expecting to land in Kent, but the weather thought otherwise."

"Then the wind and tide have brought us great honor. Let me escort you to my castle. I have rooms waiting."

"We are glad to see you and not Edward's army," Isabella says.

"Edward's army? He has no army. Some Welsh bowmen and a couple of bishops."

"We were expecting a fight, Thomas," Mortimer says.

"Now the queen is here, there will be no war," Norfolk says. "The people will flock to her."

"It's not the people I'm worried about. It's the barons."

"There's not one of them will piss on him if he is aflame," Norfolk says, thinking Isabella is out of earshot. "Not while Despenser is at his elbow. They say that man would screw the pope and crucify his own grandmother if he could turn a profit at it." Norfolk looks down the beach, at the huddle of Dutch and German mercenaries. "You won't be needing them, Mortimer. Just a good horse to ride to London."

That night she stays at Norfolk's castle at Walton on the Naze, and a courier from London brings them news. Surrey and also Arundel, whose son is married to Despenser's daughter, have vowed to stay loyal to the king.

But they are the only ones, for there is barely a nobleman or farmer in England left untouched by Despenser's greed. The crucial support comes from the Earl of Leicester, Lancaster's brother; he assumed all his estates after his death, and is now the most powerful baron in England. He is eager to avenge his death and sends messages of support.

The next day she rides through Bury St Edmunds, where crowds line the streets to greet her as their new regent. Her invasion of England soon becomes a royal procession. As Norfolk has prophesied, Edward is unable to raise an army against her. He is reduced to offering free pardons to felons; they come straight from the prison and he makes them captains in his cavalry—or that is how Mortimer tells it with a laugh.

We, Isabella, by the grace of God, Queen of England, Lady of Ireland, Countess of Ponthieu; and we, Edward, elder son of the lord King of England, Duke of Gascony, Earl of Chester, Count of Ponthieu and Montreuil, to all those to whom these letters may come, greetings.

Whereas it is well known that the Holy Church and the kingdom of England are in many respects much tarnished and degraded by the bad advice and conspiracy of Hugh le Despenser; whereas through pride and greed to have power and dominion over all other people, he has usurped royal power against law and justice and his true allegiance . . .

She had never thought it would be so easy.

Chapter 53

Gloucester Castle

Lord Thomas Wake shoves through the crowds in the great hall and reverently lays a basket at Isabella's feet. He reaches in and pulls out a severed head, gripping it by its bloody and matted hair. It is not fresh and is already turning green. Several of her ladies turn away in revulsion. The young prince takes a step back.

"Bishop Stapledon," Mortimer says.

"I have seen him looking better," Isabella murmurs.

"Oh, I don't know about that," Mortimer says. "He looks much as he always did, if you wish my opinion."

"How did this happen?"

"The mobs have taken over in London," Lord Wake tells her. "Stapledon was always the king's man, and now he has paid the price."

"Where?"

"He was fleeing to Saint Paul's, seeking sanctuary. The mob caught him at the doors and dragged him to Cheapside. There was a baker there with a knife large enough for the job."

"A mob? John, my little boy, he is held in London. He is unharmed?"

"Your grace, the citizens have made him warden of the city. He is safe where he is in the Tower until order may be restored, though no one in London would harm a hair on the boy's head."

He is still holding the king's bishop by the hair. Isabella asks that it be removed. It is attracting flies.

The news from everywhere is good. Edward has fled to Bristol, hoping to find comfort among the Welsh. His army consists of a handful of archers. Despenser is with him.

"We will have him soon enough. There is nowhere to run."

"Unless Bruce takes them in."

"The Scots?"

"They may both think it politic," she says.

In fact they do indeed head north, but they do not get far. Edward and his favorite are captured by the earls during a thunderstorm in open country in the marches. In a few weeks the king of England has fallen from king to fugitive to a prisoner of his own barons.

The war is over, such as it was. She had been in rowdier processions. In the end there was scarce a man in England prepared to stand by him.

Chapter 54

Mortimer is in a good mood. He walks in, dressed in black, his velvets set off with a gold chain, a ruby, fat as a goose's egg, on his knuckles. Becoming the most powerful man in England has been good for his humor. He looks like he is going to a wedding.

He even smiles.

There are drums in the square and the crowds are cheering. Nothing like evisceration to keep the common sort amused. It is the same manner of mob that came to see Jesus crucified, she supposes. That they hate the man is incidental, it's the entertainment they love, lots of blood and none of it theirs.

Mortimer stands by the window, beaming. She should not be surprised; he's a soldier after all, he's accustomed to brutality. But today Despenser will not be as quick about dying as even some men wounded after a battle.

She thought she would enjoy this, but now it comes to it, she just wishes they would have it done. An enemy never seems quite as formidable when he is whimpering in chains, so that you forget how he looked sneering at you when you were miserable and lying at his feet.

Another shout from the crowd. She supposes they are at this moment hoisting him up the ladder so they can do the business. She ventures a glance. They have him in some sort of nightshirt, and they have scrawled verses from the Bible on him.

Her little girls rush into the room, squealing. Eleanor and Joan have been in the elder Despenser's castle at Bristol this last year, and seem to have come to no harm from the old man. She had pleaded for his life on their account, if nothing else, but Mortimer and the barons had their own ideas about what to do with him. She felt sorry for old Hugh, but it's what happens when you choose the wrong side.

Eleanor and Joan are at the window before she can stop them. She drags them away. Where is their nurse? By the time she gets the children to the door, the people are banging the kettledrum down in the square and there is a cheer from the crowd as the Despenser is cut down, half-dead, to be butchered. She puts a hand over Joan's ears.

Eleanor wants to know what is happening. She tells them it is just a play, but Eleanor wonders: if it's a mummers' show, then why can't they watch too?

Eleanor is outraged at this unjust treatment, but little Joan sees the looks on the faces of those gathered at the window and falls silent, her face blank with fear. She allows Isabella to hustle her out without murmur.

There is a feast afterward to celebrate, but Isabella has little appetite. She should feel elated. Lady Mortimer is there and bows her head in acknowledgment, and Isabella nods in return and quickly looks away.

She thinks about Edward. Mortimer says he will come to no harm, but if even she doesn't trust the man who shares her bed, how can Edward?

The archbishop is resplendent, with a condescending smile and a large ruby ring. Richmond watches him down the end of his long nose. It is clear they don't like each other. Mortimer has his back turned, hands behind him, looking out of the window. The rest of the barons are all gathered. Now that the Despenser's quarters are decorating pikes all over the kingdom, they must decide what to do with the earthly paradise he has left behind.

The prince fidgets. He is a worrying presence for all of them. He does not speak for now, but one day he will judge them all.

"The people would like to see you resume your rightful place," the archbishop tells her.

"My rightful place?"

"With your husband. Now that the shadow has passed from the land, many would wish England returned to its former state."

"Who are these people?" she asks him.

"The general populace," he says airily, and by that she supposes he means the pope in Avignon.

"Never," she says.

"He is still your husband," the archbishop reminds her.

"In name only."

"A marriage is a marriage, one cannot differentiate."

Mortimer turns from the window. He makes a great sigh, like a teacher with a recalcitrant pupil. He leans on the table and smiles at the archbishop, but his eyes are hard. "She got rid of the tyrant for you. Now you wish to put your savior back under his fist?"

"It is what the people want," the archbishop insists. "We are in a difficult position. If the king does not give up the throne, what are we to do?"

After they have all gone, Mortimer paces the room. They have come so far, and still they do not have what they came for. Isabella stares into the fire. Go back to Edward? How can she go back to Edward now?

"We should do something," he says.

"Do something?"

"While he lives, we will never be safe."

"You mean to murder him?"

He stares at her, measuring. There is a fine curl of those red lips beneath his beard. "While he is alive, he is a focal point for rebellion."

The Lord Mortimer has not looked so handsome of late. Is it her, or is it him? Neither does he look at her with the same desire as he did before. Once the king is dead, she wonders if he will look at her at all. "I will not countenance murder."

"It might be sweetly done, without risk. There shall be no marks left."

"Edward . . ." She does not finish the sentence, is not sure what it is she wants to say. She thinks of him as he crept into her bedchamber that first night in Boulogne, kissing her forehead, tucking her into bed as if she were a niece, or a daughter. There was a kindness in him until they slaughtered his Gaveston. They had led him to this, in a way.

She shakes her head. "No."

"If he escapes . . ."

"You assured me that could not happen."

"No prison is proof against escape. Even the Tower," he adds and smiles.

Again, she shakes her head.

"Well, we must do something. If he does not give up the throne, and he is too proud to die, then something must be done. The longer he delays, the louder will be the calls for you to return to the marriage bed."

"I think that would disturb him as much as it disturbs me."

"You have to talk to him, Isabella. Go quietly, without fanfare. No one must know. But persuade him to give up the Crown to young Edward. It's the only way, else something may happen to him, with my intervention or no. I am not the only one who thinks it will be easier if there is no Edward."

She knows he is right. She nods her head. "I'll go," she says.

Chapter 55

A steward unlocks the door. Contrary to reports, Edward is being kept in some style. Better than the Tower, where Mortimer was. No drafts, a view of the garden, a good bed.

Edward jumps to his feet when he sees her. Apparently no one has warned him she is coming. He looks almost pleased to see her.

A familiar face, at least.

He draws himself up and looks at her down his nose. "Well. You are the last person I expected. Have you come to gloat?"

She removes the silk scarf from her face and nods to the jailer, indicating he should wait outside. He hesitates for a moment only, before he complies.

"Are they not worried I might take a knife to you?"

"Will you?"

"I had thought about it, once. Often, when I was king, but there seems no point now."

She comes to stand by the fire. This is not unpleasant. She had thought to find him shivering in a dungeon with a piss-soaked blanket round his shoulders. "Will you offer me refreshment?"

He has wine in a jug. Not very good wine, but better than most prisoners get. Mortimer has kept his word, or his friends have.

He looks her up and down. There were days not long past when she would have welcomed a look like that. "You look well," he says. "Overthrowing kings seems to suit you."

"You dethroned yourself."

"Really? Because this is not how it seemed when I was riding through Gloucestershire at night with Mortimer's wolves at my back."

"Come now, Edward. I washed up on a beach with a few hundred soldiers and a handful of horses and disaffected Englishmen. If the people loved their king, how far do you think I would have got?"

He shrugs, as if conceding a minor point. "Despenser overreached himself."

"No, you allowed him to do it. If you had been a true king, he could not have risen as high as he did."

He smiles. The fire makes his face appear to glow from within. An idea dawns. *Surely not . . .*

"You wanted him to make England suffer, didn't you?"

"When did England ever love me?"

"Was this all about Gaveston?"

He appears exasperated with her, a child who will not learn her letters. "You have never been in love, have you?"

"Yes. With you."

He shakes his head. "With me? You never knew me. You had a dream of something, a song in your head, and you fitted my words to it."

"How do you know you loved Gaveston more than I loved you?"

"Because I was not meant to love him, because he was a danger to me, but I did it anyway. He was my madness. He was all I could think of when I first woke, he was what I thought of when I closed my eyes. He was—"

"Stop it." She puts down her cup of wine so that she will not dash it in his face.

"England took away the one thing I loved. More, they wanted me to be something I am not, and so they tore out my heart that night they tore out Perro's. I just hated them all more. Not just the magnates, there were commoners out there that night. They threw filth at him while they led him out of the castle. All of England conspired against me."

"Keep your voice down," she says.

He looks at her in surprise. There is no one to hear. But it is Isabella who does not want to hear it. She had wanted someone to love her like that, perhaps once she thought that Mortimer would, but it seems she is doomed to disappointment yet again. She hates Edward at this moment, hates him so her bones ache, for he has had something she never will.

"You loved him more than your throne," she says.

"Will you harangue me for wanting, needing, something that I cannot resist?"

"God forbids it."

"It was God that made me want it so why should he deny it to me?"

She is astonished. How can he claim this is from God?

But Edward is not finished. "They took from me the one thing that I truly loved. He gave me what I needed! You can never do that. I loved you and honored you the best I could. Did I not? If you might turn a stone to water and drink it, then perhaps you can make of me a different man. But madam, if I am what you desire to bring you happiness, then you shall die unsatisfied. It is beyond my power to give it." There is no unkindness in how he says this. She thinks he might even put out a hand to comfort her, as he might a wounded dog.

In anticipation of it, she backs away.

"Have you ever forgiven yourself—for letting him go to Scarborough alone?"

He shakes his head. "If I had kept him with me, I might have saved him. It was all my fault."

"But why Despenser?"

"You think he was my lover, don't you?"

"Was he not?"

"Is Perro so easily replaced? If that is what you believe, then you do not understand what I felt for him. You think I just wanted a splendid pair of buttocks, is that it?"

"You wanted the Despenser just for his cruelty?"

"He was not wantonly cruel, he was cruelly efficient. There is a difference. Yes, I used him to square my accounts with England. I chose well. He was rather splendid at it, don't you think?"

The shadows lengthen in the room. The silence becomes unbearable, though Edward himself seems comfortable enough with it. She wants to tell him her girl's dreams, how she might have helped him become England's greatest king if he had but allowed her. But he is right—this was her dream, not his.

"They wish for you to abdicate the throne willingly."

"You mean *you* wish it."

"Your son will become king when he reaches the lawful age, and you will continue to live honorably."

"Until then, you will be regent, and Mortimer will be the new Lancaster. Things have turned out well for him."

"Will you do it?"

He looks in her eyes. "They won't let me live, whatever happens, Isabella. Our friend Mortimer learned his lesson when he escaped the Tower. He won't make the same mistake I made with him."

"I will guarantee your safety."

"You cannot do that." He picks up her cup of wine and drains it himself in one draft. "Look after Edward, won't you?"

"He's my son."

"And mine." He slams down the cup. "Oh, tell them I'll do it. What do I care for damned England now?"

Chapter 56

"There has been another attempt to free the king," Mortimer says.

This is the third such plot. After the first failed, they had him transferred from Kenilworth to Berkeley Castle, under the stewardship of Mortimer's son-in-law, thinking it more secure. But now, a group of royalists led by a Dominican friar called Thomas Dunheved has managed to free him, having gained entrance through a sewer leading from the moat to the inner bailey and murdering a Gascon porter called Bernard Pellet.

For a few anxious days, the king of England is loose in the marches until he is finally recaptured.

Now there are reports of armed men gathering in the Forest of Dean. Mortimer worries that there are still those in the kingdom that love him and would have him back on the throne.

"If that were true, why could he not raise an army last year when we landed at Norfolk?"

"Times change, memories are short. We cannot take the risk, Isabella."

The color rises to her cheeks. One day this Mortimer will overreach himself. They speak in whispers for an hour, his head inclined toward her, debating Edward's life.

"And what will I tell my children?"

"You need not tell them anything other than he is dead."

"The young prince will know."

"Suspicion is not the same as proof. In time he will understand that these things are necessary. He can hardly be king of England and be innocent forever."

The candle is burning down, the wax sizzles and flickers. Mortimer's face dances in the flame.

"How might it be done?" she says.

"Quietly, in the night. Do I have your approval for this?"

"No! No, you do not."

He is furious. His jaw muscles work. "Then what would you have me do?"

She turns away. She considers their position in silence and then says, in a voice almost too soft to hear: "If you do it, I want no part of it."

"It is for the prince's sake."

This hypocrisy makes her want to clout him.

"I will do what must be done then," he says and strides from the room.

That night he comes to her bedchamber and finds it locked to him. She hears him in the corridor, testing the latch, and she thinks he might rap on the door, but it seems he understands her message well enough and so finds some other warm place to rest his powerful head.

Chapter 57

The silver casket is brought in and placed on the table. Not a word is spoken. She runs her fingertips across the surface. It was a gift from her mother-in-law on the day of her wedding—a lifetime ago. Inside the casket is everything she had ever wanted and had been determined one day to have.

It is chill in the room, and she comes to stand by the fire. A log breaks in the hearth in a shower of sparks and startles her.

She thinks of him that first time she saw him, at Boulogne. So tall, so straight, her perfect knight; but no knight was ever perfect. She stares at the casket. She thought she would feel more than this.

The door opens. It is the young prince. How he has grown these last weeks. He stands straighter, and his eyes glitter.

"You have heard the news?" she asks him.

He studies her face, looking for the truth. But the truth is not as plain; there are only versions of it. "Tell me you had no part in this," he says.

"I had no part in it," she answers without hesitation.

———

The casket is still there on the table after the prince has gone. She takes it over to the window. It is a beautiful autumn day, the trees turning to gold. The sun lights her face.

She closes her eyes, brings the casket to her lips, and kisses it.

Mortimer had given his jailers precise instructions: the body was to be eviscerated, embalmed, and wrapped in linen cerecloth within hours of death, so that the bruises on the neck could not be seen. The job was done by a local wise woman who has since disappeared.

The heart was placed in a silver casket with the arms of Plantagenet and Capet in quatrefoils engraved on the lid, the same casket she is holding now.

"You see," she murmurs. "I told you that one day I would have your heart, Edward. And I always get what I want."

Epilogue

Sant' Alberto di Butrio, Northeast of Genoa, Italy

A group of riders appears above the monastery, walks their horses down the hill through the cypress trees. Two friars, working in a vineyard, watch them come. The men are knights and liveried, and the rider at their head must be an important man to have such an escort.

They do not recognize the devices on their pennants. They are not from here. The monks lay down their baskets and make their way through the vineyard to greet their visitors.

The tall monk shouts, "Can we help you?" in Italian.

One of the riders tells them, in heavily accented Italian, that they have come all the way from England. They are there at the express command of Bishop Orleton.

"You are indeed a long way from home," the friar says. "What could be so important to bring you here?"

"I am looking for an Englishman."

"An Englishman? Here?"

"You do not have any Englishmen in your chapter?"

He shakes his head. "What would an Englishman be doing in Sant'Alberto?"

"Hiding."

"Hiding?" the other friar says.

"He would have come here perhaps five years ago."

They both shake their heads. They have been gathering grapes in baskets. It is hard work, and the sweat glistens on their skin. "If an Englishman came here, we would know about it. We have been here most of our lives."

The second friar moves closer to the first. Their fingers touch. "Who are you looking for?" the first friar asks.

"The king of England."

The two churchmen laugh and shake their heads. "In Italy? You have lost your way, sir."

"The king was overthrown and murdered by his jailers."

"Then he is unlikely to be here."

"That is not the whole story. There is a letter circulating in the English court—it is said to be from the king's confessor. It claims that he escaped his jailers and that another body was substituted in order to cover it up. It further claims the body that was buried in Gloucester Cathedral was not the king but a porter who was murdered by the men who helped him escape."

"Why did this king not gather an army and take back his throne?"

"He was not popular. Some say he didn't want it anyway."

"So why are you looking for him here?"

"In the letter it says he was bound for Italy, that he wanted a simple life."

"So why not leave him in peace?"

"His son is the new king, and he wishes to leave no stone unturned."

"He fears for his throne?"

The rider gives the tall friar an appraising glance. "You are fair for an Italian."

"Not all Italians are swarthy, especially here in the north. I have German blood in me."

The Englishman smiles. "Well, it seems we are wasting your time."

"There is plenty of time here to waste. The days are long, and there is no one to harry us." He looks at his brother friar and smiles.

———————

After they are gone, he stares after them. His companion kisses him on the cheek. "Forget about them, Edoardo," he says in English. "You're safe now."

And they return to the vineyard and the lazy Lombardic sun.

The End

About the Author

Born in London, Colin Falconer began traveling in his teens after realizing that making it as a professional soccer player was simply not in the stars for him. He hitchhiked around Europe and North Africa and explored much of Asia before moving to Australia, where he freelanced for leading newspapers and magazines as well as TV and radio. Colin raised two daughters with his late wife, Helen, and volunteered in the ambulance service for over thirteen years. His travels have served as inspiration for his forty-and-counting novels in print. Ranging from vivid historical intrigues to contemporary thrillers, Falconer's work is enjoyed by a wide international audience and has been translated into twenty-three languages.